The Last Secret of the Soul

Stephen P. Smith

First Published 2025 by SP Publishing
ISBN: 979-8-3407110-4-5

Copyright © Stephen P. Smith 2025

The right of Stephen P. Smith to be identified as the author of this book has been asserted by him in accordance with the Copyright, Designs and Patents Act 1988.

All rights reserved. No part of this publication may be reproduced, stored in or introduced to a retrieval system, or transmitted, in any form, or by any means (electronic, mechanical, printing, photocopying, recording or otherwise) without the prior written permission of the author. Any person who does any unauthorised act in relation to this publication may be liable to criminal prosecution and civil claims for damages.

This book is a work of fiction. Names, characters, businesses, places, events and incidents are either the products of the author's imagination or used in a fictitious manner. Any resemblance to actual persons, living or dead, or actual events is purely coincidental.

For Margaret and Nancy – *The last secrets of my soul*

And in memory of my late friends Reg Hazel, of the Royal Engineers, who, as part of the liberation of Bergen-Belsen, witnessed the Holocaust and Esther Fairfax who, as a young Jewish girl, escaped Nazi Germany.

Who you choose to love is the last secret of the soul
—Author

1

Feitel sat on the edge of the wagon, his legs dangling out the doorway above a concrete platform. All along the train, soldiers unbolted and slid open the doors of wagons, dragged people out and kicked them away. Other soldiers held on to dogs, which strained at their leashes and growled.

With an encouraging smile, his mother grasped his hand and he jumped from the stench, the filth and the dead into a sea of people crowding onto the platform. They shuffled forward. His body took a battering from suitcases and bags: some stiff, some soft, some made of leather, others of tin.

He took a deep breath, inhaling the sweet and sticky air. 'It smells horrid,' he said, glancing up to his mother. She did not reply.

To their left, a snarling dog leapt up at a woman. She screamed, hands covering her face. Her companion, a young mother in a woollen overcoat and headscarf, clutched her baby to her chest.

'What's that big fence for?' Feitel asked, pointing ahead to a line of concrete posts covered with barbed wire. Beyond the fence was a collection of wooden huts, dark and foreboding. His mother tugged at his hand and drew him close. 'Why's your hand shaking? What are they burning in that chimney?'

She bent down and, in a quivering voice, whispered, 'We need to be quiet.' She kissed him on the forehead.

He gazed up at the chimney, stark against the crisp blue morning sky. Flames roared out of its top and thick smoke curved away, catching the breeze. 'Where are we?' Feitel said. 'Is Father here?'

She squeezed his hand and he remembered not to speak. Her matted, brown hair was hanging over the collar of her coat. She smiled, revealing her special tooth – the one with the two gold fillings.

The crowd surged, tearing his hand from his mother's. His body was jostled and he tried to fight against the wave, which carried him away. He twisted, fell and screamed for her.

A volley of gunshots peppered the air. The crowd stopped and he stumbled back to his feet. His eyes hunted for her among a sea of women, all with long brown hair and long brown coats. He trembled, his teeth chattered and his heart hammered.

'Do not push!' someone shouted through a megaphone. 'You're being lined up for work selection. Stand still. Do not push.'

For a moment, the crowd settled and Feitel heard his mother calling him. He called back, 'Mama, Mama!'

He strained his ears and, perched on tiptoes, listened out for her reply. People began to yell out in fear and he couldn't hear her. He pushed forward. The crowd was packed tight, his head and shoulders hemmed in by knees, waists and suitcases.

He called again. 'Mama, Mama!' A few people drew closer to their cases and he threw himself into the gap they made.

She called out again, her voice a bit stronger: 'Feitel, Feitel!'

He shouted back and stepped forward; people stood aside, making way for an outstretched hand. The outstretched hand became an arm, followed by his mother's face, her full lips pursed with anxiety. Her hand dropped to his and she pushed her way through.

'Oh, Feitel,' she whimpered. She dropped to her knees, held him by his shoulders and fixed her dark eyes on his. 'Oh, my boy. Oh, my dear boy.' Her voice was melodic, warm and reassuring, though her face was ashen. She drew him close and rested her trembling cheek against his.

'Where are we?' he asked.

'I don't know. I'm trying to find out. Keep close to me,' she whispered. 'Promise me you'll keep close.'

'I will,' he replied. She grasped him by the wrist.

Another burst of gunfire cracked above their heads and the person on the megaphone ordered them to be silent.

The train's engine gave out its final hisses and sighs. Feitel lowered his head and kicked a few small stones into a heap. The crowd shuffled forward and he nudged the heap. Whenever the crowd stopped, he prodded the stones into different orders. When they drew level with the engine, the final wisps of steam were swept away by the same wind that carried the smoke from the chimney.

He studied the feet of a man and woman in front of them: his were clad in black socks, worn through at the heel, while hers were bare and tapped out a nervous rhythm. The man clasped her hand. Between their ancient bony arms, he could see a line of soldiers standing, guns at the ready.

A figure, dressed in a black uniform, surveyed them. His tunic buttons gleamed and a cross lay on his breast pocket. A side parting broke his swept-back blond hair. The man flicked a hand twice to his right.

The old couple in front of them, bent with age and cajoled by the guards, shuffled away, shaking.

'Oh my god,' his mother whispered.

They were now at the head of the queue and the man glanced them over. She tightened her grip on Feitel's wrist, raised his hands and offered them up. 'Look how long his fingers are,' she said. 'He's clever with them. He's strong. I am too. I'm a good worker. I can work all day and half the night.'

The man pointed. 'You follow that decrepit couple. The boy goes over there.'

'No,' she gasped, dropping his arm and covering her mouth.

Feitel tugged at her coat. She gulped hard then bent down and gripped him by his shoulders.

'Feitel,' she began, glancing to his right, where the man was now pointing to. 'See those people? Run after them and find somebody to look after you.' His mouth crumpled and a tear leaked from his eye. 'You need to be brave. Go now.'

He did not move. She reached forward and the edge of her thumb followed the tear down his cheek.

A guard stepped forward, hooked his mother to her left with his rifle and rattled it between their arms.

'Go,' she said, pushing him away.

2

The light was fading when Feitel and a group of other new arrivals were hustled into a dormitory hut. Naked bulbs, hanging from flex, cast dingy light across the room.

Some made their way to empty bunks while others milled around, unsure of what to do. Feitel crossed towards a window at the far end of the room, perching himself on the tailboard of a lower bunk. He peered out of the window in the hope he might catch sight of his mother but, amongst the shadows, cast by powerful lights beaming from the watchtowers, all he could see were guards on patrol with their dogs. The windows of the other huts were dark, the ground between them grey and worn.

The chimney, silhouetted against the darkness, blasted out flames, lighting its upper brickwork. Smoke, pale against the sky, drifted eerily away.

A hand settled on his shoulder, pressing the coarse material of his tunic down. He glanced up. A tall, shaven-headed man smiled down at him.

'What's your name?' the man asked.

A stab of dread struck his stomach as he remembered his mother's warnings about talking to strangers. His mind flashed back to when she wiped away his tear, telling him to find somebody to look after him.

'Feitel,' he replied.

'Mine's Leon Gruner,' the man said, his mouth breaking into a smile. 'Where are you from?'

'Berlin,' Feitel replied. 'Do you know where my mother is?'

His smile faded and his eyebrows drew together. 'When did you last see her?' His voice was low and serious.

'When we got off the train.' Sensing it was somehow significant, he added, 'A man made her go a different way.'

Leon nodded like he was confirming bad news.

'Will she come back for me?' he asked, bowing his head. He scuffed his foot on the wooden boards. He hoped somehow Leon held the key to her safe return.

'Feitel,' Leon said cautiously. 'This is a concentration camp in Poland. A lot of people die here. Do you understand that?'

The agonising pain of his mother's loss pierced his chest. Salty tears streamed down his cheeks, running into his mouth.

'Do you understand?' Leon asked, offering him a hand.

Feitel sniffed, drew up his bottom lip and blinked back his tears. He pushed Leon's hand away and faced the window.

Leon said, in a lighter voice, 'Tomorrow you can come with me to where we work. We call it Canada. Would you like to do that?'

Feitel lowered his head.

'It's where we sort through the cases people carried with them on the trains,' Leon added.

Feitel swallowed a lump in his throat. Leon was being kind, tempting him with something exciting. 'Why is it called Canada?'

Leon pondered for a moment. 'A few months ago, two prisoners arrived from Auschwitz. There, they called their sorting rooms Canada, and the name caught on here. It's a country where the people are rich and free.'

With pangs of guilt for having pushed Leon's hand away, Feitel turned to face him. 'Can we go there?'

Leon shook his head. 'No.'

Feitel, realising Leon meant there was no way out of the camp, replied, 'I don't want to die.'

Leon ran his palm down the back of his shaven head. 'Let's hope you don't.'

*

Through tear-filled eyes, Feitel stared out of the window,

tracking the moon as it rose above the camp.

Late in the evening, the door swung open and a beam of torchlight reflected off the window.

'You, get to your bunk!' a guard shouted.

Feitel, realising he should have found a bed, stiffened. 'I don't have one.'

The guard pounded towards him, his tunic flapping with the rhythmic motion of his gait. Feitel's heart froze and his stomach turned icy. He spun round and his eyes flicked across the bunks in search of a bed – each was a pigeonhole rammed with people glowering back at him. The guard grasped his arm in a vice-like grip, lifted him into the air and dumped him onto the rough boards of the nearest bunk.

'Always find a bed. And face me when you talk to me.'

The guard stomped off. With an aching arm and a bruised back, Feitel slid down between the bodies and the edge of the bunk. His hip pinched as it squashed against the boards.

'That's Otto Mark's space,' a boy said. 'He'll be back in a moment and he'll have you.'

'He always sleeps there,' another whispered.

'He collects the dead, and he'll collect you,' another added.

The whispers of the boys sent goosebumps shooting up Feitel's arms.

He lay awake amidst the grunts, snorts, coughs and cries of night terrors. Tears of loss pressed against his closed eyes; he wished and prayed for his mother's arms to cradle him. He remembered his first day at school, his mother leaving him behind, the hostility of the other boys – and her warm smile greeting him at the gates at the end of the day.

The door swung open and slammed shut again. Footsteps echoed down the hut and stopped at his bunk. Two hands slid beneath him and rolled him onto the other boys. His head hit the chest of one, his back hit the boards and his feet rested across another boy.

'Get out, this isn't your bunk,' one said.

Feitel didn't move. Elbows and knees were digging into him. They made room, keeping their blankets to themselves. He closed his eyes, praying for sleep to take him away from the loneliness and the cold.

He caught a sweet, sickly whiff from Otto's clothes. He tried to place it but couldn't remember where he had smelled it before. Cocking his head, he sniffed the unwashed bodies of the boys. Otto's scent was different.

Across the hut, a man began a deep and mournful chant in Hebrew. Others joined in. He longed for sleep to steal him away.

He remembered his father's words when he couldn't sleep. 'Think through your day, Feitel. Run it through your mind from start to finish and sleep will come.'

He began by recalling when he woke on the train, his body wrapped around his mother's feet as she reached down and stroked his brow. The air was stifling. Some people wailed, some banged the sides of the train, others screamed and pleaded for water. He remembered the brief exchanges his mother had with their new companions; the sobs of a family and the hushed whispers of his mother explaining their grandfather had been taken in the night; the pungent stench of urine, vomit and excrement; the long wait before the distant hiss of the steam engine; the jerk of the train as it clunked forward; people packed in, stood upright; how it ran for a few minutes until the engine let out a final, long hiss.

He thought about the unnerving clank of the wagon doors being slid open and the terror of the guards yelling, 'Out! Get out. Everybody out!'

He remembered the colour draining from his mother's face and the concern in her dark eyes as she wiped away his tear then pushed him away. Other memories thundered and raged through his mind: the men being ordered to throw their cases on a growing pile; men being beaten for hesitating; men being beaten for protesting; the series of barrack rooms they were forced to pass through; having to strip; and the piercing shame when he saw grown men naked.

Guards had prodded and poked their bare bodies as they jogged across a yard. A man, who cut his foot on a stone then stumbled forward and yelped with pain, was punched and kicked until he staggered back to his feet.

In the next room, Feitel's head was shaved, his dark brown locks tumbling to the floor. An ice-cold shower followed, and a dousing in powder pumped from a tube by a rotund female guard. She glared, unblinking, as they coughed and spluttered. Following that, he joined a long queue where they had to bend over to be examined using a pencil-thin torch.

The tattooist with the needle came next – a thickset man with a shaven head and a striped uniform. He'd grabbed Feitel's wrist and, without looking up, whispered, 'Any news from outside?'

Before Feitel could answer, the man in the queue behind replied. He was a towering giant with a protruding chin. 'The daily roundups are getting worse.'

The tattooist had nodded in resignation. As each dab of the needle bit into Feitel's arm, they continued their conversation. When the last digit was finished, he was waved towards a desk where a haggard-faced guard wrote entries in a book.

'Name?' the guard had asked.

'Feitel Scher.'

The guard wrote it in a book, glanced at Feitel's tattoo and wrote the number in a column next to his name. 'Go and stand by the door,' he ordered.

'Do you know where my mother is?'

The guard sneered. 'You'll see her soon enough.'

Feitel rubbed his arm to soothe the sting. The man with the large chin approached the desk, gave his name and held out his arm for the guard to record the number.

The guard stared at the tattoo, checked his book and glared at the tattooist. 'That's the same number as that boy,' he said, pointing towards Feitel. 'You've tattooed the same number twice.'

The tattooist sat up straight, terror flashing across his face. 'I can change it.'

'Get on with your work,' another guard, who appeared to be in charge, ordered.

The tattooist shrank back in his chair.

'Which Jew was tattooed first?' the man in charge asked.

Terror washed over Feitel, raising the fine hairs on the back of his neck.

The guard at the desk waved an arm towards Feitel. 'He was.'

'Right,' said the man in charge. 'He can go, but that one,' he added, stabbing a finger towards the prisoner with the large chin, 'can go to the chamber. Take him there, before they close up. I don't want any confusion.'

The man was dragged away, his screams piercing the air.

They were then ordered to another barrack. The men calmed as each was allocated a striped uniform with a yellow triangle stitched onto the chest. Feitel collected a set from the smallest pile. A guard glanced down at him and spat.

He'd queued for a cap and a pair of clogs. They had run out and he shivered as a soldier was sent to find cloth caps and cloth shoes, which were emptied from a hessian sack. Once he had pulled them on and straightened his cap, a guard divided them into groups.

His group was marched to this hut, pushed inside. The door slammed shut behind them. He'd stood and gaped at the rows of hollow-eyed men packed into bunks.

3

Feitel woke in the dormitory hut, shivering with cold and covering his nose to mask the acrid stench of unwashed bodies. Otto Mark had gone, but the other boys were still in the bunk. Leon's words, that his mother was dead, crept through him, filling his veins with icy tendrils. He squeezed his eyes shut, trying to hold back the tears welling in his eyes. But the tears broke through and he began to sob.

'Shut up,' one of the boys to his left whispered, 'otherwise I'll take you to the gas chamber.'

Feitel screwed up his eyes and clamped his mouth shut to control his sobbing. He remembered his father's words – when he'd cried, *Think of something else to take your mind off it*.

A lone wasp landed on the bedframe. He flicked it, tracked its pathetic progress, then dozed for a few minutes. When he opened his eyes again, he counted the slats of wood high above the roof timbers, hoping to get back to sleep.

The door crashed open. Feitel jumped and his mouth turned dry.

'Get in line,' a guard shouted.

The boys to his left clambered over him, their feet landing on his stomach, chest and face. One of them muttered, 'Muller again.'

Feitel rolled over the edge of the bunk and dropped down, smacking his feet onto the floorboards. He shuffled forward and joined the back of the line, shaking with cold and dread in case he did something wrong. Muller strutted down the line, jabbing his finger at the men and boys as he counted. Once satisfied, he sneered and ordered Feitel and the men to file out of the hut. The other boys remained.

In the cold morning air, Feitel recognised a smell. Sweet and nauseating in the sticky air. It was the same smell that hung on Otto's clothes.

They were marched to a barrack where a line of wooden tables ran down the middle. The floor was made of wooden planks with grit, gravel and earth trodden in. The windows, covered in filth, allowed the glimmer of the camp's floodlights to filter through as squares of pale light. Cobwebs clouded the corners of the roof.

A man in front of Feitel hesitated, as if choosing which side of the tables to walk down. A guard lurched forward, striking the side of his face. The man sidestepped a second strike, then, from the table, collected a cup of dark brown liquid and a small ration of bread.

With the guard now appeased, Feitel copied the man's every move – stood back as he stood back, sipped from his cup as he sipped from his cup and lowered his head to avoid the eyes of a guard before collecting his rations. He bit into the bread; it tasted stale and was difficult to chew.

'Hurry,' Muller shouted.

Feitel jumped and panic rose in the faces of those around him. He swallowed his bread, chased it down with the coffee and wiped his mouth on his sleeve.

The man in front of Feitel glanced around. In one swift movement, he shot out his hand and transferred a piece of bread to his pocket. Feitel froze. A feeling of dread crept up from his stomach; time stood still but no shout came from any of the guards.

The men edged forward and Feitel followed, his head hung low. They filed out into the overwhelming stench of the camp. A small amount of vomit rose into his mouth which he swallowed back down.

Muller kicked and spat as he marched them to a large workshop with rows of workbenches interspersed with pillars cut from roughly sawn wood. The floor was made from planks and strewn with sawdust. Naked light bulbs hung from braided flex. Wafts of stale air teased his nostrils.

A second guard – a lean, sharp-faced man – joined Muller.

'What are we doing today?'

'Teeth and money,' Muller said.

Each man made his way to a bench. Feitel stopped, his hands clammy and his shoulders tightening, not knowing where to go until the second guard pointed him towards a row of workbenches.

He eased forward, passing three rows of workers, and reached two free benches. Terrified of making the wrong choice, he stopped, blood pounding inside his skull.

'Yes, that one,' the guard said, pointing to the bench nearest to Feitel.

4

Muller stood over Feitel's bench, a canvas bag gripped in his hand. He untied the string around its neck and tipped out wads of banknotes and coins, scraping out the final few with his shovel of a hand.

'Sort it into piles,' he ordered. 'One for each type of note and one for each type of coin. And *don't* get any ideas, boy.'

Feitel busied himself, convinced Muller's eyes were never more than a blink away from him. He made piles of different notes and piles of different coins. He pictured the coins as towering buildings and the notes as the roads below.

The bench was covered in fine grey dust and when he was finished, he scraped it into a pile. He drew the dust towards him, coaxed it over the edge of the bench and scuffed it onto the floor.

A man with a crooked prison cap and deep-set eyes collected the piles of money. 'They'll beat you for cleaning the bench,' the man whispered, 'and they'll beat you for not cleaning it. Best save your energy for the beating.'

Feitel stared ahead, unsure of what to say or do. In his periphery, he was aware of Muller approaching with a small hessian sack. He stopped at Feitel's bench, opened the drawstring around the sack's neck and tipped out the contents. A pile of teeth scattered across the bench, some white, some yellow. Each had a forked root and a gold filling.

'Remove the gold,' Muller ordered.

Feitel lifted his hand, covering his mouth to stifle a scream. He did not want to touch the teeth but he had no choice. His heart quickened as he reached forward and plucked one from the bench. It was dull and hard. His stomach churned at the yellow enamel and the long, twisted root. He swallowed back sour-tasting bile. Vowing not to touch the root, he selected a small file from the tools on the bench and attempted to prise out the sunken filling. His right hand, clasping the file, quivered each time he stabbed at the filling and, try as he might to keep the tooth steady with his other hand, it slid all over the bench.

Muller approached his bench shouting, 'No, no, no!'

Feitel's stomach retracted and a small amount of pee wetted his crotch with an unwelcome warmth.

Muller grabbed a hammer and thrust it in front of his face. 'Tap the tooth until it breaks.'

Muller dropped the hammer, sending it clattering onto the bench. Feitel jumped and, hands trembling, picked it up. Muller stormed away.

Feitel took a deep breath and waited until his hand steadied, then brought the hammer down on the tooth. The tooth broke and so began the pile of gold on his bench.

Feitel found a rhythm and worked without pause or a break. He selected a tooth with his left hand, placed it down, cracked it, added the gold to one pile and swept the enamel onto another. He learnt to judge the swing of the hammer by the state of the tooth. And when he'd become skilled, when the job no longer required thought, when his mind was no longer so occupied, the chill memories of those last moments with his mother knotted his stomach, weakening his knees.

'Don't pause, boy,' a man from behind him whispered. 'Muller is a hawk. Any change in rhythm and he'll have you.'

Feitel glanced up. Muller's eyes were upon him. He picked a tooth. It had two deep-set gold fillings – identical to his mother's. He staggered back a step. He wanted to ask somebody, to know for sure whether it was hers as his mind quivered in terror. But there was nobody to ask.

He rolled the tooth between his fingers. The two points of gold gleamed on the yellow enamel. It was similar to the fillings his father had been proud to pay for. He remembered how his mother would show him the tooth whenever he asked.

He slipped it into his pocket and glanced up – Muller was staring at him. Feitel plucked another tooth, but his hand shook so much he raised the hammer by no more than an inch. He had to strike the tooth to get Muller to look away. Shaking, he forced his arm up and pushed down hard. The hammer cracked onto the tooth.

'You!' Muller shouted.

Feitel's head shot up and, feeling dizzy, he clutched the edge of the bench with one hand.

'Yes, you,' Muller continued, pointing, to Feitel's relief, towards a middle-aged man with marks and pfennigs piled high on his bench. The man trembled and shrunk. 'What is your name?'

'Miklos Wiesel,' the man whispered.

The workshop fell silent. Tools lay motionless or were suspended in mid-air as each pair of eyes turned to the man.

Muller now stood over Wiesel. 'Turn out your pockets.'

Wiesel flinched. Muller grabbed him, pushed him to the floor and pulled a five-mark note from his pocket. He stuck his face in front of Wiesel's and yelled, 'You've been stealing!' The veins on Muller's thick neck bulged and his fist tightened around the note.

Wiesel tipped his head back but Muller caught him by the collar. The second guard joined them and Muller showed him the note. 'Squad Leader Baer, we have a thief.'

The colour drained from Wiesel's face, his hands shook, and his teeth chattered. 'That... that money is mine. It belongs to me. I-I br-brought it to the camp with me.'

'No money is yours. Jew money belongs to the Reich.'

'It is *mine*. I earned it outside.'

'Jewish money comes from theft. You ate while we starved. Now you starve while we eat. You didn't earn it outside, you stole it.' Muller tightened his grip once more and let go.

'No,' Wiesel whimpered.

Muller's face glistened with sweat. 'How do you look so well fed?'

Wiesel trembled. 'I'm not well fed.'

'You eat *more*,' Muller said.

'I *don't* eat more...' Yet his protest waned and the words tailed off.

In a second, Muller plucked his gun from its holster, spun Wiesel around and pushed the gun into the back of Wiesel's head. He cocked the weapon, the click echoing across the silent workshop. Wiesel trembled and his eyes widened.

The crack of the bullet echoed around the room, echoed off every bench, every wall, the ceiling and the floor.

Feitel raised his hands to his ringing ears. Wiesel slumped backward. Blood spread in a circular pool around him and turned the sawdust on the floor crimson, lifting specks that floated with the tide of death.

Muller straightened himself, glared at the workers and thrust out his chest. 'Work, damn you! Work!'

Wiesel's body twitched until death held it still.

A whisper came from behind Feitel. 'A man may swat a wasp in front of others, whereas alone he might let it go.' The words sounded unnatural, like those his father read out from magazines on a Sunday afternoon.

Muller kicked open the door. 'Baer, get him to the crematorium.' He pointed to two men working at nearby benches. 'You and you, carry the body.'

Feitel knew he had to return the tooth from his pocket but he hesitated, not taking the opportunity while Muller and Baer were distracted. Nor did he while the two men dragged the body, head first, towards the door. Instead, he shivered as Wiesel's cloth tunic rubbed across the floor like the sea running up a beach.

A guard was patrolling the grey ground outside – he stopped and stared at the body being dragged through the doorframe. Wiesel's tunic rode up, exposing his bare midriff. His right shoe was missing and, when his foot reached the threshold, his crooked toes and a bunion were silhouetted before they were dragged from the step. Baer exited with the men, slamming the door shut behind him.

Muller strutted down an aisle of workbenches, running a hand through his thick brown hair. 'Work, damn you! Work!' he ordered.

Each time Feitel broke another tooth, swept the enamel into one pile and shuffled the gold into another, the image of the pocketed tooth flashed across his mind. What if they had counted the teeth? What if it fell out and gave him away? He longed for another opportunity to return it but the eyes of ten thousand guards, and a thousand prisoners, willing to give him away, pierced his imagination.

As Feitel broke open the last tooth, Muller collected another small hessian bag from a bench near the door. Feitel took his chance, reached into his pocket, seized the tooth and placed it on the bench. He straightened his neck.

Muller stood over him. Feitel's hands trembled afresh, and he wondered if he'd been seen. But all the guard did was scoop the gold into the empty sack.

Muller's eyes fell on the solitary tooth left on the bench. 'Why have you stopped when there's a tooth left?'

Feitel quivered. 'I don't know.'

'Break it!' Muller shouted.

Feitel hesitated.

'*Break* it.'

'I think it's…' Feitel said, his voice fading.

'You think it's what?'

Feitel lowered his head.

'Break it!' Muller shouted again.

The workshop fell silent. Everybody was staring at him.

He remembered Miklos Wiesel and began to tremble.

'Break it! smash it!' Muller roared, thrusting the hammer into Feitel's hand.

Feitel lifted it and brought it down with one sharp tap. The tooth broke. Muller collected the two gold nuggets, poured out the new bag of teeth and ordered Feitel to continue.

*

Feitel kept his head bowed, only glancing up from his task at the bench when Baer and the two men returned. His hands throbbed and he longed for the work to end. After what felt like another hour, Muller checked his watch, nodded towards Baer and called, 'Halt!'

Feitel stepped towards the door, recoiling when he realised nobody else had moved. Muller and Baer moved amongst the workbenches, collecting the gold and money. The gold was tipped into hessian bags, the paper money rolled into bundles and banded, the coins placed into separate bags.

They were marched, at a jogging pace, to another barrack. Feitel collected a bowl of watery soup from a side table and found a place to sit.

The man opposite Feitel lifted a wooden spoon to his lips. His nails were grey and pitted and his tunic slipped back to reveal a yellow, skeletal arm. 'Turnip today.'

'Do we have a choice?' Feitel asked, and the men around him laughed quietly as if they did not want to alert the guards.

'Yes, we've a choice. We eat what we're given or we starve.'

'Is it not always turnip?' Feitel said.

'It's been cabbage for as long as any of us can remember. Turnip is a change. Drink it before the guards move us on.'

Feitel fell silent and ladled the soup into his mouth.

They were marched to the latrines then to the dormitory hut.

*

The stale air of the hut was cold. Feitel's workmates filed to their bunks. Conversations murmured as they began to settle. Otto Mark lay alone, puffing out small, misty clouds of breath.

'Where are the other boys?' Feitel asked.

Otto stared at the wooden ceiling. 'They've gone.'

'How long have you been here?'

'Mind your own business,' Otto said. He rolled over and turned his back to Feitel.

Feitel did not fear Otto. Somehow, he understood he sought solitude rather than argument.

A voice spoke from behind him. 'He's been here longer than any of us.'

Feitel swung round and was thankful to see Leon Gruner. His mouth broke into a smile.

'Anybody who's been here a few days,' Leon continued, 'is an old-timer, expert in the trains and the signs from the chimney. Otto Mark has been here longer than that. Haven't you?'

Otto didn't answer. Instead his body tensed, pulling his tunic taut across his back.

'Don't ask him what he does though,' Leon said. 'Don't ask him how come he's better fed than us.'

'Why?'

'In every hut, there's a man who has done a deal with the devil. A man might do awful things to gain another minute of life, but to gain another day, week or a year requires despicable things. Doesn't it, Otto?' He addressed Feitel: 'They can't just replace a man like that with another off the train.'

Leon's dark eyebrows and dark eyes were a perfect match. Feitel admired his confident expression.

'I want to keep this bunk,' Feitel said.

'Nobody is allocated their own bunk,' Leon said. 'But the others will get used to where you sleep and won't bother you.'

'They didn't want to share it with me last night.'

'The thing is, Feitel, a shared enemy doesn't always make somebody your friend.'

Feitel didn't comprehend what Leon meant. 'Where is Canada?'

'It's where you work.' He leaned his thin arm against the boards of the upper bunk. He smiled and added, 'It's also a country way across the sea, above America.'

'How can I get there?'

Leon chuckled and his tunic swayed over his thin frame. 'You have to head west to Berlin, then Paris, then perhaps England. There, you can board a boat for Canada. But—'

'Can we go?' Feitel asked.

Leon hesitated. 'It's not... Well, it's not easy to escape. And if we did, we'd not be free long and...'

'And what?' Feitel said.

'No, nothing.'

'Please tell me.'

Leon pursed his lips as Feitel waited. 'Well,' Leon said, raising his eyebrows, 'if you're caught, you don't get a second chance. They kill you.'

Feitel was silent for a moment, his hopes dashed. He said, 'If you could go, can I come?'

'How old are you?' Leon asked.

Feitel thought to lie, to say he was older. However, he chose the truth. 'Ten.'

Leon closed his eyes and gave a slow nod, smiling through tight lips.

5

The cold poked Feitel awake from a deep, long dream. He'd been at home with his parents but shades of consciousness had entered the story, and with it, tiny elements of unease. The hut came into focus and bit by bit the dream disassembled until all that remained was a vague set of disjointed fragments. He grabbed at a thin blanket and drew it under his chin. Its warmth gave him a moment of comfort.

Feitel recalled sweet memories of his home: the Sunday walk, collecting flowers with his mother; the train ride to the lakeside beach; the earthy pine aroma as they gained height on the wooded tracks and the musky-sweet smell of the decaying autumn leaves. With the seasons, the surroundings varied – the flowers of spring, the high ferns of summer and sweet chestnuts in the autumn.

Condensation dripped down the window, as if the glass itself was melting. Feitel waited, breath held, while droplets gained weight and took off downwards, pooling on the lower frame. He reached up to his cheek, gathering up his soft skin with the edge of his finger. He remembered his mother wiping away his tear when they said goodbye.

The hut door crashed open. Guards ordered them into a line. One guard marched up and down, stabbing a finger at each prisoner as he counted them. When he was satisfied, he gave the order for them to file out.

They crossed the open ground, a line of guards passing to their right. One broke off, scuffing his way towards Feitel. The other guards sniggered as Feitel flinched and recoiled from him.

'Nobody is going to hurt you here, little boy,' one guard said, a man of around twenty with blond curls protruding from below his cap.

'What are you frightened of?' a darker-skinned guard

said. 'Not us, surely?'

'I expect he misses his mother,' the first guard said, his tone mocking.

The darker-skinned guard sneered. 'You'll see her soon enough, Jew boy.'

Their voices grew distant as they moved away and Feitel's pounding heart settled. He remembered his mother's wise words: to take a few deep breaths whenever he was frightened. He sensed her presence. He glanced around at the foreboding grey of the camp.

They passed through the breakfast barrack – he recognised the cobwebs and dirt of the day before. Today, the bread was a bit fresher, the coffee warmer.

'You'll get used to it,' a voice whispered. Feitel looked over his shoulder and was relieved to see Leon. 'It's a lucky day today.'

'Was yesterday the worst it can be?' Feitel said.

Leon raised his eyebrows and pursed his lips. 'No, my friend. No. We're lucky to have breakfast two days in a row.' He ruffled the cap on Feitel's head.

Feitel remembered his mother's last words to him. *See those people? Run after them and find somebody to look after you.* Feitel straightened his cap and half smiled.

When they left the breakfast barrack, Leon pointed to the barbed wire surrounding the camp. 'Keep away from that.'

'Why?' Feitel said.

He pointed to the towers. 'The guards will shoot anybody that goes near it.'

He tried to stay with Leon but, beyond the breakfast barrack, they became separated as the guards prodded and cajoled the prisoners. He searched for Leon in the array of heads and bodies until an icy blast of wind struck his face. He bowed his head and followed the feet of the man in front. When they reached the draughty interior of the workshop, his eyes darted around, seeking Leon out.

Amongst the gaunt, drawn faces, he caught sight of him, a brief glimpse of his ears and the side of his head. Joy surged through him but, not wanting to attract the attention of the guards, he dropped his gaze and surveyed the tools, the dust and the scores on the bench he remembered from yesterday. He longed to be anywhere other than here.

He fought back tears. The bench of Miklos Wiesel was empty. A solitary figure hesitated at the door. His narrow, shaven head stood tall on his slender shoulders. His tunic cuffs were rolled back and his long hands and thin fingers rested on his thighs.

Baer pointed him towards the empty bench. Feitel wondered why the new man had been chosen. Feitel prayed the guard would not silence him with a bullet like they had with Miklos Wiesel.

Feitel admired the distant figure of Leon across the workshop. He stood with his back straight and his head held high amongst a sea of dropped shoulders and bowed heads.

Muller and Baer moved around the room issuing orders and assigning work. Feitel hoped he'd be spared teeth and money. His palms turned sweaty and he slipped his hands inside his pockets, checking for illegal contraband.

Muller emptied a basket of clothes onto his bench. 'Buttons and fasteners in one pile, cloth in another.'

Feitel picked up a dusty pair of black scissors and snipped off buttons, cutting away the material around the fasteners. Sometimes the cloth was easy to snip, other times it buckled within the scissors and he had to learn to hold the material taut when he snipped.

After about an hour, he glanced around at the nearby benches and was relieved his pile of buttons and fasteners had grown bigger than anybody else's. He took a deep breath, then wondered if this was wise, whether he should slow down and not risk being singled out by the guards or disliked by his neighbours. At the bench next to him, deft fingers separated the cloth from the back of the fasteners.

Panic snatched at his stomach – he'd been leaving the material attached. He scooped the pile towards him and glanced around. With rapid finger movements, he unpicked the material from the fasteners and removed the cotton from the loops of the buttons.

When he'd caught up, he patted his pockets in case a button, a fastener, a hook or an eye had slipped into one of them. He continued checking his pockets until he had to chant silently to himself in an attempt to stop. But the urges became stronger and, each time Muller's gaze was averted, he checked his pockets.

Around midmorning, Muller glared at him and shouted, 'You!'

The men in the workshop stopped, as if they were holding their breath.

'Yes, you,' Muller shouted, pointing at Feitel. 'Don't stare at the others; stare at your work.' With that, he smashed his fist onto the nearest bench, causing the man working there to stagger back.

One by one, the men resumed their tasks until the cacophony of scraping and tapping returned. Feitel lowered his head and pressed his groin against the bench but was unable to stem a trickle of warm pee which dribbled down his leg, wetting his shoe. Panicking that it might show, he continued to press against the bench and busied himself with the scissors.

As he pulled another garment from the pile, an erratic recollection of his mother's wardrobe flew through his mind. In the chaotic mix of his memories, each of her garments disappeared until he could only recall the last dress she wore. He frantically sifted through the pile of clothes, wondering if he'd be brave enough to keep a button.

His mother's dress was not there, not amongst the coats, the trousers, the shirts, the blouses or the dresses.

*

In the early afternoon the door of the workshop creaked

open. The heavy face of a guard was sandwiched between his helmet and his collar.

Muller strutted over to him and nodded, tight-lipped, as the messenger whispered to him. Straightening himself up, Muller turned to face the workers. 'Put down your tools and make your way to the parade ground.'

Unsure of where the parade ground was, Feitel followed the other men filing out from behind their workbenches.

The sky was grey outside and a light wind forced an icy breeze through his tunic. Men spilt from the other huts and congregated in the open area next to the main camp gates.

The guards goaded, pushed and prodded them into a tight crescent around the front of two army lorries with long bonnets.

The lorries had split windscreens – gigantic eyes frowning over the flared nostrils of their broad wings. Wooden planks, forming a platform, were perched between their roofs. A noose dangled from the branch of a tree that stretched out over the top of the lorries and the platform.

The guards used their rifle barrels to tip up the head of anybody who dared to look down. A soldier in an important-looking uniform climbed a ladder to the platform. Two guards followed, pushing and prodding a dark-haired man ahead of them, whose face was dominated by a claw-shaped nose.

'For those of you who don't know me,' boomed the soldier, his voice carrying unaided across the silent witnesses, 'I am the commandant of this camp. I've ordered you here to witness what happens to a man who breaks the camp rules. This man had a privileged job in our kitchens.'

A guard grasped the man's chin and jerked it back, revealing his Adam's apple.

'This morning, he stole a loaf of bread,' said the soldier. 'He has stolen the food from your mouths and for this he will be punished.'

Feitel wondered how the man had stolen food from his

mouth.

The commandant stood aside. The two guards pushed the man towards the rope. The man dug his heels into the platform, trying to resist, but the guards grabbed his arms. He was straightened up and the rope placed around his neck. The guards tightened the noose, crushing his Adam's apple, then bound his hands and ankles. His eyes were filled with terror, widened and staring.

The guards stepped back. The commandant spoke again, this time addressing the prisoner: 'Do you want to say you're sorry before the sentence is carried out?'

The man was silent for a moment. He spoke in Yiddish. '*Violence is the henchman of prejudice—*'

'Shut up,' the commandant shouted. Stabbing his finger towards the crowd, he added, 'Otherwise I'll hang them all.'

The man fell silent and stood, hands bound. Feitel rubbed the back of his neck, imagining the roughness of the rope drawn against his own skin.

As the commandant and the two guards descended the ladder, the lorries were started and their engines revved up. The condemned man shook and vomit erupted from his mouth.

With grating gears, the two lorries reversed and the platform tilted and tumbled away. The man's feet kicked out in a frantic search for the planks. When the rope jerked tight, his body came to an abrupt halt, recoiled and settled. His hands rose, as if he were trying to free himself. His head tipped forward and his body shook. He twisted and slowed until Feitel could not tell if the movements were the last vestiges of life or the breeze.

A patch of wet expanded around the man's crotch, trickled down his trousers, dribbled over his foot and onto the planks that lay strewn across the ground.

6

A whisper circulated through the workshop that it was snowing. Feitel glanced at the window. Snowflakes sank to the ground in the fading afternoon light. He returned to his task and, as Muller switched the lights on, he again checked his pockets in case a buckle, button or fastener had found its way there.

He worked until the tools on his bench trembled with the vibrations of an approaching train. Its whistle pierced the air as it clunked to a halt.

Muller straightened his back, checked his watch and shouted, 'Halt.'

The men downed their tools. Wagons concertinaed together with haunting rumbles. A moment of silence was shattered by a barrage of noise as dogs yelped, feet pounded and wagon doors slid open. While a megaphone blared orders to disembark, Baer directed the workers to form a single-file line.

Muller strolled back and forth, striking and kicking until the men were lined up. He gave the order to move, and Baer opened the door.

They filed from the workshop into the cold night air and marched in a line past the train, which was spilling its cargo of wretched people onto the snow-clad ground. A guard, dressed in an immaculate tunic, held a pistol against a boy's head.

A woman, dressed in a thick overcoat, pleaded with the guard. 'He's only a boy.'

The pistol glinted under the stark floodlights. The air cracked with a bullet and the boy dropped at the woman's feet. She buckled to her knees; the guard grabbed her collar and wrenched her away. Half standing, she swung her arm and smacked him on his right cheek.

'My boy, my boy! Why did you kill my boy?' she

shrieked, thrusting her bent arms up and down. 'My boy, my boy! Why did you kill him?'

Her screams echoed off the huts, off the fence and off the train. The guard allowed her to repeat herself one more time, then raised his gun to her head and fired. She buckled to the ground, her torso draping over her son.

Feitel held his breath as the guard wiped the end of his gun, returned it to its holster and brushed down his tunic. A firm hand gripped his shoulder.

He flinched but a voice reassured him, 'Don't worry, Feitel. It's only Leon.'

*

The dormitory hut filled with men returning from their work. Leon followed Feitel to his bunk and propped himself up against its wooden frame.

'Why did that man kill the lady and her boy?' Feitel asked, looking up.

As a man clambered onto the top bunk, Leon took his cap off and straightened it in his hands. 'It isn't easy to explain.'

'Why?' Feitel said, puzzled.

Leon pondered this. 'Were you and your family called names?'

'Yes,' Feitel replied, lowering his head.

A few men stopped their conversations and listened.

'By people who weren't Jewish?' Leon said, his voice suggesting there were more questions to follow.

Feitel nodded.

'Were your people made to live away from those people?'

'My father refused to move and was taken away,' Feitel said. 'I hid with my mother in our basement.'

Leon raised his eyebrows. 'How long were you there for?'

Feitel shrugged. 'I don't know. I had two birthdays.'

Leon nodded. 'The thing is,' he said, returning to his original train of thought, 'it began with name-calling, then we were made to live apart from everybody else, then they started to kill us. That's how hate works.'

And the men who were listening nodded.

7

Distant explosions rumbled through the night, and men whispered that American planes were bombing German cities to the west. Feitel managed to drift back to sleep, waking before dawn, gripped by hunger and cold but warmed by a dream he had had about his mother. Although he knew she was dead, he could still sense the warmth of her soft touch as it met the tear rolling down his cheek.

He wondered if she could still feel his tear when death came. Lying on the bunk, he rubbed his damp eyes, and in that instant the camp stole from him the memory of which eye had spilled a tear. He thought hard but he could not picture it. His skin still tingled with her touch, although the memory of which cheek it was had gone. His mind threw up a wall. The harder he tried to remember, the more the wall grew until misery jabbed and pitted his stomach.

He lowered himself from the bunk. His arms ached from the previous day's work and he was weak from lack of food. He crossed to the window to see how much snow had fallen and gazed out onto a thick blanket of white. He remembered the erstwhile excitement of childhood when his mother allowed him to play outside, never caring how soaked he became from a sleeve or boot full of snow. And how his father chastised him in mocking tones before drying him off. He'd take him outside again to build a snow cave in a bank behind their house. As they snuggled inside the cave, his father would tell him how, in the last war, they kept warm by making snow caves in the trenches.

His focus returned to the dawn light of the camp and the joy of remembering slipped away. He flicked through the memories again, the snow, his mother, his father, until they faded and all that remained was the pain of remembering.

He wiped his misty breath from the window. A line of

men, walking in single-file, crossed the snow between the huts. The third man to the end dropped to the ground, balanced on his knees and twisted onto the snow. The second from the back stooped to help him but was pushed on by the boot of the last man: a guard. As Feitel tried to make out what had happened, the hut's door swung open and Baer shouted at them to get ready.

The workers in the hut shuffled towards the door, Feitel joining the back of them.

Muller followed Baer into the hut and strolled up and down the line three times, making his daily count.

'Four missing,' Muller called out while Baer examined the bunks and counted the dead.

'Four dead,' Baer said, confirming Muller's tally.

Muller pointed to the two men at the head of the queue. 'You and you, help Squad Leader Baer.'

He opened the door and the rest of them filed out, one by one, across the snow. The rays of the morning sun shone through the barren trees into the camp.

Feitel shivered, the cold biting through his tunic. They marched, passing the place where the man he'd seen from the hut window had sunk to the ground. It was marked by a line of blood, ending in no more than a few dots. There was a mix of footprints and a depression where his body had been dragged away.

By Feitel's foot were the imprints of a small bird and a half-smoked cigarette, sunk into its own snow grave. With each wisp of wind that crossed the camp, the tip of the cigarette glowed with a red ember.

Feitel counted the line of men in front of him, counted the sticks of arms swinging in baggy sleeves, counted the stooped heads and shoulder blades that poked through the striped material until he recognised the protruding ears of Leon Gruner.

A mute baton of unease passed through the line of men

as they were marched past the workshop to the main gates. Muller stopped and spoke to the guard: a conversation Feitel could not hear. The guard clicked his heels, nodded and called to his fellow gatekeeper to open up.

Feitel tensed as the wire-clad, wooden-framed gates buckled against the snow. His feet ached from the icy ground. Snow-covered rail tracks stretched into the distance; he shuddered at the thought of what lay ahead.

Muller ordered them to keep moving and, as they traipsed through the gates onto the snow-clad train tracks, he pointed to a line of shovels propped up against a snowdrift. 'Clear the tracks.'

Each prisoner took a shovel until only six remained: one for each of the dead and one for each of the two men who had helped Baer remove their bodies.

Muller offered them no plan. It was simple work, the snow light and fluffy. Each scrape of the shovel left the rails coated in no more than a fine powder. Feitel, relieved by how easy it was, worked his way along the line of men until he reached Leon.

'Careful,' Leon whispered, as Feitel caught the end of his shovel. 'We don't want to attract Muller's attention.' And with that he pulled a piece of bread from his pocket, tore it in two and handed one half to Feitel.

Feitel peered at the bread. 'Where's it from?'

Leon spoke in a hurried whisper. 'The man next to me died in the night. I took it from his pocket. Take it, it's yours.'

'What are those black things on it?' Feitel pulled a face.

Leon studied it. 'Only lice. Shake it, they'll come off.'

Feitel hesitated.

'They won't hurt you,' Leon added. 'Quick, eat it before Muller sees you. We didn't get supper or breakfast.'

Feitel shook the bread and stuffed it into his mouth. His jaw ached as he chewed and swallowed. 'Why didn't we get breakfast?'

'There's no reason why. Some days we do and some we don't,' Leon whispered. 'There's never enough to feed everybody.'

'Will we go back to the workshop later?'

'I don't know,' Leon replied, scraping a rail track with his shovel. 'I was worried when they marched us past it. Sometimes when men are marched out of the camp without breakfast they're never seen again.'

'Oh.'

'I'm sorry, Feitel. I wish it could be different. I always imagined that if they were about to kill us, we could all overpower the guards.'

'Why don't we?' Feitel said.

Leon smiled and ruffled Feitel's cap. 'We'd all need to act at the same time. It'd be impossible to plan. Our only plan is hope.'

They fell silent and continued to shovel snow. Feitel, worried Leon was cross with him for being ungrateful for the bread, thought hard until he found a question to test his mood.

'Can we escape from here?'

'I doubt it,' Leon said. 'Our clothes are thin, the day is bright, Muller has a gun and the camp has dogs. But we can dream.'

'Does it snow in Canada?' Feitel said.

Leon smiled. 'Only in the winter.'

Feitel chuckled. 'Which way is Canada?'

'Follow the tracks. They lead west.'

'All the way?'

'No, but if you ever get the chance, follow the tracks. They'll get you to Berlin. That's a start. Maybe you could find your old house.'

Leon glanced towards Muller. 'Watch out.'

Muller glowered at them. 'Silence!'

Feitel staggered backwards. Leon grabbed his shoulder and steadied him.

Muller's hand went towards his holster, but he was interrupted by Baer returning with the two men who'd taken the dead to the crematorium. 'What took you so long?' Muller asked, scowling.

'We had to make two trips,' Baer said, above the scrape of shovels and the soft thud of snow landing in piles, 'and there was a queue at the crematorium.'

'Why didn't you leave the bodies outside?'

Baer shook his head. 'Not in the open. The commandant doesn't permit it.'

Muller gave a sarcastic sniff but said no more while the two men, each now armed with a shovel, joined the lines. As they cleared snow, Feitel followed Baer's gaze along the track, along the pine-needle canopy until the track swept left and out of sight. The rich blue sky was framed by snow glistening on the high branches of the trees. A small amount pattered onto the ground like quiet applause.

'Don't stand and stare, work!' Muller ordered.

Feitel began to shovel.

8

A low rumble came from the direction of the camp. Feitel stopped scooping the snow and leaned against his shovel. Leon placed a hand on his shoulder.

'What is it?' Feitel said.

'I think it's a lorry,' Leon whispered.

'Is it coming to get us?'

'I doubt it. It'll be another hour before the light fades. It's best we keep shovelling.'

Feitel copied his friend and scooped snow from the tracks. The growl of the lorry drew closer and a stir went through the men. One by one, they straightened their backs as the lorry, straddling the right-hand rail, ploughed through the piles of snow they'd heaped by the tracks.

It pulled to a halt in front of the men, brakes grating, its wheels caked with snow. The engine ran on for a few seconds, the bonnet shuddering. Feitel coughed as whiffs of hot oil caught his nostrils.

Not a bird, man or a shovel could be heard. The men fixed their eyes on the two figures positioned to the driver's right: the commandant and a short dark-haired man in civilian clothes.

The commandant stepped from the passenger side.

Muller clicked his heels together. 'Heil Hitler.'

'Heil Hitler,' the commandant replied before signalling for Muller to follow him.

They crossed the tracks and dropped down the slope to the soft flat snow edging the woods.

As Muller and the commandant conversed, the driver wound down his window. Feitel sniffed and for a moment, burning tobacco masked the sweet, sticky stench of the camp. The driver glowered at the men. He lifted his right hand to his neck and, with his hand lying flat, made a throat-slash gesture.

Muller climbed back up the bank, his right leg sinking deep into the snow. Baer stepped forward to help him but Muller flicked away his outstretched hand. After hauling himself up onto the tracks, he ordered the men to get into line. The men fell in and Baer paced along, counting them while Muller helped the commandant up the slope.

Before Baer could finish his count, Muller shouted, 'Walk in silence to the back of the lorry.'

Leon hesitated.

'Walk!' Muller ordered, kicking snow in the direction of the men.

They hurried to the back of the lorry. It was the smell that first struck Feitel – not the sickly smell of the camp, nor the woody odour of the driver's cigarette, nor the heavy fumes from the lorry. Instead, it was a smell that he hadn't expected: soup. Three galvanised vats, dented and dirty, stood above the dropped tailboard.

Some of the soup had spilt in transit and splashed onto the outer sides of the vats. Feitel did not care – the watery liquid was sustenance.

The men were fair and equal; no order was needed. When each had taken his turn, the soup was divided into half ladles so nobody was denied a second scoop.

When the soup was finished, and the vats tilted so that every last drop had been poured and drunk, Muller ordered them into line. 'Walk past the truck to the tracks ahead.'

As Feitel passed the driver's door, the cigarette end was tossed into the snow. Before it could melt its own grave, the men scrabbled for it. The victor rewarded himself with several puffs before the crowd murmured for their share.

At the front of the lorry, Muller shouted, 'Stop! Turn and face to the right.'

The short, dark-haired man in civilian clothes had alighted from the passenger side and was busy erecting a tripod.

'Baer,' Muller continued, 'spread them at regular intervals and bring the smallest to the front.'

Feitel trembled; his mouth turned bone-dry. Was this the end? Would he, at the front, be shot first?

Leon whispered, 'It was a trick. The soup was a trick.'

'Silence!' Muller shouted. 'The commandant wants a photograph of you clearing the tracks.'

Leon exhaled a deep sigh.

The dark-haired man attached a camera to the tripod, adjusted the lens, slid a plate into its midriff and flicked the black cloth over his head.

Muller ordered them to bend forward and shovel, only calling a halt when the man raised his hand from under the black cloth, and said, 'That's it.'

He dismantled his camera apparatus, placing the tripod and camera in the lorry. He hauled himself up into the cab while the driver remained still, hands clasped to the wheel.

The commandant climbed inside the vehicle and showed his thanks to Muller with a raised hand.

Muller snapped his heels and saluted. 'Heil Hitler.'

The driver started the engine, which gave a lazy, low growl. The silence of the tree-lined tracks was broken by the angry revving of the engine as the driver thrust the lorry back and forth through a turn.

Baer and Muller entered into conversation. 'The sun sets in an hour,' Baer said. 'That means we'll march them back in the dark.'

Muller stood between the tracks, legs splayed, surveying the line of workers. 'We'll now stop for the day. Follow me back to the camp. Squad Leader Baer will follow from the rear. And there will be no meal this evening as the commandant was generous enough to bring food to you.'

9

After they had cleared the snow on the railway tracks, Muller led the march back to the camp. Feitel shivered as an icy wind tore into his legs.

'Try and walk on the sleepers,' Leon whispered, 'otherwise the stones will dig into your feet.'

Feitel glanced up, grateful Leon was carrying both their shovels, one across each shoulder. 'Why didn't the man who took our picture wear a uniform?'

'I would say he was one of us,' Leon said. 'Jewish, but with Nazi friends who are allowing him to live.'

'He didn't have a gun either.'

'He still shot us,' Leon joked, and Feitel chuckled.

Each time they rounded a bend in the track, Feitel prayed the camp gates would appear. Twice he caught the camp's putrid scent before the stench became so sharp he could taste it.

When the camp came into view, Feitel exhaled a sigh of relief. Snow had drifted against the wire fence and their workshop and the dormitory huts were silhouetted against the greying sky.

A murmur of relief rippled through the prisoners as they passed through the gates and cast their shovels into a pile.

Something whistled above their heads and, a split second later, their workshop exploded in a mass of splintering wood and shattering glass. As the men dived to the ground, Leon gripped Feitel's arm and dragged him down.

A sharp and sweet whiff of burnt sulphur rose high in Feitel's nostrils. 'What is it?' he asked, taking short breaths.

'A shell,' Leon said, panting. 'Somebody fired a shell into the camp.'

Guards rushed out of the huts and gazed up at the sky. Others sprang out with handguns, shouting ceaseless orders. Doors opened, slammed, crashed on their hinges. Men poured out. Dogs barked as the prisoners staggered back to their feet in silence.

Baer shifted his legs, as if unsure of which way to run. 'What was it? Where did it come from?'

Muller surveyed the sky, his eyes wide with fury. 'It was a shell. It came from the east.'

A guard on one of the watchtowers faced away from the camp. Holding his binoculars in his gloved hands, he surveyed the area. 'Russians!' he shouted. 'About ten miles away, maybe fifteen.'

More orders were shouted and guards burst out from the huts, armed with trays, baskets and armfuls of paper, hurrying towards the crematorium.

*

Feitel tucked his hand into the sleeve of his tunic and wiped away the condensation on the hut's window. He pressed his nose against the glass. Outside, a group of guards received instructions, nodded and dispersed. The crematorium's chimney, silhouetted against the night sky, belched white smoke. Bright embers glowed and drifted to the ground. From the buildings near the chimney came the piercing shrill of a drill and the repeated dull thump of a hammer being taken to masonry. The camp lights were out, the watchtowers abandoned and the guards' quarters – which on a normal evening echoed with laughter and singing – remained silent. The gates were shut but the guards who protected them could be made out as patches of shadow moving against the wire.

Leon strolled over to Feitel. 'There's a theory that men gather the relics of their life when the end is near. See how the Nazis destroy theirs?'

'Are the Russians coming?'

Leon bit his lip and nodded.

'What will that mean?' Feitel said.

'Perhaps freedom,' Leon said in a measured voice.

A man with crooked teeth and dark hair, sitting on a bunk next to the window, shook his head. 'Perhaps death. Look at the Nazis and how they cause chaos with such an air of organisation. It's as if they planned it.'

'Did they know the Russians were coming?' Feitel said.

'I expect they knew,' Leon replied, 'but no Nazi would ever admit it.'

'There's a train arriving,' somebody called out from the other side of the hut.

The train whistled. Its wheels slid to a halt, screeching above the din of the guards as they destroyed evidence. The train gasped a weary sigh of steam, then shouts and arguments pumped like violent fists. Leon forced open the window, cocking an ear to the night air.

'What are they saying?' the man with the crooked teeth asked.

Leon batted his arm up and down to silence him. The hut fell silent too. It was some minutes before he closed the window and addressed the hut. 'The guards ordered the train to leave. The officer in charge of it argued the prisoners must be accepted, explaining he had nowhere else to take them and no means to kill them. The officer from the camp said he couldn't exterminate them now as they're smashing the gas chambers. They fetched the commandant and he's ordered them to fill the huts. I suppose that'll dilute down those who know what else goes on here. He's hoping the Russians will buy the story that this is only a forced labour camp.'

'What's happening now?' the man with the crooked teeth said.

Leon turned back to the window. 'The gates are open and they're being led into the camp. The guards are splitting them into groups. I guess a group per hut – we're going to be crowded… They're even allowing families to stay together.'

Feitel felt a warm glow of hope. Could he escape with Leon?

The door of the hut opened, revealing a line of dishevelled new arrivals. A guard shouted at them and they filed in, inching their way down the aisles of pigeonhole bunks. They pressed against the walls, huddled on the floor, leaned against the roof supports and perched on the edges of the bunks. The snow they trod in formed puddles by the door, dampening the boards by the bunks.

The new people sought the advice of the long-term prisoners. And for the first time, the hut contained the soft voices of frightened women and the wails of crying babies.

Feitel looked at the women and babies. If they were no longer killing women and babies, he and Leon might be spared too.

'What happens here?' one arrival asked. He was a middle-aged man with a long beard, wearing a heavy knee-length coat.

'We work and die here,' Leon replied. 'We don't know what will happen now – today is different.'

Feitel was proud his friend was the one making the explanations.

'How is it different?' the man said, rolling his eyes in their sunken, wrinkled sockets.

'A shell landed in the camp,' Leon said. 'It's sent the guards wild. They've allowed women and babies into the huts and they are smashing the gas chambers. They believe the Russians are coming.'

Whispers circulated around the hut, petering out into an uneasy silence.

'You're alive. Why aren't you pleased?' Leon said.

'Over the last days,' the man said, 'we've heard dreadful stories about the Russians. Rapes and murders.'

Leon was tight-lipped. 'This is the first time they've let

an entire train of people stay in the camp. Because of that Russian shell, every one of you avoided the selection procedure.'

'Selection for what?' a woman said. She was parked on the floor with her back to a bunk, cradling an infant whom she struggled to pacify at her breast.

'Death,' Leon said.

The word hung in the air, then some of the new arrivals gasped. Feitel watched as Leon waited for them to settle down and continued, his words slow and considered. 'Only a few of us get to work here. This isn't a labour camp. It's a death camp. Those who work here are employed in the business of death.'

An older woman, wearing a felt skirt, half covered by the remains of a fur coat, spoke next. 'You mean, we'd all have been killed if it hadn't been for that Russian shell?'

Leon furrowed his brow and pursed his lips. 'One or two of the men and boys may have been spared for work.'

Feitel flicked his eyes across the new arrivals. They all stared at Leon, wild-eyed.

'How long would they have kept us alive for?' the man with the sunken eyes cried.

'You want me to say weeks or even months? This is a production line. Do you hear that wrecking noise? That's the guards smashing the gas chambers. If you don't believe me, ask him,' Leon said, pointing to Otto Mark.

The man with crooked teeth repeated Leon's words. 'Ask him.'

Another said the same, and soon 'Ask him' became the repeated whisper from the shaven-headed men. Otto stiffened as the whispers grew into cries and shouts.

Otto opened his mouth and spoke, but his words were drowned out.

Feitel, desperate to hear what Otto had been doing, shouted, 'Be quiet!'

Leon raised a hand and the chanting whittled away until no more than a solitary voice said, 'Ask him.'

When silence fell, so did Leon's hand.

'You wish to speak?' Leon said, directing this at Otto.

'I've never killed anybody,' Otto said, folding his arms. 'I was made to carry the bodies from the gas chamber to the crematorium, that's all I ever—'

'What about pulling out the teeth with gold fillings from the corpses?' Leon said.

'I don't know anything about *that*,' Otto replied. 'Anyhow, you'd all have been dead within the hour. You don't queue in the camp. You queue on the train.'

10

In the early hours, the hut door flew open with a violent crash, the silhouette of Muller looming in the open doorway. He stepped inside, followed by Squad Leader Baer and a woman, who was wrapped in a coat similar to the one Feitel's mother had worn.

'All you workers, form a line at the door,' Muller ordered. 'Those of you who arrived last night, stay where you are.'

'By whose authority?' a man called out from one of the bunks.

The hut seemed to take a collective breath. Feitel bit his lip.

'By whose authority?' Muller shouted. He drew his Luger and stepped around the people to reach the man who had dared to question him. 'By whose authority?' he repeated, dragging the man from his bed.

The man fixed him with a defiant stare. Muller lifted his gun and fired a single shot into his neck.

The newcomers gasped and recoiled as the man sank to the floor, blood pumping from his throat in rhythmic gushes.

Feitel gulped down vomit that had risen in his throat. His hands trembled and his heart thumped.

Muller returned to the door, waved his gun in the air, and shouted, 'Move!'

The men gathered in a line, caution spread over their faces. Muller sneered and fired a second shot into the air, shattering a light. The glass tinkled to the floor, and the echo waned. Muller strutted around the hut with his chest pushed out, peering into each bunk. When he got to Otto Mark's, he stopped. Otto glared back at him.

'You, get into the line,' Muller said, his eyes bulging.

'I don't work for *you*,' Otto said.

'You do now.' Muller pressed his gun into Otto's ribs.

Muller shoved Otto to the back of the line then joined Baer and the woman by the door. Muller kicked it open and ordered everybody to follow. When Feitel stepped outside, the prickling snow whipped into his face. The sweet sticky reek of the camp had morphed into the earthy odour of paper being burnt in the crematorium.

Muller marched them to the camp entrance, stopped and spun around. 'Baer, you can't bring your wife.'

'Greta *is* coming with us,' Baer said.

'That's not possible.'

Feitel willed Muller to allow her to come. She might be more sympathetic to them than Muller and Baer.

'I can follow of my *own* will,' Greta said. 'There's no rule against that, is there?'

'She's your responsibility,' Muller said. 'If we're caught, I'll tell them she's a Jew.'

'Very well, but it's the Russians we fear,' Baer said. 'You must have heard the stories. We can't leave the women behind.'

Muller sneered. 'What stories?'

'Oh, come on,' Baer said, raising his arms in exasperation. 'The rapes and the reprisals. We've all heard about it.'

Feitel remembered the new arrivals speaking of the Russians raping and murdering. He guessed what rape meant, dreading what might have happened to his mother before she was murdered.

Muller fell silent for a few moments. 'I need to go back home for a minute. Wait here.' With that he set off, his boots squeaking in the fresh snow.

'Looks like more company,' Baer said.

'How many children does he have?' Greta asked.

'Three, I believe.'

'A march from the camp will be no place for children.

Will it?'

'No, but this will be no place to leave children.'

Feitel huddled close to Leon. He took a deep breath as his friend's hand settled on his shoulder.

Greta spoke again. 'I'm not looking forward to marching in this snow.'

Baer opened his mouth to reply but a muffled gunshot, coming from the direction that Muller had gone, left him wide-eyed and silent.

Greta grabbed her husband's arm with her gloved hands. 'Oh no, he's not...' A few seconds later, another shot rang out. She winced. Two further shots followed in quick succession. 'Oh Karl, he hasn't. Not his children and his wife.'

Karl Baer was silent.

*

Leon grasped Feitel's hand, drawing him close.

'What's happened?' Feitel asked.

Leon spoke in a whisper. 'Muller's killed his family.'

Fear flooded through Feitel's body. 'Why?'

'So the Russians don't get them.'

Baer raised his torch, picking out the panting figure of Muller as he returned.

Greta gasped. 'You haven't... How could you?'

Muller's mouth was half open.

Feitel glanced up at Leon who was staring, wide-eyed, at Muller.

'We could have taken them,' Baer said, piercing the silence.

'Why didn't you leave them in the camp, amongst the new arrivals?' Greta asked, her voice tight with anger.

Muller scoffed. 'And leave them to the Russians?'

'Better than what you've just done—'

Baer squeezed her arm and she fell silent.

Muller gave the order to move off, passing through the

camp's gates. The wind had smoothed the piles of snow they'd cleared from the tracks earlier. The distant torchlights of other parties danced in the darkness.

Feitel reached up for the cuff of Leon's tunic. His friend took his hand and they kept pace with the rhythmic shadow of the heels of the man in front.

'You said to follow the tracks,' Feitel whispered.

'Yes, I did,' Leon replied, squeezing Feitel's hand with his long, thin fingers.

'Why didn't any of the new people come with us?' Feitel said.

'The commandant wants to tell the Russians that it was just a labour camp. We know different so they want to hide us. The new people are still in their own clothes. That'll support the commandant's story.'

The beam of Muller's torch picked out falling snowflakes and Feitel found a rhythm stepping between the railway sleepers. After a few hours, the prisoners whispered their complaints: some suffered with their knees, some with their hips and all with their feet.

Muller stumbled, and his torch cut out. He stopped and banged the torch twice into the palm of his hand. The light came back on, bringing the train tracks into view, cutting a swathe through the forest.

As Muller spoke to Baer, the line of men halted, shuffling with unease. Feitel rubbed his stinging ears, tucked his hands inside his tunic and shivered with the piercing cold.

'Where are you taking us?' a man from behind said.

'Silence!' Baer yelled.

The man called back, 'There's no destination, is there? Just death.'

'I said silence!' Baer shouted. 'When I say silence, I *mean* silence.'

Muller drew his pistol from under his coat and paced

along the line of men. 'Who disobeyed Squad Leader Baer's order?'

Nobody gave the man away; nobody pointed to him or said his name. But a barely perceptible shuffle, a step, created a space until the man's darting eyes shone in the light of Muller's torch.

Muller's arm thrust out like a boxer's punch, plucking the man from the line. He spun him around, pushing him to the soft snow on the flat land below the track. The man cowered in the spotlight of the torch. His right arm covered his face; his left sank into the snow. Muller leapt down the bank – light tore at the trees as he heaved his arm up and down, clubbing the man's head with his torch.

It was dark when Muller had finished, his torch extinguished. His boots crunched in the snow as he made it back to the rails. Between deep breaths, he cursed until the torch came back on. He swung the light around, allowing it to hover over the half-buried man. His head was smashed, leaking blood and brain. Shaking, Feitel's hands became clammy as he swallowed back vomit.

'Never disobey an order,' Muller shouted, his forehead glistening with perspiration. 'Never.'

Nobody spoke, and in the silence, Greta Baer took her husband's arm. The quiet was broken by Muller himself.

'You lead,' he said, pointing towards the Baers. As they set off, he waited for the prisoners to pass before following up the rear.

Leon tugged on Feitel's hand and hurried him forward, dodging in and out of the men in front. 'We need to move closer to the Baers.'

'Why?' Feitel whispered.

'The Baers are at the front and Muller is at the back. I don't want to be near him.'

Within half a minute, after sidestepping everybody in their way, Leon had steered them to the front. As they tucked in behind the Baers, Feitel lowered his head and eavesdropped on their conversation.

'Muller's a pig,' Greta said.

Her husband lowered his head and did not respond.

'What did he say to you when we stopped?'

Her husband drew in a breath. 'He's worried about what'll happen if the Russians catch us with Jews. He's going to start killing the stragglers at the back so we can travel faster. I believe he's on the verge of killing them all.'

'What's going to happen if we arrive at the next camp *without* them?' Greta said.

'We may well be shot for disobeying orders.'

'So it's the lesser of two evils,' Greta said, her voice quivering with worry. 'He's a liability. How are we going to survive this?'

Baer shook his head. 'I don't know.'

Greta was silent for a moment, deep in thought, before replying. 'What if you shoot Muller and let them go free? We could injure ourselves and give ourselves up to a patrol, saying we were hit by shells.'

'We'd need to find a German patrol,' her husband said. 'I don't fancy the Russians, with or without the Jews.'

'What about the Americans or the British troops?'

'I don't believe they've got this far yet.'

'Could you kill Muller?'

'I don't know,' Baer whispered. 'I've never killed anybody.'

'Well, we either kill him or hope things turn out all right for us,' Greta said, before stumbling. 'Blast.'

'What?'

'I stubbed my toe against a sleeper.'

'Lift your feet higher and place them down flat.'

Feitel flinched as a gunshot cracked from the back of their column.

Greta froze and said, 'Oh my god. True to his word…'

11

During the night, three further shots pierced the air and with each one Leon squeezed Feitel's hand. 'We must keep up,' he whispered.

Blood soaked images of Muller's killings swept through Feitel's mind. Miklos Wiesel in the workshop, the man he shot in the neck before leaving the hut then the man beside the tracks. He imagined his wife and children, lying dead. He knew they had to get away, but the thought of fleeing with Muller pursuing them was terrifying. They must stick close to Greta.

As the night gave way to the first greys of dawn, a cold blast of wind scurried in from the east. The rail track was now on a raised bed in a wide channel that cut through the trees. A line of fence posts bordered each side, snow capping each with a dome of white powder.

'How long have we been walking?' Feitel asked.

'I don't know,' Leon replied. 'Six hours, perhaps.'

Feitel shivered. 'I'm tired.'

'We can't fall back,' Leon said. 'We'll be shot. Don't give up now.'

'It's cold.'

'It's only cold because the wind's picked up.'

'Halt,' Muller ordered from the back of the line. 'Piss against the fence.'

They descended the slope; snow squeaked and crunched beneath their feet. Feitel glanced back, catching sight of Greta Baer as she disappeared down the other side of the bank. Leon gripped Feitel's hand, keeping him afloat.

At the fence, Feitel fumbled inside his trousers. 'I can't find it. I'm not going to be able to pee.'

Leon stood to his left. 'Hold your hands over it to make it warm.'

All Feitel felt was the wind carrying a warm spray of pee

from the man to his right. Muller shouted that they had had enough time.

While they made their way back up the bank, he fired a shot into the air. He shouted orders to the Baers to take the rear and kill any stragglers. He then took the lead with purpose in his step. Leon, with a strong grip on Feitel's hand, guided them towards the back.

They trudged on for an hour. The dim light of dawn became the light of the day; the outlines of the forest became distinct trees. Ahead, parties of Jews appeared between the tapering rails, making their way to the same unknown destination. The light brought the distant thud of shells and the drone of far-off aircraft.

They reached a level crossing where a road lined with barren trees crossed the tracks.

Muller turned to face the men. 'We'll stop here for twenty minutes.'

With the sun on their backs, they sat and rested. The trees swayed, bowed and embraced in the breeze. Next to them lay a corpse, half buried in the snow with its right hand sticking up. Snow had caught in the fine hairs of its wrist and glistened in the sunlight. Feitel turned his head, feeling sick.

Leon pulled some bread from his pocket and passed Feitel a piece which he slipped into his mouth. Others did the same and munched on what bread they had smuggled.

Muller, leaning against a level crossing sign, fixed them with a stare.

'You, Baer,' he said. 'Get that bread off them.'

'But—'

'Do as you're ordered. Take it.'

Feitel gulped down his bread.

Baer jumped up, snatched Leon's bread then strolled up and down the line. Nobody refused to hand over his bread, however nobody was asked to turn out his pockets. When

Baer reached the end of the line, Muller ordered him back.

'Split the rations in two. Half for you, half for me.'

'What about Greta?'

'She's your responsibility.'

Baer handed over half and lowered himself down beside his wife, handing over the other half. He held nothing back for himself. She stuffed the bread into her coat pocket and smoothed down her long dark hair, wiping the morning mist away. Feitel's mind caught an image of his mother in their basement back at home, smoothing down her long dark hair. Her loss bit deep. They'd left the camp where he'd last been with her.

'I can't eat in front of them,' Greta said, shaking her head. 'Not when it's their food.'

Muller sneered. 'You're soft. What does it matter if you eat it in front of them or eat it later?'

'Have you considered I might want to give it back to them?' she said.

Muller snorted and turned his head towards Baer. 'Your wife's as soft as you are. I don't believe you've ever killed a Jew, have you? If I ordered you to shoot a Jew, say that Jew,' he added, pointing to Otto Mark, 'you'd not have the courage to do it.'

Baer was quiet.

'Go on, shoot him. Be my guest,' Muller taunted.

'He's done good work for the camp,' Baer said.

'What about him?' Muller replied, pointing to a man sat behind Leon with a nose glowing russet red and eyebrows crusted in ice.

'No,' Baer whispered. 'There's been enough killing.'

Muller shook his head. 'You're yellow.'

Baer remained silent and motionless. Greta slipped her hand inside her husband's coat, drew out his gun and tucked it inside her own coat. She stood, took a few paces and stopped behind Muller. Feitel fixed his eyes on her, willing her to pull the trigger but panicking she might miss, unleashing Muller's wrath. She pursed her lips. Horror crossed her face as a gust of wind rushed through the trees.

Muller tilted his head. He stood. 'Right, we'll take the road, and I'll shoot anybody who makes a break for the trees. If you want to try to escape, keep near the Baers. They won't shoot you.'

Muller bunched them close together. Leon grasped Feitel's hand and led him onto the road, keeping them no more than a step behind the Baers.

'It didn't go off...' Greta whispered to her husband.

'You mean you pulled the trigger?'

'Yes, but nothing happened,' she said.

'The safety catch,' he cursed.

'Oh God,' Greta said, 'and I believe he knew. I don't know if I'll get another chance.'

'Best give me the gun back,' he said.

She slid the gun from under her coat into his gloved hand. The cold metal squeaked against the leather as he returned it to his holster.

With a pit of fear in his stomach, Feitel looked to Leon. He pressed his lips tight and nodded – he'd seen it too.

*

Leon held Feitel's hand tight. They scuffed their way through snow, cut their way through drifts and detoured around sheets of ice. The morning passed and the length of their shadows marked the transition from morning to afternoon. Feitel's legs grew weary and he began to slow.

'We must keep up with the others,' Leon whispered.

'I'm tired,' Feitel said.

Leon tightened his grip on his hand, pulling him along.

The scream of an approaching aircraft engine pierced the air. Greta grabbed Baer and clung to his arm. Feitel looked up. The belly of a plane sat below the trees with its wings ruffling their tops. The blades of its single propeller drew up the snow, making the others disappear in a grey whirlwind of spindrift. The plane twitched and its machine guns let out shrill bursts of fire. One wing dipped below the trees while the other skimmed over the tops of the trees on the opposite side of the road.

The snow swirled and peppered Feitel's eyes, blasting and stinging his face with its icy spindles.

'Get down!' Leon shouted.

A further three short bursts of gunfire followed. Leon thumped into Feitel and he buckled to the ground, flattening his face against the snow.

People screamed in pain. Leon did not move, did not speak. Feitel fought the weight of his friend, which pressed him into the ground, squeezing the breath from his body. A surge of relief swept through him when Leon began to stir, allowing him to wriggle free.

'It's gone,' Leon said, sitting up. 'Are you all right?'

Feitel spat out snow and coughed – the air was sulphurous. 'Yes, I'm all right,' he replied, pushing off the ground to raise himself up.

'That was close,' Leon said.

Feitel brushed damp snow from the neck and cuffs of his tunic and looked around. The spindrift had settled; bodies lay scattered on the ground. The snow bled scarlet. Ice crystals were captured by a crimson flow of blood.

At the back of their group, Baer knelt, tending to his wife. He exhaled a piercing shriek, fell forward and kissed her.

'It was a Russian plane,' Leon said.

The plane disappeared and it continued to draw up snow in its wake. The howl of its piston engine faded amid short raps of machine-gun fire.

Feitel cocked his head, unsure if he could still hear the plane or whether its sound just hung in his ears. People rose from the ground, and for each one who sat or stood, another groaned with pain or lay motionless. Baer still knelt by his wife, going through her pockets and transferring items to his.

A low, breathless voice whimpered, 'Baer, Baer. Help me.'

'That's Muller,' Leon whispered.

Baer staggered up, stepped over the corpse of Otto Mark and picked his way to the head of their group. Muller raised his body and pointed to his legs. Baer straightened himself up and, glaring down at his superior, drew a pistol from his greatcoat. He took a step back, stretched out his arm and, with a stony stare, pointed the gun at Muller's midriff and fired.

Muller screamed in pain and clutched his stomach. 'No, Baer! No.'

He writhed, his torso bent forward, hands grasping at the wound as blood bubbled out between his fingers. He slid his right hand into his coat, fumbled around and pulled out his gun. With his left hand clutching his stomach, he twisted and pointed it at Baer. His hand shook as he released the safety catch.

Fearing Muller, Feitel willed Baer to fire again.

Baer gazed down at the gun and its erratic movements, then at Muller's determined face and furrowed brow. Baer fired again, hitting him clean between the eyes.

'Come on,' Leon said. 'Baer's not watching us.'

'What?' Feitel exclaimed. Leon yanked his arm, tumbling them down a short slope at the edge of the road. They landed in soft snow, banked against the pitted trunk of a pine tree.

'Lie still, dead still,' Leon said. 'It'll be dark soon and this is our best chance.'

'Are we running away?' Feitel whispered.

'Yes, we're running away.'

'Where to?'

'Canada if you like,' Leon said.

'Just you and me?'

'Yes, just you and me,' Leon replied.

Feitel took deep breaths, the cold of the snow pressing through his tunic. His heart began to settle. He was away from Muller, away from Baer. It was just him and Leon now. And they had a plan.

After a few minutes, Leon half stood, pressing his hand into Feitel's back. 'Stay still,' he said as he clawed his way back up the slope and peered over the top. After a few moments, he whispered, 'Baer is rounding up the living.'

'Is he looking for us?' Feitel asked.

Leon craned his neck. 'Shit!'

'What?'

'He's walking along the edge of the road, checking the woods,' Leon said.

Feitel tensed and sweated, his shoulders taut. As Leon slid back down the bank, snow tumbled over his head. He made to brush it away but Leon's hand stopped him. 'Stay still.'

'How far away is he?' Feitel asked.

'Not far. Keep still.'

Feitel resisted every temptation to wriggle or look up.

Baer's voice called out, 'Get back on the road.'

Feitel raised his head but Leon gripped the back of his neck. Feitel panicked and yelped in pain as his friend's knee pressed against his spine.

'Keep still,' Leon repeated, relaxing his knee.

Terror sucked the breath from Feitel's mouth. He made to sit up. Leon's hand pressed harder on his neck and he winced, waiting for a bullet to come their way.

A shot rang out and reverberated around. Feitel tensed, waiting for the pain. When none followed, he relaxed and began to fidget, reaching out towards Leon.

'It wasn't for us! For heaven's sake, *stop* wriggling. Baer wasn't talking to us. Settle down.'

Feitel complied.

'Baer is organising the survivors, ordering them to march on,' said Leon.

12

'Are you asleep?' Feitel asked. It felt like ages since they'd dived off the road and hidden.

'It's too cold to sleep,' Leon whispered. 'It's getting late and we need to find shelter.'

Feitel cast his mind back to when it snowed in Berlin and the fun he'd had with his father. 'We could build a snow cave.'

'Build? I thought you dug one,' Leon replied.

'It's easy,' Feitel said, pleased to impart knowledge. 'You pile snow against a deep bank and dig.'

'It'll be dark soon. We'll search for a spot tomorrow, away from the road. Let's dig in here for the night, as deep as we can.'

They hollowed out the snow until Feitel's fingers, numb with cold, scraped at the earth of the forest floor. They lay down and wriggled to get comfortable.

'It's still too cold,' Leon said. 'I've got an idea. Wait here.'

And with that Leon clambered from the hole and slipped off into the darkness.

The cold seeped into Feitel. He brought his knees up to his chest and shivered. With every crack of a twig, every distant cry of an animal and every patter of snow falling from a branch, he thought his friend was returning. His mind wandered back to the camp and to his mother. Screwing his eyes up, he tried to remember which cheek she had wiped his tear from, but still the memory would not come.

Raising himself onto his elbows, he wondered where Leon was. An icy breath of wind caught his face, and the cold from the ground chilled his body.

After a further ten minutes, Leon ploughed into the snow hole from the direction of the road. He nudged Feitel to one side and thrust a piece of stiff material into his hand.

'Stretch this under us,' Leon said, raising his body.

Feitel raised his buttocks and tugged at the material, shuffling it underneath.

Leon lowered himself and pulled another piece of material over the top of them. 'This is Muller's coat,' he said, patting it down around them. 'The bastard owed us. And we're lying on Mrs Baer's. There are still a few bodies up there but everybody else has left.'

The coats smelled earthy and damp. Feitel shivered until the warmth of their bodies filled their makeshift bed. He stretched out his leg and his foot met the freezing night air. He whipped it back in and tucked it under his other leg.

*

Feitel shivered and blinked as the dawn light cast a warm orange glow across the forest floor.

'What are we going to do?' Feitel said.

'I need to think,' Leon said, handing over three dried biscuits. 'Eat these.'

'Where did you find them?'

'They were in one of Mrs Baer's coat pockets. I checked Muller's but the shit must have eaten all the bread he took from us.'

'I saw Baer emptying her pockets,' Feitel said.

'He must have missed the inside pocket. He missed this too,' Leon said, pulling a gold dental filling from his own pocket. 'I expect he stole it from the workshop and gave it to her to carry. It might be worth enough to get us on a train to Paris. That's if we make it to Berlin first.'

Feitel stared at the filling, convincing himself it was too big to be one of his mother's.

'Have you had your biscuits?' Feitel said.

Leon hesitated and replied, 'I had mine when I took the coat. That's why I took so long.'

Feitel guessed Leon hadn't eaten, but he still stuffed the

dry and tough biscuits into his mouth. He coughed as the crumbs tickled his throat.

'Steady on,' Leon said. 'That's precious stuff.'

Feitel swallowed and explained how they could build the snow cave.

Leon smiled and nodded.

'Can we build it now?' Feitel said.

Leon shushed him and said, 'Keep your voice down. There are voices coming from the road. Listen.'

Feitel cocked an ear. 'I don't know what they're saying,' he whispered.

'That's because they're Russian,' Leon said, 'It means we're behind Russian lines.'

'Shall we give ourselves up?'

'I don't know how they'd treat us. I prefer to dream of Canada. You can imagine anything in your dreams, big or small. One thing they can't do is take dreams away from you.'

The murmurs of conversation and the crunching of soft snow drew closer.

'*Myertviye yevryei*,' was repeated a number of times.

'Dead Jews,' Leon whispered. 'I only understand a bit of Russian but I reckon they're sorry for killing us.'

'Why did they shoot at us then?'

'Because,' Leon said, 'I expect they thought we were German refugees.'

'Are we safe now?'

'I don't trust the Russians. If they find out we're here they could do anything. They might shoot us to cover up the killings.' Leon stiffened. 'Lie still. They're right above us.'

Feitel held his breath, catching a whiff of cigarette smoke and the murmur of Russian voices.

'One of them,' Leon whispered, 'said it's a good job there are no survivors.'

'But—' Feitel began.

'Shh, they're really close,' Leon said.

One of the Russians laughed; another made a comment. There was more laughter before the voices drifted away.

'Feitel,' Leon said, his voice low and measured. 'It'll be too dangerous on the road. Your idea to dig a snow cave is good. If we can get warm and comfortable, we could stay put until we figure out what to do. Can you wait while I find somewhere to do it?'

Feitel nodded.

'Good. Be ready to move when I get back.' With that Leon slid from under the coat and jogged, half bent, into the trees.

Feitel lay for a while before he rolled forward and brushed the frost off the greatcoat. His hand caught on a dark sticky patch of blood. Feeling sick, he rolled up the coat, packed it under his head and rocked on his buttocks to free Mrs Baer's coat. It was a dark fawn colour, knee length and made of a thin material with a crisscross pattern on its chocolate-brown buttons. He flicked them one by one until he felt a deep pain below his fingernail. He shook his hand and brushed off the twigs, frozen leaves and a small fir cone that clung to the back of the coat. Three neat holes punctured the fabric.

The snow under the nearby trees crunched as somebody approached. Feitel's heart skipped a beat.

'It's only me,' Leon called out in a half whisper, treading his way back. 'I've found a hollow where the snow has built up on one side.' Leon gathered up the coats and took Feitel by the hand. 'Best we run. We don't want to be out in the open for any longer than we have to be.'

They darted into the gloom of the forest, buffeted by branches that sprung from the trees.

*

Feitel peered into the hollow Leon had found and pointed

to the snowdrift built up against one side. 'We start by using sticks to dig a tunnel,' he said, remembering how his father had taught him to build a snow cave.

Leon's eyes flicked around the sides of the hollow, stopping on a thin branch that protruded from the snow. He stepped towards it and sank down, up to his knees in the snow. Feitel snorted with laughter.

'Not a good start,' Leon said, laughing while freeing himself. He stepped towards the branch, grasped it in both hands, dug his right foot into the snow and tugged. The branch snapped off and he fell flat on his back.

Feitel snorted with laughter again.

'You'll bring a Russian with all that noise,' Leon said.

Feitel froze with worry. 'Can they hear us?'

'They will if you keep laughing,' Leon said, rocking forward to half pull himself up.

Leon stood and snapped the branch into two pieces.

'Your spade,' he said, handing one end to Feitel, 'I'm afraid it isn't up to the standard of the ones we used to clear the tracks.'

Feitel needed no persuasion as he began his work. He scraped at the snow, flicking it through his legs.

Leon chuckled. 'You're just like a dog.'

Feitel glowed with pride and dug close to the ground to keep the roof of the snow cave thick. Whenever he slowed, Leon took over until the hole widened and Feitel crawled in. Lying on his stomach, he scooped away the snow in front of him, flicking it onto his back for Leon to dust away. Every few minutes, Feitel hauled himself forward and, when his feet were in the tunnel, he rolled onto his back, jabbing the stick upwards to raise the height of the ceiling. Snow trickled onto his face and he spat out the bits that dropped into his mouth.

As the roof formed, he smoothed it with his hands and gathered up the loose snow, throwing it down the tunnel.

Leon scooped it out and packed it onto the roof with a succession of thuds.

Once Feitel could sit up, he stopped and rested.

'Let me have a go,' Leon called.

Feitel crawled back down the tunnel and swapped places with his friend.

Leon's feet disappeared into the tunnel. 'It's quite a hollow you've made,' he called.

'Scoop out the snow and push it down to me,' Feitel said.

Leon used his feet to push the snow down the tunnel. Feitel scooped it out and packed it on the roof.

'That should be enough,' Leon called. 'Can you pass me the coats?'

Feitel pushed them up the tunnel, crawling behind them until Leon's outstretched arm grasped at the material and dragged them into the cave.

'Welcome to our home,' Leon said. 'You've done well.'

Feitel grinned but he knew Leon could not see him in the dim light.

Leon plugged the tunnel with Mrs Baer's coat, packing it tightly with snow. He snuggled down next to Feitel and spread Muller's greatcoat over them.

Feitel's wet tunic clung to his skin, his teeth chattered and his chest pulled tight with the chill. He shivered and huddled close to his friend. 'What will we do in Canada?'

'You'll have to learn English and go to school,' Leon replied.

'What will you do?'

'I'll find a job and earn money.'

'Will we have a house?'

'I expect so. It's a rich country with lots of wood for building houses.'

'Don't they burn down?'

Leon chuckled. 'I believe they make the fireplaces out

of stone.'

'What about the chimneys?'

'The chimneys too I expect,' Leon said, patting down Muller's coat.

'How will we get there?'

'First we have to make it to Berlin, from there to Paris, then on to England. It'll be a long journey.'

'I'm tired,' Feitel moaned.

'Try and get some rest and stay warm.'

*

When the dim light faded into night, Leon tucked Feitel's body into his own for warmth. For the first time since he'd been separated from his mother, Feitel felt safe. He dozed, then woke and willed the night to never end. When the dawn light came, casting vague shadows across their snow cave, Leon stirred and loosened his embrace – Feitel's mind raged back to his arrival at the camp, when his mother was torn away from him.

They left their snow cave and stretched their legs. Passing lorries rumbled by on the road. Light snowflakes floated down from heavy clouds. Feitel tipped back his head and caught some in his mouth.

'What shall we do?' Feitel asked.

'Let's get back in the snow cave, it'll be safer. We also need food,' Leon said. 'I'll go out tonight and be back before dawn.'

'Can I come with you?' Feitel asked, following Leon back to the snow cave.

'No, I might have to travel far and you'll get tired. Don't worry, I'll come back.'

They spent the rest of the day dozing and playing 'Twenty Questions', changing it to 'Guess the German City in Five Questions'. Leon allowed Feitel lots of free guesses and, when the light faded, declared him the winner.

13

'It's night-time now,' Leon said, sitting up in the snow cave and readying himself. 'I'm going to go in search of food. Are you hungry?'

'Yes, starving,' Feitel replied.

'I'll return before dawn.'

'Okay,' Feitel said, trying to sound brave.

'Don't worry, I'll be back,' Leon said, unplugging the tunnel of their snow cave.

As Leon crawled away, the extra space filled with freezing air. Feitel shivered and plugged up the hole with Mrs Baer's coat and huddled into Muller's.

Longing for his mother, he rolled himself into a tight ball. He screwed up his brow and scrunched his eyes, stemming the flow of tears. His skin tingled as he imagined her finger running down one cheek then the other. Her face flashed before him in the darkness.

'Leon is looking after me, Mama,' he whispered. He dabbed his face with the rough material of the coat and mopped his wet cheeks.

Feitel counted to ten, a hundred, then a thousand. He counted backwards from a hundred, forwards to ten, and gave up altogether.

He thought of the camp. The neat piles of coins he'd sorted in the workshop. He wished he had some to give to Leon.

*

Feitel woke to a scratching from the entrance to the tunnel. His scalp prickled and his heart quickened. In the dim morning light, Mrs Baer's coat was pulled away. Before he could move, something crisp and dry was pushed into his hand.

'It's just some stale bread, I'm afraid,' Leon said.

'Where did you get it?' Feitel said, relieved.

'From a body on the road. Go on, eat it.'

Feitel bit into the bread. It was rigid and he had to tear into it with his teeth. 'Are you eating yours?'

'No, I ate it on the way back. I was that starved.'

Feitel chewed on the stale bread, wondering if his friend had really eaten.

Leon waited for him to swallow the last piece. 'It's going to be a bright day. Let's stretch our legs.'

Leon crawled out, flat on his stomach. Feitel followed, blinking in the bright light. The snow glistened under a rich blue sky. The small hollow was surrounded by thin trees loaded with ice crystals sparkling in the morning light.

A long-nosed lorry, in military khaki, flicked past the trees. Leon dived to the ground, pulling Feitel with him.

'We can be seen from the road,' Leon whispered.

'Is it a German or Russian lorry?' Feitel asked.

'I reckon it's Russian,' Leon said. 'Lie still and be quiet.'

*

Three days passed during which Leon went out by night and they laid low by day. His scavenging trips grew longer and he slept by day, shivering as he clutched his stomach. The food he found was poor – stale bread, one potato and a rotten apple. Feitel was certain that Leon was not eating. Each time he asked, Leon said he had eaten his share while he was out. He tried to share his food with him, but Leon said no, insisting that Feitel eat it right away. He knew Leon was being kind, protecting him. But guilt gnawed at his stomach as he could see hunger was gnawing at Leon's.

On the fourth night, Leon returned with only a piece of leather, ripped from the seat of an abandoned car. He showed Feitel how to chew on it, creating saliva, until it became moist enough to swallow. On the fifth night, he did not go out.

'We need to move,' he said, 'or we'll starve.'

'I want to stay *here*, with you,' Feitel said.

'Me too, my friend, but there's nothing left to scavenge here. I found a barn last night, where people were staying. People like us. They don't have much food. However, it's a step closer to Berlin. We can head cross-country which cuts a mile off the road.'

'Do we have to go tonight?' Feitel said.

'No, we'll go tomorrow after dark.'

*

The following day, as the late afternoon light gave way to the shadows of dusk, Leon, who was sitting outside the snow cave, wove the tails of Muller's greatcoat together with a piece of fence wire.

'What are you doing?' Feitel said.

'I'm making a sling for my back to carry you to the barn in.'

'I can walk.'

'No, the snow is too deep and it's too far,' Leon replied, laying the coat down on its back. 'Come and lie down in it.'

With a heavy heart, Feitel lay down on the coat. Leon buttoned him in and hoisted him onto his back.

'You all right?' he asked.

'Yes,' Feitel said. 'But what about Mrs Baer's coat?'

'We'll have to leave it. Right, hold on, off we go.'

Leon managed no more than ten paces before Feitel sank to the bottom of the greatcoat.

'This is no good. Can you straighten up?'

Feitel clawed his way back up. Leon took two more strides before Feitel slipped back down again.

'Try and hold on tight,' Leon said. 'Tip forward when we go uphill and back when we go downhill.'

Feitel grasped the inside of the coat. 'I'm ready.'

Leon set off again. A chill wind ripped through the coat, and they found a rhythm. Leon stopped only to brace himself against the wind or to shift Feitel's weight.

The air in the coat turned stale. Feitel's cheek, pressed

against his friend's back, became hot and his right foot went to sleep. He pushed down with his left foot and it plunged through the wire bonds, crumpling Leon to the ground.

As he righted himself, Feitel said, 'Is it far?'

Leon hesitated. 'About an hour.'

*

Desperate to help, Feitel perched on the wire bonds and hung on, allowing Leon to make progress. But his friend was weak and he knew he was the cause of it.

On an uphill stretch, Leon cursed and dropped to his knees.

'Shall we rest?' Feitel whispered.

It was a long while before Leon replied. 'No, it's too cold. We need to keep moving.'

'We could dig another snow cave.'

Again, the pause was long and the answer not what Feitel wished for. 'No. It isn't far and the barn is better shelter.'

Leon struggled to his feet. Feitel forgot to hold on and they tilted, then slumped to the ground. Feitel, thankful Leon did not complain, held on tight while his friend righted himself.

They carried on for a few minutes with Leon's breath labouring under the burden of Feitel's weight. The wind picked up, ripping away the warmth from within the coat. Feitel shivered and his chest became tight.

They fell, tumbled and slid. 'No!' Leon shouted, his voice desperate. And as Feitel clung to the coat, Leon thumped the snow and sobbed, 'No, no, no!'

Snow got inside the coat, which Feitel spat from his mouth. Blood thumped inside his skull, blocking out sound. He lay still, dread creeping up from the pit of his stomach, as if he were dangling over a bottomless chasm.

Leon attempted to stand but slipped back to the ground and became still.

Feitel shook in the piercing cold. 'Leon,' he whispered, patting his friend's back.

'I need to rest,' Leon replied.

Leon's back rose and fell with each breath and Feitel slipped into a broken sleep.

He woke to silence and the cold piercing through his thin tunic. Placing an ear to Leon's back, he listened for his breath – he could hear none and his friend was still and cold. He tried to wriggle but the coat pulled taut across his back.

An owl hooted. Something rustled nearby and snow slipped off the trees, pattering to the ground. Still Feitel could not make out if Leon was breathing.

He thrust his bottom back against the coat, hoping it would tear open. It held fast.

Leon stirred the stir of a beast waking from its winter slumber.

'Are you okay?' Feitel asked.

Leon did not answer but scrabbled, collapsed, then scrabbled again before lifting Feitel back into the air.

'How far now?' Feitel asked.

Leon still did not answer and it was as if his friend were no longer there, as if he rode roughshod on the back of a wild creature. Feitel clung on, trying to stop his feet from slipping through the woven tails of the coat.

Bound like a prisoner, Feitel gulped deep breaths. He clung on, wringing his hands; they were in pain from the cold. His chest ached as it bashed against Leon's back.

*

Leon stopped and kicked against something solid, stamping each foot twice. Feitel sighed, realising this was their journey's end.

The breeze had gone, voices murmured and candle fumes pricked deep inside his nose. He was lifted off Leon's back, the buttons of Muller's coat were unpicked and faces behind the candles gazed down at him.

They were now in the barn.

A cup of water was lifted to his lips. He took a few sips then was given a square of stale cheese.

14

Feitel stirred, aware of voices murmuring in the barn. He folded back the coat, and the chill air nipped at his legs. Leon slept next to him on the barn floor. His tunic top, stained with the colours of the forest, had ridden up at the waist.

Feitel raised himself onto his elbows. He figured this must be the barn Leon had spoken of. The dull light of the morning sneaked past a door adrift from its latch and cast shadows on the earthen floor. Horse tackle and long baling forks hung from iron bars set into the stone walls.

People with matted hair and grubby clothes propped themselves up against the walls; others hunched forward or lay on the ground. As people woke, they greeted each other, some with a nod and others with a few words.

A voice boomed from his left. 'Your father sleeps well.'

Feitel turned towards the man. A bottle nose, with a net of red veins at its tip, hung in the middle of his face.

'I've barely slept a wink on this hard floor,' the man said. He added, in clipped tones, 'My name is Abraham. What's yours?'

Before Feitel could answer, a man of around forty with a receding hairline crossed from the other side of the barn and knelt beside Leon. He rolled him onto his back, revealing Leon's blue lips and half-open eyes.

The man felt for Leon's pulse and shook his head. 'He's dead. Hypothermia. I've seen it before.'

Abraham nodded as if he'd made the diagnosis himself.

Pain clutched at Feitel's stomach and sent a burning sting down his legs.

The man stood and returned to his spot, speaking to a woman whose long mud-streaked hair edged a kind face. They spoke in whispers before they came back over. She dropped to her haunches. 'Do you understand what's happened?' Her eyes were dark and caring. 'That your papa is dead?'

Feitel's mouth turned dry and he was unable to speak. He managed a single nod.

The man searched through Leon's pockets and found the gold filling that had been in Mrs Baer's coat pocket when she died. Feitel was worried he'd be told off for having such riches.

The man passed it to Feitel. 'Looks like your father lost a filling.'

He continued searching Leon's pockets, pulling out a tatty envelope. A small photograph slipped to the floor. He picked it up and examined it. 'Is this you?'

Feitel took the picture – Leon and a woman stood either side of a boy, hands resting on his shoulders. Feitel shook his head but slipped the photograph into his tunic pocket and pulled Muller's coat over him.

*

Feitel became aware of people moving around and figured he must have slept. He raised himself up onto his elbows and surveyed the space where Leon had been.

'They took your father outside,' Abraham said. 'It's wretched what men must do.'

Feitel glanced up at him. The strength drained from his body.

'What's your name?' Abraham asked.

Feitel lowered his head and fidgeted with a button on the coat. He reminded him of the man who used to deliver groceries to his mother, but without the coldness of Abraham's eyes.

'Come, boy,' Abraham said, patting the space next to him.

Feitel moved and sat next to Abraham, but the weight of grief bulged within him. He wrung his hands together, longing to be alone to remember Leon.

'I held my grandfather's hand when he died,' Abraham said. 'It was peaceful, a relief really. He was old – a month from being ninety-three. That's a good age, isn't it?'

Feitel blinked away a tear.

'My mother died in hospital. She had cancer. A nasty, nasty way to go. Your father had it easy, going in his sleep. I've seen worse, a lot worse. Last week, we had dysentery in here. Two died in a mess of blood and shit.'

Feitel was bitten by despair.

Abraham added, 'I was in the last war – not that the Nazis take any notice of that. You should have seen the way the men died in the trenches. By the score, killed fighting or taken by disease. Think of the men who went to the gas chambers, knowing they were about to die. It chills you, doesn't it? Yes, your father had it easy, going in his sleep. No fuss, no fear.'

The man who had attended to Leon glowered from across the barn. 'Shut up,' he shouted.

'I beg your pardon?' Abraham said.

'The boy doesn't want to know how lucky his father has been.'

'Why not? I'm trying to comfort him.'

'The boy will be upset. It doesn't matter how he died.'

'What do you mean, it doesn't matter how his father died? Of course it does. It'd be awful for the boy to know he died in fear or agony.' Abraham lowered his voice and glanced towards Feitel. 'Take no notice of him, boy.'

However, Abraham did shut up and Feitel slipped to the ground, tears pressing against his eyes. He yearned to be anywhere but here – on the road, in the camp, but not here. He trusted nobody. People slouched with no purpose, no routine and nowhere to go. The camp had had anticipation, breaking the boredom and sorrow. The road to Berlin would have a purpose. He tucked Muller's coat around him and shivered as he drew his legs up to his chest.

*

Feitel stirred. A gunshot cracked in the distance.

'How far away do you reckon *that* was?' a woman said, panicked.

'It might only be poachers,' a man replied.

'No, not in this weather,' another said.

'Is it Russians or Germans?' the woman said.

'Perhaps it's a farmer.'

'Perhaps it's a farmer who doesn't want us in his barn!' the woman said. 'He might betray us to the Russians.'

'Be quiet. Lie still and snuff out the candles,' a man whispered.

The barn fell silent for around ten minutes until a few people began to whisper and fidget. Others hushed them. Feitel lifted the coat from his head as a bullet cracked over the roof. A series of heavy feet pounded around the outside of the barn, stopping next to the door.

'It's Russians—' a man began, propped against the opposite wall.

Hushes silenced him.

'God save us,' a woman shouted.

Feitel's stomach drew tight. The door crashed and swung on its hinges, slamming against the wall.

'No!' a man shouted.

Feitel could not see who it was. The glare of a torch rounded the room, picking them out one by one. He squinted when it caught his eyes.

'*Nyet,*' the torch-holder said. He turned away, revealing the broad back, uniform and helmet of a Russian soldier.

The voices and thuds of boots streamed away.

A man stood and closed the door. 'They were searching for somebody. We'll have to be careful who we let in.'

*

Feitel woke, blinking in the early morning light as a draught of cold air teased his face. A man wearing dirty pinstriped trousers stood outside the barn door, peeing into the snow. Hunger gnawed at Feitel's stomach. He threaded his arm inside his tunic and stroked his aching tummy.

Abraham's voice boomed across his shoulder. 'Stay with me, boy. We can find food together and make our way to a city.'

Feitel tensed.

'I noticed you had a nice piece of gold. I know about gold. We'll buy food with it and find a place to stay.'

Feitel faced the man and caught the coldness in his eyes. He groped in the pocket for the gold filling – it was gone.

Abraham nodded with a faint smirk. 'I took it for safekeeping.'

The man who had tended to Leon interrupted them. He glared at Abraham as he held his hands out towards Feitel, offering him a stained china cup and a piece of bread.

'I'm sorry the bread's stale. It's all we can spare.'

Feitel took it, tore off a piece and chewed. It tasted dry and a faint musty odour teased his nose. He moistened it with sips of stale water, rammed the rest into his mouth and swallowed. He swilled his mouth and drank down the water, tipping his head back to drain every drop.

'You were in the camps,' Abraham said. 'I can tell by your tunic. They were a convenient place to stuff us inconvenient people.'

Before Feitel could respond, a call came from outside that the thaw had come. The barn became a murmur of plans.

Somebody asked, 'Is it melting much?'

A voice from outside replied, 'The snow's dripping from the roof.'

Abraham smiled at Feitel and gathered up his belongings. 'Now we can leave. We must get moving before we're caught.'

With a sense of foreboding, Feitel spread out Muller's

coat, laid the sleeves flat across its front and flattened the wires binding the cuffs and the tail. He folded it across the middle and folded it again, forming a neat cube.

Others discussed their plans and gathered their meagre possessions into bundles and battered cases. Most mentioned Berlin, estimating how far it was and the number of days it would take to get there on foot. Others spoke of trains, carts and trucks they might board along the way.

Abraham circled the barn, saying goodbye. Feitel shivered, feeling as though somebody had walked right through him. He waited until Abraham was on the far side of the barn, with his back to him, then bundled Muller's coat under his arm and made a dash for the door

At the door, the man who had tended to Leon said, 'Where are you going?'

Feitel froze, blood thumping against the inside of his head. The woman sitting beside him glanced to the door; her encouraging smile gave him permission and her raised eyebrows gave him action. He darted out and sprinted into the cover of the trees.

The forest floor was covered in leaves and twigs and, as Feitel ran, his feet plunged into muddy, icy water. He slackened his pace and, with his shins and feet aching from the cold, headed towards higher ground where sunlight beckoned through the trees.

At the top, he stood on the edge of a tree-lined, snow-dusted field which sloped down towards a road. A convoy of people trailed amongst their handcarts, bicycles and bundles carried under their arms, on their backs or dragged along by bits of rope.

The legs of his tunic, wet with mud, stuck to his skin as he made his way down to the field. At the bottom he climbed a gate and stopped by the edge of the road. Horse-drawn carts, led by old men, pitched and rolled with each rut. Where there was no man, a woman led, and when there was no horse, a man pulled at the shafts.

A German army lorry with its wheels caked in icy brown sludge menaced its way through the parting crowds. Its horn blared and its gears whined, adding to the soundtrack of the road. In its wake, a woman, stooped with age, stepped from the crowd, two cooking pots hanging off her back. They rocked and rang the rhythm of her feet like a set of out-of-tune bells.

Sorrow hung everywhere; the trees leaned forward as if in mourning. He pictured his mother's face, Leon's tall frame, and fought back the tears.

The air swelled with a squadron of Russian planes peppering the road with machine gun fire. A shell exploded in an adjacent field, vomiting earth and snow while the people dived for cover.

Feitel leapt into a ditch, his chest thumping onto its muddy floor. Some people screamed, others wept over the dead, and those who lay wounded hollered in agony or stayed silent, waiting for death. Amidst the cacophony of cries, Feitel made out two voices:

'Why did they not evacuate us sooner?'

'Did you not hear the wireless? They banned us from moving so the troops could use the roads.'

Where had these people been evacuated from? It couldn't be the camps; they didn't wear striped tunics.

With mud seeping into his cloth shoes, he set off along the road.

*

In the early afternoon, Feitel came across an elderly woman and a freckle-faced teenage girl kneeling over a corpse. They both lowered their heads, kissed its forehead. With their heads still bowed, they half stood and rolled it into a shallow roadside grave. The corpse came to rest on its back, revealing the wizened blood-streaked face of an old man.

The woman removed her woollen hat and bowed her

wrinkled head. Hands shaking, she stood for a moment then helped the girl cover the body with earth. They snapped a piece of birch in two and fashioned a simple cross.

A cart lay nearby, burnt down to its axle, and a mutilated horse lay dead with its eyes staring at nothing. A group of black-haired gypsies, dressed in tatty suits, lingered nearby and, when the woman and the girl had finished, asked if they could cut the horse up for its meat.

He trudged on, passing other crosses that marked roadside graves. The fields were littered with abandoned tanks alongside gun carriages and burnt-out lorries. He stamped on frozen puddles, ripped up shards of ice and sucked on them to ease his thirst. Where blades of grass poked through the mud, he plucked them out and chewed on them.

When the grey afternoon sky gave way to the shadows of dusk, people entered the woods and bedded down for the night. Others went in search of barns.

Feitel spotted a cluster of fir trees on the opposite side of a ditch brimming with icy water. He leapt across and sank down, wrapping himself in Muller's coat.

He woke during the night, his stomach aching with hunger. Those who slept nearby groaned and sighed while trying to make themselves comfortable on the hard ground. He shivered and pulled the coat closer as the stars made a million pinpricks of light against the night sky.

*

Feitel woke at dawn to find somebody dragging the coat away from him. He hung onto it for a few seconds until the material slipped through his hands. Cold swept over him and beat against his chest. The robber, a sallow youth, fell back and stared at him. They both made a grab for the coat but the youth was too quick and scurried off, bundling his prize against his chest.

Feitel stood, dabbing away his tears with the dirty cuff

of his tunic. He headed back towards the road and cursed as his legs plunged into the icy water-filled ditch. He grabbed at the bank and hauled himself out, collapsing onto the sludgy earth. Water drained from his shoes. The sodden cloth of his trousers clung to his legs and his heart wrenched in misery.

A woman wheeling a bicycle, packed from front to back with belongings, stopped and peered down at him with disgust. 'You need to change those clothes, boy.'

He did not reply. He had already realised his tunic made him stand out.

Feitel staggered up; the bitter wind tore at his chest. He glanced along the road and rejoined the stream of people heading for Berlin. He stopped at each abandoned car to search for clothes and food. Some stood intact, out of petrol. Others rested on their flat tyres, burnt out or broken by a shell. He searched them all – none contained food but some offered a few coins in the glove box. He slid these into his tunic pocket, next to the photograph of Leon. He tore a piece of seat leather from one car and chewed and sucked on it.

Another car, which from a distance was no more than a black dot, had its exhaust pipe dropped to the ground, its rear window smashed and a rear door open. It rested at an angle with its front left wheel turned into a ditch, leaving its rear right wheel hanging above the ground. The boot and roof were dotted with a line of neat bullet holes. Save for the torn-out front passenger side, it looked as if a giant needle could thread the car back together.

Stepping away from the stream of people on the road, Feitel pushed his fingers into the tread of the raised wheel and spun it. It rotated, free of its brakes, free of the road. He shoved it hard. It clicked as it spun a half-turn, then came to rest.

Feitel peered into the cab, hoping to find food or a few

coins. His heart jumped and acidic bile rose into his throat at the sight of the driver's mangled body, pressed into the steering wheel with eyes staring out across the fields.

He stepped towards the ditch but froze in rigid terror – the body of a small boy lay at the bottom of the gully, head cocked at an impossible angle. He wore a jumper, a shirt, trousers and shoes.

Feitel glanced around. Nobody was paying him any attention. He slipped down the gully and stood staring in the hope that somehow, time might undress the boy for him.

With a racing heart, he slipped off the boy's shoes, kicked off his cloth shoes and slipped on the new ones. He took a deep breath, closed his eyes and dragged the jumper over the boy's head. He unbuttoned the shirt and tugged it free, unbuttoned the trousers and yanked them away. Gathering the clothes against his chest, he reached for the car door and hauled himself up the bank.

Feitel's eyes flicked back towards the boy. The legs and torso were pale and smooth, his nipples pink and flat. Vomit rose into his mouth and he coughed, spat and spewed.

He cleared his mouth and ran until he buckled against a gate and slid, panting, to the ground. After catching his breath, he climbed over the rails and slipped behind a tree. With trembling hands, he changed into the boy's clothes.

He pulled the photograph and the coins from his tunic and pushed them into the trouser pocket. His fingers brushed against some other coins which he withdrew and counted.

Climbing back over the gate, he rejoined the road – warmer in his new clothes. He patted the money and the photograph of Leon in his pocket. He set off along the road, the bitter taste of bile still hanging in the back of his mouth.

*

That night, Feitel found a wooden barn with a rust-coloured

galvanised roof. He crouched in a corner while others bedded down. The earth floor had a dusting of hay. He gathered a few strands, chewing on them to pacify the hunger that gnawed at his stomach. He slept on and off as people snored, stirred and spoke in whispers. In the early hours, army trucks rumbled by in the safety of darkness.

When morning came, he pocketed a few strands of hay and joined the stream of people on the road. He plodded over ruts brimming with murky water. In places, the column of people diverted along fields to avoid the worst of the ankle-deep mud.

He passed through a small town where an unscathed church spire stood amongst looted shops and the blackened shells of buildings. The drone of airplane engines returned.

'Russians!' came a shout.

Moments later, people fell. The crack of machine gun bullets flung up divots of earth. Feitel dived into the roadside ditch, covering the back of his head with his hands. Only when the planes had passed and the machine-gun fire became distant did he scramble back onto the road.

A few people were tending to the grief-stricken. Others darted between the corpses, looting what they could. Feitel sprinted over and joined in – he'd learned the time of death was measurable by how much a body had been picked over. He managed to collect a few more coins, a half-eaten apple and more hay.

15

Three days passed. The snow turned to mud, blurring the boundary between the road and the fields. People slid, slipped and sank to their knees, thumping the muddy ground with despair.

Trucks passed and cut deep ruts in the mud, leaving behind the pattern of their tyres to become overrun by water. Other trucks followed and crisscrossed the troughs, forming mighty puddles. Rivulets formed between the puddles and poured into ditches, which became torrents of water, holding the story of a mile of road.

Feitel kicked through the mud and water. Whenever he reached a dry patch, he'd empty his shoes and ring out his trouser legs.

When the light changed, and the afternoon hinted dusk was nearing, Feitel searched for somewhere to bed down for the night. He followed a group of women who turned off the road and crossed a field to an open-fronted barn. It was clad in corrugated tin, red with rust. Bales of hay had been pulled away to make room to bed down. Relieved to escape the mud, he slumped down in a corner and rubbed his clothes with handfuls of hay.

Feitel munched on the hay, careful not to catch an eye or attract a comment. He slipped his hand into his pocket and stirred the coins then pressed Leon's photo tight against his leg. He did not look up when people arrived but instead studied the reaction of others for any sign of danger.

*

At first light, he returned to the road and hobbled on a painful blister until his feet got used to walking again. The road dried as it twisted its way uphill. With the longer days, the bird numbers swelled and the chorus of caws, chirps and songs grew louder.

Come late afternoon, with the sun still warming his

body, he reached a track that branched off to a farm building. Feitel followed a small group of people to its open front. Beams and trusses supported a tin roof. Excrement was piled and splattered against the left-hand wall.

A lean, sharp-faced man had his back to a bale of straw. He cast his eyes towards Feitel, cocked his head to one side and raised his eyebrows. Feitel's heart jolted and panic shot through him – it was Squad Leader Baer.

He darted back to the road and was about to walk on when he was unnerved by the thought that Baer might catch him up. He needed to wait for him to leave first, needed to keep behind him. Glancing around, his eyes settled on a grass slope that overlooked the rear of the building. He jogged halfway up it and rested his back against the grassy slope. Away from Baer and the pungent smell of excrement, his heart began to settle.

The grass was sharp and pierced through his clothes. He wriggled until he got comfortable.

The grasshoppers clattered their wings and called their shrill pulses. A lone cuckoo answered and other birds swooped, collecting the last insects of the day. The air chilled and he raised his knees to his chin, wrapping his arms around his legs.

The grass grew damp and the distant murmurs of the travelling people gave way to the sounds of the animals that grazed, called and rustled.

Throughout the night, Feitel stirred with cold until the glimmer of dawn woke the birds, which called and roused one another with their song. His eyes opened and the calm thoughts of his sleep slipped away like melting snow from a barren tree.

The sun rose above the slope; its rays warmed the top of his head and burnt through the dawn mist. In the fields below, farmers and their womenfolk toiled, keeping their animals away from the stream of dishevelled people who trod the road. The stream had no head; it had no tail. People joined it from where they had been lying for the night. Its dark mass tattooed the road, weaving its path and its contours.

The damp grass seeped between Feitel's trousers and jumper. He pushed himself up by the palms of his hands, wiped them on his trousers and allowed the sun to warm his back.

At the bottom of the slope lay the farm building. Years of sun had yellowed the white walls. The tin roof, red with rust, extended over the south-facing gable. Below, a scythe leaned against a moss-covered stone water trough.

He counted the corrugations of the roof. He made it fifty-seven. He covered one eye and counted fifty-six.

The occasional lone figure, a couple, or a mother with her children emerged on the far side of the building and made their way across a trampled path to rejoin the road. None of them was Squad Leader Baer.

A lean woman, hair streaked with grey, appeared, and made her way to the trough, standing side-on to Feitel. The sun glinted on the ripples as her hand caressed the water's surface. She took off her coat, unbuttoned her blouse, glanced around and slipped it off. She splashed water under her arms, around the back of her neck then up and down her arms. Bending forward, she lifted handfuls of water to her face. Her breasts dangled above her starved stomach.

Feitel's body tingled and his penis pressed against his trousers. He recalled the chatter of older boys on synagogue youth trips. How catching sight of a naked woman appeared so important to them. He'd heard his parents late at night, their shaking bed and the soft moaning. Now, hands quivering with shame, he willed her to turn and face him. Instead, she dabbed herself dry with her coat, slipped her blouse back on and followed the path to the gap in the hedge. On the road, she disappeared amongst a sea of bobbing heads. His penis went limp, but his body still tingled. Nobody was here to admonish him, but the shame of his thoughts bit deep.

He breathed easy when the lean figure of Baer emerged from the farm building and headed towards the road. Feitel stood up and, with sore feet and aching shins, jogged towards the building.

The moss-covered trough was full of cloudy water. To its right stood the scythe, its handle riddled with woodworm, its blade dulled by rust.

Feitel broke the surface of the water with his lips, wetting his dry mouth and throat. He sucked up large mouthfuls, only stopping when the cold water made his stomach ache.

He rejoined the trail and, as the sun rose high in the sky, he made out the distant shapes of people joining from a side road.

Beyond the junction, the ground thundered with a convoy of Russian lorries ferrying tanks on low-loaders. Feitel pressed himself into a hedgerow to avoid being run over; others ducked down in the ditches.

A man in a grubby suit, carrying a bundle tied up with string, staggered with exhaustion into the path of a lorry. The lorry didn't slow. He was rolled over and crushed beneath its wheels.

Soldiers threw small metal objects from the open back of the rear lorry. Feitel scooped one up and, turning it over in his fingers, recognised it from pictures in the newspapers his mother bought – it was the Iron Cross. He ran his fingers over its ribbon, around its four tail-like fins, and followed the contours of the swastika at its centre.

An older man stared at him. In panic, he threw it to the ground.

Feitel followed the path of the convoy over the brow of a hill. Below, a town straddled the road. Soldiers unhooked guns from the trucks and wheeled them around to face the buildings.

Shells flashed, whizzed and exploded. Buildings shook, and masonry spewed out in clouds of dust. One by one, the buildings collapsed across their middles and toppled.

People halted. Feitel stopped with them, catching the smell of burning on the wind. They stood for two hours as the town was ransacked to screams and bursts of machine-gun fire peppering the air.

When the Russian convoy moved on, columns of smoke swallowed up the silent ruins and rose up.

The procession of people made their way down the hill towards the remains of the town. A woman of around thirty, with brown shoulder-length hair, ran towards them – one eye was swollen and half closed, the other flitting wildly. Fresh bruises brushed her cheeks, and dried blood hung from the corner of her mouth.

'They raped me! They raped me!' she shouted. 'They burnt our town, shot the party officials and strung up the men.'

The people marched on, heads bowed.

'You pigs! You pigs!' she sobbed. 'Why won't you help me?'

Feitel stopped, but she passed him by, retelling her story. Nobody helped her. He followed the road into the torn town and picked his way through broken china and smashed furniture littering the main street. Others scavenged the bodies and sifted through the debris. Smoke stung his eyes. The stench of burning rose high in his nostrils until he choked and sneezed.

He stepped over a sewing machine, round a half-crushed piano, and stood staring at the body of a woman, stripped, with a slit from her genitals to her stomach. He took a deep breath and bolted away, treading on debris and bodies until he reached a low wall. Resting a hand against its stone capping, he caught his breath.

He coughed and hacked, blinking until his eyes stopped stinging from the smoke. A line of men sat with their backs to a wall, heads slumped forward, throats cut and their shirts scarlet with blood. He lowered his head and ran again, stumbled, tripped, then righted himself until the road became the one he was used to.

The sun slipped lower, casting shadowy tendrils across Feitel's mind. He made his way a mile out of the town, found a barn, and threaded his way through those already bedded down. He slumped to the ground in a free corner and scanned around for Baer. Satisfied he was not there, he tucked his head into his knees and let his mind sway through its course until his eyes edged shut.

He lay still throughout the night, drifting in and out of sleep while others sobbed and whimpered in terror. Men soothed women and women soothed children. As dawn came, people spoke in murmurs, sorted their possessions and drifted off towards the road.

He dozed, opened his eyes, and the barn was empty. Weariness pinned him to the ground and he slept until he stirred at the drone of distant aircraft.

The door opened and he blinked in the light. A woman stood silhouetted in the doorway – he recognised her. She had run from the town, screaming about what the Russians had done.

Her hair, dishevelled, torn and matted, was draped over a tattered black jumper. Her dirty green flannel trousers were ripped from waist to knee, revealing a scraped and blooded leg.

Feitel raised himself onto his elbows. She flinched, her good eye widened and her mouth opened. She glanced him over and settled down in the straw a few feet away.

He made his way outside. A trough full of clear water lay next to a fence running alongside a track. He lowered his face and broke the surface of the ice-cold water with his lips. It tasted fresh and he gulped down mouthfuls, chased by a day's thirst, until his stomach hurt.

The ground around the trough was covered in a loose scattering of hay. He raked up a handful, dipped it in and held it under until his wrist ached from the cold.

He slipped back into the barn through the half-open door and stood over the woman, holding out the hay, which dripped water onto her trousers.

She took it and wiped her face. 'Thank you. Where did you get the water?'

He stepped out the door, waited for her to join him and pointed towards the trough. She crossed to it and cupped water over her face and hair.

Feitel settled down in the barn again, his back to the wall. When she returned, she sat next to him. 'Where are you from?' she asked.

His lips turned down and he shook his head.

'Are you a refugee? They've been passing through for weeks – we've been hiding our food...'

She looked deep in thought.

'Now I'm a refugee too,' she added, sobbing. 'There's no more town left. You saw what they did.'

She was silent for a few minutes before speaking again. 'What's your name?'

He did not answer.

'Well, mine's Elisabeth.'

*

Feitel remained seated next to Elisabeth. As the afternoon passed, the barn filled with bedraggled and weary people, who seemed thankful for a place to bed down for the night. A young man, perhaps in his early twenties, with an angular face and a wide smile, spoke to Elisabeth. 'Where are you from?'

She looked thoughtful. 'A town to the east.'

'How did you get those bruises?'

She closed her good eye and shook her head.

'Where are you going?'

'I'm taking my son,' she said, opening her eye and glancing towards Feitel, 'to his grandmother's house. My husband is waiting for us there.'

The man gave her a wan smile and moved to the opposite side of the barn.

Feitel beamed, elated to be described as her son. But, wanting Elisabeth to himself, he was glad that the man had moved on.

'Sorry I said you were my son. I wanted rid of him. Men only want one thing.' She hesitated, then lowered her voice. 'My husband is dead. He was killed in the war with Russia and I don't have a son.'

Night fell and the sounds of the barn changed to snores, grunts and the hooting of a distant owl. As Elisabeth sobbed and convulsed in her sleep, Feitel settled down to watch over her.

When the new light of dawn seeped into the barn, people became restless, whispered to one another, then rose and set off for the road.

After they'd left, Elisabeth spoke to him again. 'So, you watched over me all night.'

Feitel prickled with embarrassment.

'Have you lost your mother? You want me to replace her, huh? Or do you stare at me because you want a piece of what the Russians had? You're too young, my friend.'

Tears pricked his eyes and he lowered his head, allowing them to tumble down his cheeks. And when he could not hide his sobs, her breathing mellowed and her voice softened.

'I'm sorry, boy. It's not you. I know you mean well.' She was silent for a moment and Feitel sensed her mellowing further. 'Come along with me. I'm going to try and get in at a farm.'

She led him out of the barn and up a rutted, grass-centred track away from the road. She took his hand, and he wrapped his fingers around her fingers and nestled his palm into hers. He remembered his mother's last words to him. *See those people? Run after them and find somebody to look after you.* Could Elisabeth be that somebody?

They crossed the brow of a hill and below, where the ground levelled out, stood a long timber-framed house with an undulating thatched roof. Wisps of smoke meandered from a chimney. Chickens fussed and pecked in the front garden. An old woman in a scruffy woollen coat and a red headscarf scattered grain from a wicker basket held in the crook of her arm.

'This is the farm,' Elisabeth said. 'I used to come here with my mother for eggs.'

Feitel tightened his grip on her hand, wondering what had become of her mother. As they approached, the woman stopped.

'Who are you?' she said, taking a step back. 'We don't want refugees up here.'

'Anna, it's me, Elisabeth. Martha Seeler's daughter.'

The woman studied her and her face brightened. 'Oh, Elisabeth,' she said, stepping forward. Elisabeth dropped Feitel's hand and rushed to greet her. They hugged. Anna stepped back and, holding onto Elisabeth's arms, took in her dishevelled appearance. 'What's happened to your face, your clothes?'

Elisabeth lowered her head. 'It was the Russians.'

Anna tensed. 'They don't know you're here, do they?'

Elisabeth shook her head.

'You weren't followed?'

'No.'

Anna took her by the arm. 'You'd better come in.'

Feitel, unsure if he was meant to follow, tagged along

behind, trailing after them into a higgledy-piggledy kitchen which was a mass of furniture, cooking pots and game birds hung from the ceiling. In the corner, a black pot of soup simmered over a blazing fire. The warmth enveloped him, reminding him of the times his mother had wrapped him in a blanket and cuddled him on a cold winter's evening.

'Sit down,' Anna said.

Elisabeth pulled out a chair from under the long wooden table and gestured for Feitel to sit down. He sat down opposite a bowl of peeled potatoes. Elisabeth pulled out another chair for herself.

'Ernst is up at the barn,' Anna said, ladling soup into two bowls. 'He'll be back soon.'

'Can I help?' Elisabeth asked.

'Just help yourself to bread,' Anna replied, nodding towards a loaf on the table.

Elisabeth cut two slices, passing one to Feitel. 'Tuck in.'

It smelled sweet and tasted warm and doughy. Anna carried the soup bowls to the table and handed him a spoon. Feitel stared at his steaming bowl as the warm aroma of beef and vegetables teased his nostrils.

Anna glanced at Elisabeth's face then made her way across the kitchen. 'I'll get something for your eye.'

Feitel scooped up a spoonful of soup and took a sip. The flavours erupted in his dry mouth, sending a dash of warmth into his stomach. He took another spoonful, slurping it back. The taste took him back to his mother's cooking. Again, he remembered her words to find somebody to look after him. Could it be Anna?

Anna opened a cupboard. 'I've got some iodine somewhere.' She fumbled around, pulling out a bottle and a cloth.

'Tilt your head back,' Anna said, unscrewing the cap from the bottle.

Elisabeth leaned back on her chair, tipping her head

back while Anna dabbed the iodine around her eye, turning her skin a reddish-brown.

Feitel finished his soup. Swathed in the warmth of the kitchen, he shut his eyes and slipped into a half-sleep while Elisabeth explained what the Russians had done to her and her town.

*

'That's Ernst coming back,' Anna said.

Feitel stirred from his half-sleep and opened his eyes. The door opened and an old man with thinning grey hair and a weathered face pulled off his boots and hung up his coat.

'Ernst,' Anna began. 'It's Elisabeth.'

Ernst's eyes brightened and became alarmed as he took her in.

'The Russians attacked her – destroyed her home and the town,' said Anna.

'They haven't followed her?' he asked, concerned.

'No,' Anna replied. 'They're miles away.'

'That's good. Does she need a doctor?'

'I think she'll be okay after some food and rest. Can she stay?'

Ernst nodded. 'We could use some help on the farm.'

'Thank you,' Elisabeth said.

Ernst pointed towards Feitel. 'Who is this?'

'A refugee,' Elisabeth said.

'He's a Jew,' Ernst said, his voice full of panic. 'We can't take in Jews. We'll be shot for hiding him.'

'The war is over for Germany,' Anna said. 'It's the Russians who are here now.'

'If he's caught, he might betray us,' Ernst said.

'He doesn't speak,' Elisabeth said.

'He's got to go,' Ernst said. With a raised arm, he added, 'You can stay but get rid of him.'

Feitel raced out the door, scattering the chickens as he

made his way back towards the track. Elisabeth followed, calling after him, 'Wait, boy! Wait! Please.'

He stopped and swung round to face her.

'Don't go that way. I'll show you a better way. Come with me. It's not a trap. There's a better way.' She stretched out a hand. 'Come on,' she whispered. 'I'll show you.'

He took a nervous step towards her, encouraged by her smile. He reached for her hand and allowed her to lead him. They followed a path to the back of the farmhouse and onto a rough track into a wood.

The trees were in bud and birds chirped, whistled and sang their shrill tunes. In places, Feitel and Elisabeth had to stoop down to avoid low branches. At other times, they had to edge their way around moss-ridden fallen trees. The woodland floor was littered with snowdrops that bowed their heads and nodded in any passing breeze.

When they broke free of the wood, the track cut across a circular field, leading to a row of trees on the horizon.

'There's not much kindness left,' Elisabeth began. 'Anna and Ernst are kind and they will look after me.' Her grip loosened on his hand.

He bowed his head.

'I'm sorry, boy. I need to stay with them. They can offer me a bed, food and work. When something like this happens, you want to know the world can still be a nice place.'

They continued until they reached a point where the track crossed a railway line.

'Are you going to Berlin?' Elisabeth said.

Feitel nodded.

'See these rail tracks? Follow them. They're flatter than the road. Mind the trains, if there are any. You can rejoin the road where it crosses this railway in about twenty miles. Then it's thirty miles to Berlin – two days at the most.'

He did not move.

'I'm no use to you,' she said, shaking her head. 'I can't be your mother.'

Tears welled in his eyes.

'Go on,' she said, giving him a gentle shove towards the tracks.

He moved a few paces and glanced back.

'Go on,' she said.

He carried on for half a minute until Leon's words came to him: *If you ever get the chance, follow the tracks.* He looked back again and she'd gone.

16

Feitel trod on the sleepers as he sauntered along the railway track, sometimes leaping to take two at a time. He balanced on the left-hand rail and, with his arms outstretched, covered about a mile before slipping off. He continued on the stone ballast, returning to the sleepers when his feet throbbed from the uneven stones.

No trains or people passed and when dusk drew in, he searched for a place to bed down. He peered into the trees that lined the rails. Terrified of what lay beyond, he continued until he found a trackside hut next to an iron water tower; it was made of rough brick with a tiled roof. The stiff door gave when he pushed it, revealing a cold and musty interior.

He kicked the door shut after him and lowered himself onto the cold earth floor. With no straw to keep him warm, no hay to eat and nobody else to give him warmth, he tucked his legs against his chest and shivered.

He could still taste the doughy bread and the beef soup. He thought of Elisabeth at the farm, picturing her sitting in the warm kitchen. Animals called and grubbed around in the woods, and branches groaned in the blustery wind. He trembled, ready for the door to be prised open at any moment.

After about an hour, distant thuds rumbled and boomed like a far-off thunderstorm. He drew his knees in tight against his chest and rested his chin on them. Cold terror spiralled in frosty coils down through his chest and through his shaking legs.

He prayed for the piercing cold of the night to pass, for the sun to rise and for the birds to sing the dawn. Rain drummed on the roof.

When, after many hours, the first bird called, he stood, opened the door and circled the hut. The daylight was his friend; the woods were no longer menacing. Hunger stabbed at his stomach.

A leafy bush next to the hut was awash with snails, stretching their bodies to move from leaf to leaf.

Feitel knew what he had to do. He waited for a snail to be at full stretch, grabbed it and turned it over. He hesitated and it pulled itself back into its shell. He plucked another and bit its body off. It sat cold and slimy on his tongue. Grimacing, he chewed it to make sure it was dead, then swallowed it down. It tasted like the chicken and mushroom pies his mother made.

He ate three more snails, munched on fresh shoots of grass and studied the water tower: a tank, on four iron stilts with a leather hose dangling down. He ran, leapt at it, clung on and swung from side to side.

With a sudden jolt the hose dropped, operating some mechanism above. Water gushed from the end, soaking the lower half of his trousers. He let go and his bottom slammed into the ground as the leather hose jerked back into the air. The mechanism above made a mechanical clank.

A small group of crows took off from the woods, squawked in terror and circled in the blue sky.

Feitel's knees buckled – he expected soldiers to come running. None materialised.

The leather hose dripped and the earth beneath it was awash with water. He pressed his lips to the ground and drank.

The track buzzed. In the distance a spiral of smoke from an approaching train appeared above the trees. With a quickening heart, Feitel stepped back into the woods, sank to his haunches and hid. The rhythmical low thud of the train's pistons slowed until the engine drew level with him. It stopped and exhaled steam like it was sighing from the effort of its journey. The wooden wagons, set on metal frames, clanked and groaned to a halt until only the gentle hiss of the engine filled the air.

A man with a peaked cap and wearing blue overalls, taut across his bulging stomach, jumped from the cab. He grabbed the water tower's hose and passed it to another man, clambering towards him along the side of the engine.

While both the men were distracted, Feitel slipped a hundred metres along the side of the trees. He crouched down, his legs shaking – the wagons reminded him of the ones they'd travelled to the camp in.

A door slid open and a German soldier, wearing a tin hat and a greatcoat, grabbed hold of the wagon's edge and peered along the train.

'We've stopped for water,' he said, addressing some bored soldiers, huddled up with blankets over their legs.

A few nodded and grunted.

Feitel, with terror pulsing through him, continued to creep along the edge of the woods, away from the open wagon door. Between each wagon, people huddled on the couplings in groups of twos or threes. Realising this could be a quick way to Berlin, he stumbled along the edge of the trees, searching for a free gap between the wagons.

They were all taken and when the train lurched forward, and the couplings pulled tight, he stopped and straightened himself up. The wagons began to pass by.

When the rear of the train came into view, a few gaps appeared between the wagons. He darted forward and scrambled up onto a coupling, clinging on tight as the train gathered speed.

17

Feitel pushed his back against the wagon, wedging his feet against the coupling. The train gathered speed and icy draughts sprung from below as the countryside flickered past. It reminded him of a film his mother took him to see during one school holiday. Ash from the train's firebox swirled overhead, grey like scraps of paper.

He lowered his head and closed his eyes, hoping the train was bound for Berlin. He recalled Elisabeth's words that it was twenty miles until the train track crossed the road, then another thirty to Berlin. He opened his eyes, scanning for the road. After some time had passed the train whistled and he caught a brief glimpse of a road crowded with people. Thirty miles to go.

Bit by bit, the farmland yielded to buildings, hamlets and suburbs. When the train slowed, he caught better sight of the buildings, some in ruins, some intact and others being patched up by women and old men.

The train came to a halt at a station and the air was pierced by shouts, wagon doors sliding open and a burst of gunfire. He craned his neck to look along the side of the train. Some soldiers fired in the gaps between the wagons; others charged towards the back of the train.

Running towards him.

He pulled his head in and peered out the other side of the train: people emerged from between the wagons, hurrying towards a dusty road full of refugees. Soldiers' boots pounded along the platform behind him. He had to run, now.

He slipped off his perch and, heart thumping, sprinted away. When he reached the road, he dived into the throng of refugees. Panting hard, he mustered up the energy to walk. He glanced behind him and was relieved that no soldiers followed. Wafts of something burning caught his nose and tickled the back of his throat. Rising smoke clouded the distant skyline.

He gulped deep breaths and his heart calmed. He tuned in to conversations estimating how far the centre of Berlin was, what the city might be like and what food they might eat. One old man, bent over and dragging himself along by a stick, grumbled about air raids, bombs and flashes that had picked out Berlin by night.

No soldiers or convoys passed. The only vehicle was a battered car from the 1920s which, when it reached a hill, stalled, with steam hissing into the afternoon air. Feitel helped a group of men and boys push the car. When it reached the brow of the hill, the driver turned over the engine and coaxed it, stuttering, into a steady roar. As he wove it amongst the people, who were sniffing the oil-fouled air, a red-faced man who had helped push it muttered, 'He could have given one of us a lift.'

Below the hill lay Berlin, forlorn and grey. Plumes of smoke drifted skywards. Some suburbs were alight, glowing orange against a sea of destruction. Feitel realised this must be the air raids.

As the afternoon slipped into evening, Feitel entered the city's suburbs, passing factories and grander houses. Some were intact, others in ruins. He mingled amongst soldiers, refugees, people who had returned from work, people searching for food, and others who just wandered.

The road switched between concrete and tarmac. Rain swept in, his trousers clung to his legs and he scooped water from puddles to drink.

A line of German army trucks rumbled past a row of smashed houses. Some had gable end walls, still intact, pointing skywards like aged fingers. Most houses had their fronts blown out, exposing bedrooms with high-hung fireplaces where nobody could now set a fire. Ceilings, floors and partition walls had been torn away, exposing the décor in rough frames: patterned pink for a bedroom, lime green for a lounge, black and white tiles for a kitchen. What was once only glimpsed through an open curtain was there for all to see.

Destruction was everywhere; the torn buildings of his home city offered no hope, comfort or refuge. He remembered his mother's words at the camp gates: *Find somebody to look after you.* But everybody was preoccupied. Nobody raised a head, spared him a glance or smiled.

In the gaps between the remaining buildings, people worked in chain gangs or cowered in makeshift shelters while others scavenged for wood. Feitel stopped as a group of men wrestled for ten minutes to free a fallen beam and argued for another ten over how to divide it.

Feitel sauntered on. The sky darkened and the crescent of the waning moon silhouetted the ruined buildings. He stood on a street corner, shivering in the cool night air. All was quiet.

The people had shrunk away. The buildings that stood were barred and unfriendly, the fallen ones sinister. There were no barns to seek refuge in, no ditches with soft grass to settle down on – the ground was harsh, undone, upturned and uprooted.

He trudged on, unsure of where to rest. He tried to remember relatives, their addresses, but it was all vague.

A siren made him stop. Moments later, the low drone of distant propellers and piston engines swept in from the west. As the droning grew closer, it crammed into Feitel's head – he raised his hands to his ears and swallowed to change its pitch.

A succession of searchlights flicked on and punched the air like sky projectors. Whether vertical, to the left or to the right, each hunted out a bomber. Some moved and twisted until they locked on to a plane. Ammunition with tracer bullets rattled towards the enemy aircraft, pounding out its own rhythm.

Explosion after explosion, until the blasts grew so frequent he was unable to keep up. He followed a searchlight that had locked on to one aircraft. The plane dropped and corkscrewed but was unable to outwit the beam and the torrent of chasing shells. A brilliant flash, and flames shot across the plane until one wing and the fuselage were alight. It bore around to the west then flew straight. He followed its progress until it exploded, broke up and rained from the sky.

His ears stung. Bombs whistled to the ground, flashed and exploded. He hurried towards a row of standing buildings and jogged up a flight of grand steps to a front door. He knocked, and knocked again, until his knuckles stung with pain.

A gruff-looking man, huddled in the corner of the porch, spoke. 'Nobody will answer. Clear off.'

He hurtled back down the steps and up the flight to the porch of the house next door. A bomb landed in the next street; a wave of air pressure threw him against the door. He shook with terror as he sank, cowering, onto the cold stone step.

Feitel drew his knees to his chest, his damp trousers pulled tight and cold against his legs. He rested his head and shoulder against the door. Three bombs fell in quick succession. *Crack, crack, crack.*

Engulfed by the blaring noise, he pushed his fingers into his ears. Warm sticky blood wetted his fingers. He drew his legs up tight and tucked his chin between his knees. He rocked back and forth, desperate to take himself to another place.

As the drone of the planes faded into the distance and the great searchlights petered out, his eyes grew heavy. He blinked and caught the burning vista of the skyline. As he slipped into sleep, the scenes flicked through his mind.

18

Feitel woke, stretched out his arms and straightened his back in the confines of the doorway he'd sheltered in. The city smouldered. Smoke spiralled and the pungent acrid smell of burning rose high in his nostrils.

An army lorry bounced along on the street below, spitting stones from beneath its tyres in the half-light of the new day. Its engine whined and its gearbox crunched as it disappeared around a corner.

Now he was in Berlin, his mind drifted to the dream he and Leon had of reaching Canada: Leon would find a job, they'd get a wooden house, and he'd go to school.

The bell from a passing ambulance shook him from his thoughts. He stood and buckled forward, exhausted from hunger. He grabbed hold of a stone balustrade to steady himself and descended the steps.

On the street, people emerged from houses and makeshift shelters to start their day amongst the strewn rubble of the city.

His stomach growled, his legs shook and he made it his goal to stagger between the streetlamps. Some still stood, others were half bent over or broken. Many were torn out of the ground as if a wild storm had raged through a forest.

At the first street corner he came to, his legs buckled and he gripped a lamppost. He straightened himself up and faced a side road. Wafts of warm, fresh bread drew his attention to a line of people queueing out of a bakery door. A row of baskets in the window display were lined with nothing more than crumb-covered paper. He sauntered to the back of the queue where a small pile of bricks had been stacked amongst broken roof tiles.

The queue edged forward and he rummaged in his pocket for the coins he'd collected on the road. People speculated about implausible prices, yet nobody forsook their place in the queue.

The opposite side of the road was flattened, exposing the backs of the buildings beyond. Feitel made out a distant bed and a washstand.

In the bakery doorway lay a bundle of newspapers, tied tightly with string and boasting headlines in large black type. People brushed past them on their way out, clutching their loaves of bread.

Inside, the bakery was deep and narrow. At the far end, a man dressed in blue trousers and a blue and white striped apron opened a metal door in the wall. A frail old woman pushed in a tray of dough and the man shut the door.

At the head of the queue stood a glass counter with shelves of scattered cake crumbs on thin grey paper. The baker, a broad-shouldered man with a stern mouth full of crooked teeth, glowered down at him from behind the counter. Behind him sat the bread, lined up in neat rows on three wooden shelves.

Feitel placed two of his coins on the counter. The second made a slapping sound.

The baker glanced at them and raised his eyebrows. 'Any cigarettes?'

Feitel shook his head.

'Alcohol?'

He shook his head again.

'Booze, drink, schnapps?' the baker asked, curling his lip.

Feitel drew the remainder of the coins from his pocket and added them to the two on the counter.

'Always the way,' the baker said, raising his eyebrows. 'There'd be no queue if everybody handed over the right money first.'

A woman sneered behind Feitel. 'You don't want to feed us. You just want to profit off us.'

The baker did not look up. 'You've not seen the price

of flour and yeast. I have to pay extortionate amounts before I see your money. You'd complain if I went out of business.' He surveyed the coins, took a loaf from the shelf, cut off a third and handed it to Feitel. 'You're lucky. I'm generous today.'

Feitel hurried out of the shop, ramming some of the bread into his mouth. He scurried away, fearing the rest of his bread would be stolen before he could eat it. He rested at a street corner, coughing and spluttering as he forced bread into his mouth. Hunger prevented him from savouring the doughy taste.

When he'd chewed and swallowed the last piece, he looked along the street. Rows of buckled bodies in torn and dusty clothes lay side by side. A rotund lady with a wrinkled face, wearing a green headscarf and a black shawl, picked her way between the corpses. She shook her head at each until she stopped at one and nodded. An official-looking man stepped forward and made a note on a clipboard.

Feitel backed away, skin tingling and hot with sweat.

*

Feitel headed towards his home, passing through more streets of bombed-out houses. Grubby people picked through the rubble, recovering the odd pot, pan or piece of wood to burn. He stopped at each corner to reassure himself he was heading in the right direction.

He recognised a small tree-lined park where his father had taken him to play on a Saturday morning. Before him lay his street, with its road strewn with rubble from the jagged remains of the houses.

He picked his way through the debris, gazing up at the hollow remains. He stopped and peered into the rough circle of a bomb crater. Sections of the road lay at angles, water gushed from a fractured pipe, and layers of different-coloured soil revealed the archaeology of the city. A lone rat scurried through the debris before vanishing amongst a heap of shattered street cobbles.

He edged his way around the hole and looked up. The clear blue sky gleamed through the high windows of shattered buildings. Small bits of masonry tumbled and scattered, creating puffs of dust in their wake. People rummaged through the debris while others piled bricks into stacks.

A voice shouted from behind him. 'You!'

He swung around and faced a soldier who was stabbing a finger towards him.

'Don't stand around,' he shouted, pointing towards a line of older men who were passing bricks to each other to be stacked. 'Clear those bricks.'

Feitel hurried towards the men. They made room for him to join them and he took a brick from the man in front, passing it on to the man behind. As he passed brick after brick, his hands became rough and bruised.

After a few minutes, the man in front of him winced, straightened and grasped his back, then left the line. Feitel stepped forward and took his place. This happened every few minutes until he found himself at the head of the chain, proud to be choosing the bricks to pass on to the men behind. He enjoyed seeking out the best bricks, sometimes from a heap, other times scattered one layer deep on the road.

Then the brick he was about to pick up rose as if an invisible force had pushed it from below. He stopped, eyes flying wide. The man behind him, with a stern unshaven face drawn tight across his cheekbones, also stopped. The other men gathered around.

A circle of bricks toppled away and a dark crescent formed around the edge.

'It's a manhole to the sewer,' somebody said.

Two men bent forward and grasped the thick metal lid. The last bricks slid away and one dropped down the hole.

There was a waft of rotten eggs and a distant splash.

The bony hand of a skeletal figure appeared at the rim – its nails yellow, flaking, chipped and dying. It was followed by a man's face, blinking in the bright sunlight as he peered up at them.

'Is the war over?' he said, his voice quivering.

The circle of men shook their heads.

'The Nazis are still here?' he asked, revealing toothless gums.

The men nodded and his eyes grew wild.

'But they've no real power now,' whispered a cloth-capped man.

Another man glanced to where a soldier stood amongst a group of boys whose oversized uniforms hung pitifully from their shoulders.

He lowered his voice. 'Do you have food?'

The man who had glanced at the soldiers shook his head. 'None to spare.'

'I thought so. We've nothing to trade.' His lips were cracked, a mixture of dried and bright new blood. His skin, the colour of chalk, and a tatty beard, failed to hide his sunken cheeks.

'Are there more of you?' the cloth-capped man asked.

'Yes, come and see,' the man from the sewer replied, nodding towards the ladder he was standing on.

At first, no one took up the invitation, until the cloth-capped man stepped forward. Another man joined him, then Feitel followed and descended into the dark. The sharp rust of the worn rungs dug into his palms. Feet splashed below and a warm draught caught his legs. He was about to tread into the Berlin underworld of the sewer.

Distant drips of water sent eerie echoes down the tunnels. The man from the sewer lit a candle and there, on a line of rickety chairs or lying on the wet bricks were around a dozen men. Some were dead, others stared through their sunken eyes and gaunt faces. All had scruffy beards, their upper lips folded in.

'Who are they, Joseph?' one of the men said, perched semi-naked with stick-like legs. His voice was a husky whisper.

'Just people clearing the rubble. They say the war is still going on.'

'We've heard the bombings,' the seated man said. 'We've been hiding for many months. Perhaps years, we don't know. We brought money and all the valuables we could with us. We traded it for food, then we traded our clothes and the gold from our teeth. We ran out and the people we traded with didn't come again.'

'They didn't betray us to the Nazis but instead to death,' Joseph whispered. 'I had a job, a trade. I was a tailor. Look at me now.' He fell silent before adding, 'I believe I'm twenty-seven.'

A thunderous roar echoed through the tunnel.

'That's the sluices,' Joseph said. He waited for the noise to finish before asking, 'Can you bring us food?'

'Yes,' replied the cloth-capped man. His promise sounded as empty as the drips of water coming from the curved brick ceiling of the sewer, which plinked onto the water below.

Feitel climbed back to the surface. One of the brick-pickers grasped his hand and helped him out.

'Starving Jews,' the man behind him said, hauling himself out of the manhole. He shoved the manhole back in place. The chain of brick-picking resumed and nothing more was said.

As the afternoon sun cast its long shadows, the soldiers made their way past the bomb crater and turned out of sight. The men straightened their backs and, after bidding each other farewell, picked their way through the rubble. Feitel stumbled his way through the remains of his street.

The ornate trees that once lined the pavement were shattered and smashed, their trunks pitted by flying masonry. He stopped by one with a distinct curve in its trunk and remembered how he used to gaze down at it from his bedroom window, waiting for his father to return from work with his thick coat in the winter or his jacket in the summer, but always in the same black hat. He'd wait until his mother called him down for supper – giving them a few moments undisturbed.

He leaned back against the tree. The ground-floor façade still stood, its blown-out windows revealing mounds of rubble beyond. On the floor above, only the brickwork of one window remained – a section of its shattered frame still hanging by the thread of a solitary hinge.

Feitel wiped his eyes with his sleeve as misery jabbed his stomach. This was once home, with Mama and Papa. He took a deep breath and headed to the right of his ruined house. An L-shaped wall of stacked bricks, a bit taller than him, jutted into what was once the side path. He edged around it, squeezed through a gap, and found himself standing on the wooden basement doors.

19

Feitel stepped back from the wooden double doors of the basement, brushed away a few strewn bricks and dragged them open. It felt too easy but he'd opened these doors many a time to play and had spent his last two birthdays with his mother, hiding behind them.

He peered down the stone steps into the darkness, the familiar musky smell of the basement teasing his nostrils. He stepped in and closed the doors behind him, blocking out the bright light of the day. As he descended to the flagstone floor, he counted the familiar eight steps.

He brushed his hand over the simple wooden table on which his mother had prepared their meals. He found bread and cheese. He tore off a piece of each and rammed them into his mouth, causing him to cough and gasp.

To the left of the table he made out the hooped end of his iron-framed bed. He pressed down on the thin mattress and the springs pushed back. He swept his hand over it, thankful for its familiarity, until his fingers brushed against something he did not recognise.

With his heart fluttering, he patted around to discover its shape and texture. Only then did he realise it was a felt hat with two pom-poms that tickled the palm of his hand. He lifted it up and dropped it back onto the bed.

Feitel returned to the table, running his hands over it again. He brushed against the cold tapered form of a water jug. With trembling arms, he dragged it to the edge of the table and managed to lift it to his lips. Water trickled over his chin then over his chest and his shirt. He managed to gulp two large mouthfuls before he had to let go, slamming the jug back onto the table.

Feitel stretched his hands above his head and stepped forward, allowing his fingers to brush against the damp gritty bricks of the lowest point in the ceiling. Knowing this was where the two parallel arches of the ceiling met, he turned left, using the low point of the ceiling to guide him to the chimney breast, located in the centre of the basement.

He wiped his hands on his trousers then patted his hands around the chimney breast, searching for a small shelf of books belonging to his mother. They were still there, perched above the fireplace where his mother dared to boil water for washing. He dabbed his eyes as he remembered his mother bent over the fire. Who was staying here now?

Beyond the chimney breast the two roof arches were partitioned by a short brick wall. A bed was tucked into each alcove, one his mother had slept on and the other a spare.

A deep cough came from the direction of his mother's bed. Feitel froze, panic rising.

'Who's there?' a man's voice asked.

Feitel did not reply.

'I said who's there?'

A match struck, flared and rose to the wick of a candle. When the flame settled, light danced off the walls, revealing a young man sitting on the bed.

'Who's there?' he said again.

Again, Feitel did not reply.

The man leapt off the bed and, candle in hand, staggered towards him. Feitel's breathing became rapid, the sulphurous whiff of the burnt match filling his nostrils. The man's eyes glinted in their sockets – two handsome arches at the top of a neat nose dividing boyish dimpled cheeks. The candle flickered and danced, casting eerie shadows against the walls.

'Who are you?' he asked.

Feitel remained silent. The man grabbed Feitel's left arm and held the candle to his face.

Feitel's head tipped back, his body swelling with the same trepidation he'd had in the camp.

'What are you doing here? What do you want?'

Feitel stared back at him.

'Answer me, darn you!' The man loosened his grip. 'How did you know to come here? How did you know about this basement? Have you been here before?'

Feitel nodded.

He tightened his grip on Feitel's arm again, shook him. 'Don't tell anybody I am here.' He raised his voice. 'Nobody. You've not seen me. Okay?'

Feitel nodded, wild-eyed.

'You'll have to stay until my girlfriend and her sister return. Don't go out until then.'

Feitel nodded again. The man loosened his grip, straightened up and returned to the bed. The candle flicked its shadows across the arched roof and picked out a rusty metal meat hook screwed into the high point of the arch.

As the man blew the candle out, Feitel slumped on his bed, pushing the felt hat to one side. The mattress smelled mustier than when he'd last slept on it – the day the police came.

After a few minutes, the man spoke again, his voice pleading. 'You won't give me up, will you?'

Feitel tried for words.

'You're a quiet one.'

Feitel tried again to find words, but nothing came.

'Do you know what a deserter is?' the man said, his voice tinged with panic.

Feitel, unnerved by the man, straightened himself up.

In a quiet, shameful voice, the man added, 'It's somebody who leaves the army when they're not allowed. I'll be executed if I'm caught.' The words hung in the air and Feitel did not know what to do with them. The man lit the candle again and paced, head stooped, towards Feitel.

Standing over him, he said, 'Do you understand what being executed means?'

Feitel nodded.

'I do believe you do,' the man said, his voice calm. He returned to the bed and snuffed out the candle.

Feitel tucked his legs into his chest, rubbed his shin for warmth and, as fragmented images dashed through his mind, slipped into sleep.

*

Feitel woke to the doors being opened. He sat up straight, wiping dribble from his cheek. His heart thumped and blood pounded inside his skull. In the light of the new evening, two women, one blonde, one brunette, descended the steps and lowered the doors behind them.

The brunette woman spoke. 'Hans. Hans, are you there?'

'Yes,' Hans replied.

'Oh, thank God,' she said, fighting back tears. 'When we saw the bricks on the doors had been moved, we feared the worst. You won't believe what's going on in the city centre.'

'What?'

'Boys who don't volunteer for the SS are being hung from lampposts, and when they run out of lampposts, they're using trees.'

The blonde woman spoke, breathless. 'The wireless is reporting that Hitler has come out of his bunker to talk with boys volunteering to defend Berlin to their death. Volunteering my boot. That's what you get when the men are captured, dead or fighting elsewhere.'

'Or deserted,' Hans added.

'Marianne, can you do the candles?' the brunette woman asked. She glanced towards Hans. 'Please don't go and defend the city. It's futile. There's so much damage and you might get hung for being a deserter. You've got to believe us.'

'As shameful as I feel,' Hans said, 'I'm not going to leave this basement.'

Marianne raised her eyebrows. 'Both you and Hitler, hiding in their bunkers.'

'I know,' Hans said.

'I've brought the newspaper,' the brunette woman said, 'but it's the same propaganda being pumped out on the wireless.'

The candles cast shadows that flicked and danced across the room. Feitel recognised the women. Sisters. Gertrud and Marianne Binz who lived at the other end of the street. His mother used to stop and chat with their mother before she was snubbed for being a Jew.

'We have a visitor,' Hans said.

Gertrud stiffened and glanced around. 'Where?'

'On the bed, by the table.'

Feitel tensed as Marianne stepped towards him. She held a burning candle which shone into his face. 'You're Feitel Scher.'

Feitel nodded.

'Where's your mother?'

He lowered his head.

Gertrud joined her sister. She wrinkled her nose. 'He's so thin and dirty, but it's him, all right.'

Marianne spoke again, her voice soft. 'Have you been in the camps?'

Feitel nodded.

'Is your mother dead?'

He nodded again, fighting back tears.

'We can't afford to feed another—' Gertrud said. She broke off into a deep cough.

Marianne did not rush to answer; instead she waited until Gertrud had stopped coughing and regained her composure. 'Have you no compassion?' Marianne said, her voice low. 'Anyway, we've no choice. If he's caught by the Nazis, he might betray Hans.'

'You can never trust a Jew,' Gertrud said, her voice rich

with spite.

Feitel cowered against the wall.

'Gertrud!' Marianne said. 'This *was* once his family's basement. It'd be wrong to throw him out and if we look after him, he'll have no reason to betray Hans. He's got to stay.'

Hans sighed, sounding relieved.

'We all know what's happening out there,' Marianne continued, pointing towards the basement steps. 'Hitler's turning on us now the war is all but lost. They're blaming us, the German people. They don't want us to survive.'

Gertrud settled next to Hans on the bed. 'It's so awful in the city centre,' she sobbed. 'We saw soldiers round boys up, ferry them away in trucks and rope them up any way they could. They're left to hang, dangling in the air. The terror in the boys' eyes is horrid. They struggle. Their hands are tied behind their backs as they die.'

Feitel shuddered as he remembered the hanging in the camp.

Hans spoke next. 'So you volunteer and die by the bullet or don't volunteer and die by the rope.'

'Hmm. That's about right,' Gertrud said.

Hans sighed. 'Any news of the Russians?'

Feitel held his breath.

'Days away apparently,' Marianne called, now standing at the table. 'There's talk they go on drunken rampages.'

A few moments of silence followed before Hans said, 'Did you bring food?'

'Only some bread and a few potatoes,' Gertrud whispered. 'It took all our money to get that. I'd better go and fetch water before it's too late.'

20

Gertrud returned with two jugs of water and, as the light from around the basement doors slipped into a dim glow, then faded altogether, Marianne lit another candle. She sliced and chopped food on the table, dishing it onto three plates. She took two across to Gertrud and Hans. Feitel stared at the third, still on the table. Tears pricked his eyes. He presumed it was for Marianne and he would go without.

Marianne returned to the table and picked up the plate. 'Here's yours,' she said, flashing Feitel a smile. Her blonde hair was swept-back from her temples revealing a slim face, high cheekbones, full lips and neat white teeth. He shuddered as he remembered the gold fillings in the camp and the men in the sewer with their missing teeth.

He took the plate of raw potato and a small slice of bread and stuffed the food into his mouth.

As Marianne prepared food for herself, Gertrud sat next to Hans. Her face was longer than Marianne's, her teeth and ears larger, her chin more pointed.

The siren wailed and Hans said, 'Bang on time. Those Brits and Yanks are excellent timekeepers, I'll give them that.'

The grating wail of the siren became the drone of engines. The drone of engines became crashing bombs interweaved with the fury of anti-aircraft guns.

The basement shook as a bomb landed nearby. A fine layer of dust fell from the ceiling and tickled Feitel's face. Gertrud shrieked and Hans comforted her.

'They're closer tonight,' Marianne whispered, propping herself up on Feitel's mother's bed.

A heavy explosion shook the ground, followed by an avalanche of masonry crashing down outside.

'Christ, that was *close*,' Marianne said. 'I didn't think there were any more buildings to come down!'

'Hans,' Gertrud said, taking short breaths, 'what about the entrance? The doors. What if they're covered? We'll be trapped. Nobody will know we're here.'

'Don't worry,' he replied. 'There're no buildings left near the doors to come down.'

'What if the rubble we piled up to hide the entrance has collapsed? We'd be trapped. Nobody knows we're here.'

Hans hesitated. 'I'll go and check.'

Feitel tracked the candle as Hans lifted it from its alcove and made his way towards the steps. Another crash roared from outside. The candle flickered as a wave of air pressure burst into the basement. Hans stopped, his legs poised in mid-step, the candle holder gripped in his hand.

Another explosion rocked the basement, followed by a further crash of falling masonry. Feitel curled up on his bed, clutching his legs and shaking with terror.

'Stop it! Stop it!' Gertrud shouted. 'Why don't they stop it? We're *not* the wicked people.' Amidst wheezy breaths of terror, she coughed and hacked until phlegm gurgled in her throat.

More bombs thumped around the basement.

'What's to become of us?' Gertrud sobbed. 'If they're doing this to us before they arrive, heaven knows what they will do when they get here.'

Hans placed the candle at the bottom of the steps, climbed up and pushed on the left-hand door. Cool air flooded through the basement and the candle flickered and stabilised. Feitel took a deep breath, exhaling slowly, as his mother had told him to do when he was scared.

'It's okay,' Hans called. 'It opens.'

'Thank Christ,' Marianne said.

Gertrud jumped up. 'I'm going to wait outside.'

'No, you are *not*!' Hans said.

'I'll feel safer outside in the garden. There's nothing there to fall on me. And if the doors get blocked, I can dig you out.'

'Stay here,' Marianne said. 'Please.'

'I'll take my chances – if a ten-ton bomb falls on me out there or in here, I'd still be dead. No shelter is safe against a direct hit. We know that, don't we? We hear the stories. And outside, I'll see it coming. I'll dodge it.'

Hans gathered the candle up and stood facing Gertrud. 'Don't. Please.'

She pursed her lips.

Hans spoke again, his voice tender. 'Take care out there.'

Gertrud raced up the basement steps, banging the doors shut behind her. Feitel let out a long breath.

'Why didn't you stop her?' Marianne said.

'Her eyes. She was so frightened,' Hans replied. 'I do believe she'd have cracked if she'd stayed down here.'

'Well, go after her,' Marianne ordered.

'I can't. What if I'm caught? I'm a deserter, remember.'

'You shouldn't have let her go,' Marianne said.

'There was no stopping her and I don't believe she's in any more danger in the garden than in here.' He was quiet for a moment. 'I know what it's like to feel desperate to get out.'

*

Feitel's heart settled and his breathing calmed as the explosions and the throb of the aircraft's piston engines faded into the distance. He wondered what might happen next. Where this would end? It appeared there was no hope in Berlin, but Canada felt like a far-off dream.

'We've been spared,' Hans said, climbing the steps to open the doors. 'Gertrud,' he whispered.

Gertrud came to him and he took her in his arms.

'What's it like out there?' Marianne called out.

Gertrud slipped out of Hans's arms. He stood aside and she entered the basement. 'The sky is lit up with stars, tracer bullets and fires. If this wasn't the death of Germany, it'd be quite beautiful.'

'You okay?' Hans asked.

'Yes. You should see the planes weaving to avoid the shells. I saw one drop out of the sky in flames. When the bombs land, there's a white flash. It changes to red and orange as it burns. I reckon one of us should always be outside during the raids.'

Marianne scoffed. 'What, for the view?'

'No, stupid,' she replied, raising her eyebrows, 'to dig us out.'

'Oh, you were sounding rather poetic, that's all.'

'Relief, I think,' Gertrud said. 'We should move the bricks further back, so if they fall down they won't cover the doors.'

Feitel decided he'd help do that. He was uncertain of Gertrud, but if he could get her to like him then perhaps she'd be kinder.

'That'd be a lot of work,' Marianne said.

'And people from the road could see us,' Hans added.

'Oh, it doesn't matter,' Gertrud said, peeved.

'I understand your fears—'

'No, no, it doesn't matter,' Gertrud repeated.

Hans sighed.

*

Feitel lay curled up on his bed, hoping the candle would be left to burn all night. After about an hour, Marianne rose from her bed, licked her forefinger and thumb then squeezed the life from the flame. The image of Marianne, the chimney breast and the arches of the basement's recesses remained imprinted on his mind. He blinked and it fragmented like a dream on awakening.

He longed for the warmth of a blanket and for his mother to be there to tuck him in. He recalled her tender kisses to his forehead, telling him to stay quiet while she slipped out in search of food and water. And how he used to lie trembling, terrified that she might not come back.

When she returned, her expression would seem empty. He'd watch her spread food on the table. *Where have you been?* he'd ask. She always responded with a thin smile.

It was his job to empty the slops bucket. She'd wait at the hatch as he hurried across the garden, struggling with the weight of the heavy bucket.

For all his memories, he knew her ghost remained in the camp, and by coming back he had found only the two sisters he barely knew and Hans, a stranger. He tried again to recall which eye his mother had wiped his tear from when she'd said goodbye to him at the camp – still it would not come.

Gertrud's whisper, coming from the bed she shared with Hans, broke the silence. 'There are rumours of death camps.'

'Where?' Hans asked.

'Out to the east. There's a woman at work who takes a chance and listens to the British wireless broadcasts. Apparently, Winston Churchill has promised that those responsible will be brought to justice.'

'I expect it'll be the Russians who'll arrive first,' Hans said.

'They'll blame us for everything,' Gertrud replied, her voice full of panic. 'We'll pay.'

Feitel lay quietly with an ear to the mattress and an ear to the conversation. Part of him hoped for praise; part of him expected familiar words of hate. And when their voices fell silent, soft moaning began, so similar to the sounds that once came from his parent's bedroom, some two flights up, now an unknown point in the sky.

21

Feitel woke to birds chirping out the dawn chorus. He reached out for the boards that edged his bunk. There were none and he remembered he was back home in his bed, no longer in the camp. He rolled onto his front and gazed at the dim light seeping through the cracks in the basement doors. He remembered a game he had played with his mother: whenever the light grew, or faded, through the cracks in the doors, he'd guess the time. She'd check her watch and tell him how close he was.

The watch had fascinated him but he was only allowed to handle it if he promised not to change the time or wind it up. The numbers, which he counted by moving his finger from one to the next, were sharp, clear and white against the black dial. They resembled a circular railway and he imagined a train as it ran around with people getting on and off at each number. He told his mother this and she had said, 'Is your train on time?'

He liked everything about the watch face: the name 'DERSI' printed between the ten and the two, the tiny second hand in its own dial, and the hour and minute hands with peapod-shaped tips that glowed in the dark.

*

Feitel lay still as Marianne and Gertrud rose, discussing their plans for the day – things to fetch, things to avoid. He hoped they'd leave while Hans still slept, so he could do what he needed to do.

They stood at the table, just above his head. A knife rasped through bread, water was poured and the woody smell of cheese tempted his nose. They chewed and swallowed before Gertrud spoke.

'I'm not that hungry. I'll leave the rest for Hans.'

'Come on, we'll be late,' Marianne said, in a low voice.

She led the way up the steps. Gertrud followed, closed

the doors behind them and, with a few soft thuds, covered them with bricks.

Feitel waited for a few moments, his heart thumping, before he got up and made sure Hans was still asleep. He tiptoed to the table, groped for the bread, cut a slice for himself then a large chunk that he rolled into his jumper. He crept up the basement steps, pushing hard against the doors until the bricks toppled away and the doors opened.

Hans gave a light groan. Feitel scrambled out into the daylight, shutting the basement doors behind him. He replaced the bricks and made his way out into the street.

The street was a mess, yet a different mess to the one he'd left behind yesterday. A party wall, which had stood in jagged memoriam to the buildings it adjoined, had collapsed across its midway point. Its bricks were easy pickings for a line of workers, who passed them from man to man then on to a queue of carts waiting to be filled. By each cart stood an old retainer who eyed up its horse and the load of bricks. When the retainer figured it was about as much as the horse could manage, he set the beast to pulling it. A man or two pushed against the tailboard to set the wheels free and, with the horse taking up the slack, the same men steadied the cart until it reached level ground.

Feitel picked his way through the fallen buildings, avoiding the soldiers. At the manhole cover to the sewer, he knelt and rolled the bread from his jumper, placing it on some fallen bricks. He ran his fingers around the thin gap between lid and the rim and tried to prise it open with a roof tile. It crumbled and snapped at the slightest pressure.

He grabbed a broken brick, tapped on the metal, then leaned sideways, steadying himself with his right hand as he lowered his ear to the cover. He tried tapping again. Fearful of the soldiers, his stomach tightened with each clink.

Feitel rested for a while; no sound came from below. The sun beat on his neck, and the sky was a rich morning blue. He glanced towards a crater where two soldiers with their backs to him peered into its abyss.

They turned and strode towards him. He grabbed the bread and retreated, climbing up the rubble-strewn heap that was once his home. He peered into the back garden and made out the bank where he and his father had built the snow cave.

Feitel hurried down the mountain of debris and made for the basement, removing the bricks and opening the doors before entering. Shutting them behind him, he skipped down the steps to the table. A cold hand gripped the back of his neck. He dropped the bread and every muscle in his body turned rigid.

Hans then grabbed Feitel's shoulder and spun him around. 'Where have you been?'

Feitel's stomach tightened and his heart drummed inside his chest.

'Where have you been?' Hans repeated, shaking him. 'Did anybody see you?'

Feitel shook his head and tried to take a step back.

'Were you followed?'

With his knees quivering, he shook his head again.

'Don't go out alone,' Hans said. He flared his nostrils and loosened his grip. 'You'll attract people to the basement.'

*

Feitel found the lump of bread he'd dropped and placed it back on the table. He lay on his bed and allowed his mind to drift back to the crowded bunk beds in the camp.

Hans's voice cut into the silence. 'There won't be any bricks on the doors. They'll know one of us has been out – Gertrud will be cross and Marianne will worry.'

Feitel's stomach knotted with the dread of Gertrud's wrath.

'You could empty the bucket.' Hans's words hung in the

air. 'I mean, if you took the bucket and emptied it, Gertrud might not be so cross. Marianne will say you were being helpful and didn't realise about leaving the doors uncovered.'

Feitel did not reply.

'Will you do that, boy?' he pleaded. 'I don't know where you've been but the girls will insist on knowing.' The words hung in the air, as if they were echoing around.

Feitel stood and fetched the bucket. He remembered the many times he'd done this chore for his mother. 'You need some fresh air,' she'd say, then add in an unsteady voice, 'Be quick and run back.' For him it was a daring night-time adventure.

The galvanised handle of the bucket dug into his hand as he struggled to carry it up the steps. He shoved open the doors then carried the bucket across the garden. He tipped it up and tapped the base, making sure the waste slipped out. He sprinted back to the basement, closing the doors behind him.

'Thank you,' Hans said as Feitel replaced the bucket and settled back onto his bed. 'If you need to venture out again, go for the day with Gertrud and Marianne.'

Feitel lay on his bed and wriggled, making himself comfortable. He counted to sixty in his head, then counted three thousand six hundred, and with that he figured he'd waited an hour. He missed playing with his mother, the stories she'd make up and her silly voices when she read to him.

Hans began to snore. Feitel stood up, crossed to the chimney and patted around for the row of books. At the end of the shelf, his hand brushed over a candle and a small book of matches. He tore one out and lit the candle. The flame grew into a teardrop, casting a cone of shadow against the basement wall.

He leaned into the chimney and held the candle up to

the shelf. There was a small brass pot with a few coins, a bunch of small keys and a fruit knife. The books were still there, though he'd outgrown the children's books. The adult ones looked difficult. A red volume, with gold lettering on its torn spine, caught his eye. He tugged at it, pulling it free. The same gold lettering was on the front cover. *Wörterbuch: Deutsch-Englisch* – a German-English dictionary. He remembered Leon's plan to get a job in Canada while he learnt English and went to school.

Feitel settled down with his back to the chimney, the candle resting between his feet. He opened the dictionary and a letter fell out, dropping onto his lap. It was written in dark blue ink on light blue paper, dated 1939, and was addressed to his mother from a cousin in Paris.

He tucked the letter inside the back of the dictionary, then looked up words he knew and tried to memorise the English equivalent, imagining how it would be said. When he ran out of words, he opened the book at random, learning the English counterpart of the words he recognised. When he grew bored of that, he thought of phrases, looking up each word.

In what felt like the late afternoon, Hans stirred. 'What are you reading?'

Feitel stopped.

'You don't say much, do you? I thought you could never shut little boys up.'

Feitel blinked and bit his bottom lip.

Hans strode over, took the dictionary from him, and glanced over the cover. 'You wish to learn English? You're an optimist, my boy. A pessimist would learn Russian.' He snorted with amusement.

The basement doors began to open. Hans flinched and passed the dictionary back, picked up the candle, blew it out and stood it back on the shelf. The smoke of the dead flame caught in Feitel's mouth and he coughed as he returned to his bed.

Gertrud and Marianne entered the basement, shutting the doors behind them.

'Hans, are you okay?' Gertrud called.

'Yes,' he replied.

'Have you been out?'

'No, it was the boy,' Hans said and, without pausing for breath, added, 'he emptied the bucket. He was trying to be helpful but I've told him not to do it again.'

Marianne lit the candle and Gertrud glared at Feitel. 'Were you seen?'

Feitel backed away.

'I hope for your sake you weren't. You could have signed Hans's death warrant.'

Feitel lowered his gaze. On Gertrud's left wrist, she wore a thin watch with a raised metal edge and a leather strap – his mother's. He hadn't noticed it before – perhaps she had put it on at work? As Gertrud moved her arms, the watch's hands glowed and appeared to dance through the air on their own. His skin tingled. His mother couldn't have been wearing it when the police came and took them from the basement.

'There's no harm done,' Marianne reasoned.

Gertrud swung around, her face turning red. 'Why don't you ever back me up?'

'All I'm saying is there's no harm done. Did you empty it in the back garden?' Marianne said, turning to Feitel.

He nodded.

'And you came straight back?'

He nodded again.

'I told him,' Hans said, 'if he wants to go out, he needs to go with you and come back with you.'

'We have to cover the doors with bricks when we go out,' Marianne continued. 'Leave the bucket to us next time.'

'It's always *us*. We always empty the bucket,' Gertrud said. 'We use the toilet at work and don't even shit in the bucket.'

'You'd rather Hans or Feitel did it?' Marianne said.

Feitel slunk into the corner.

'No, it's took risky for Hans to go out and I don't trust Feitel not to give the basement away. But it's not fair. It's bad enough with Hans's, but there shouldn't be Jew shit in there too.'

'This war isn't fair,' Hans said. 'Don't forget, I'm cooped up in here all day.'

'If you'd *stayed* and fought,' Gertrud said, 'you wouldn't have to be.'

'And I'd be dead.'

Gertrud tensed. 'I hate you both. You twist my words.' She darted to the table, grabbed the water jugs and shot up the basement steps, flinging the doors open.

Marianne crossed to the table. 'I hate this war too,' she whispered, 'and hang on, who's cut the bread? It'll go stale if you cut it. Just cut it when you need it.'

Hans joined her at the table. 'I don't know what to do about Gertie.'

Feitel slipped the dictionary under his mattress as Marianne tidied the table.

'She's feeling the strain,' Marianne said.

'And she's developed that horrible cough,' Hans added.

'TB is rife in the city,' Marianne replied.

'Do you think it's TB?' Hans asked, alarmed.

Marianne pondered this. 'Actually, I think we'd all have it by now if she did. It's probably the dampness of this basement. And don't forget she smoked until cigarettes became difficult to get hold of.' She cast an eye down to Feitel. 'What's that book you've got there?'

For a moment he was back with his mother, here in the basement, as she prepared a meal.

'Don't look at me like a lost little boy! What's the book?'

'It's a German to English dictionary,' Hans said. 'I told him he's an optimist. He should be reading a Russian one.'

'You're not wrong there,' she said, snorting. 'They're digging trenches to protect the main roads into Berlin.'

'Are troops manning the trenches?' Hans asked.

'Just the boys I believe.'

Feitel wondered what boys these were. A pang of fear gripped his stomach as he wondered if he'd be expected to man a trench.

Hans nodded.

'Apparently,' she added mischievously, 'it takes all day to dig a trench but it'll only hold the Russians up by an hour and a quarter.'

'How so?'

'One hour to stop laughing and a quarter of an hour to bridge it.'

'That's the joke going around, is it?' Hans said.

'It's gallows humour out there,' Marianne replied.

'Any news of where the Russians are?'

'Bernau,' she said.

'My god, are they that close?'

'It makes your hair rise in horror, doesn't it? I doubt even Doctor Goebbels could deceive us now. "Our glorious armies are standing firm holding a line of impregnable strength".'

Hans sniffed out a laugh.

Feitel cast his mind back to the stories he'd heard about the Russians, then poor Elisabeth, on the road, running away from them. He hoped she was still with Anna and Ernst, sitting in their warm kitchen, eating fresh bread.

'What other news?' Hans asked.

'Our armies are being smashed. Refugees from East Prussia and across the Oder are pouring into the city. They sleep in the open and complain about the Russians.'

'Is it not dangerous talking about it? In the open, I mean?' Hans said.

'Not anymore. The irony is we had to lose the war to gain free speech. Okay, you'd not go up to a party member or a soldier and say it, but everybody has had enough of Hitler and knows we're paying the price.'

Gertrud returned, slammed the doors shut and dumped the jugs on the table.

'You okay?' Marianne asked.

She ignored Marianne and settled on her bed, coughing and sobbing. Hans comforted her as the sirens howled and the night was broken by the crash of distant bombs.

Feitel lay awake late into the night, willing the bombs to remain distant. His stomach tightened at the thought of the Russians coming.

22

Feitel woke with the grey morning light, his mind half aware of Marianne and Gertrud talking and half still in a dream where he walked through the streets of Berlin, unable to find his way home.

'I doubt any of them will be there anymore,' Marianne said.

A light breeze, from the open basement doors, chilled his face.

'It's worth a try,' Gertrud replied.

Feitel wondered what they were talking about.

'It feels a bit mean,' Marianne whispered. 'As if we don't want him.'

'Hmm,' Gertrud said. 'It's already hard enough getting food. It'll be easier if somebody else takes him on.'

Feitel opened his eyes.

Gertrud held a small book bound in pink cloth – his mother's address book.

'Is this yours?' She thrust it towards him.

He nodded, raising his hand to take it.

Gertrud jerked it away from him. 'In that case, you can come into the city centre with us and try and find somebody you know.'

He lowered his head and stared at her grey cloth shoes with flower-shaped buckles.

Marianne joined them and took the book. 'We'll be going to work,' she said, flashing him a kind smile. She opened it and glanced through its pages. 'If you can't find anybody, wait for us in the park on the corner of the street.' She gave him an encouraging smile. 'There are a few Schers who have addresses near to where we work. We'll take you there and get you started.'

He took the book from her. Gertrud handed him a slice of bread and a glass of water. The water tasted warm and stale, and the bread was cold and tough. The sisters slipped their coats on and gestured for him to follow.

Outside, they passed through the bombed-out streets, heading towards the centre of Berlin. Half listening to their conversation, Feitel gripped the address book so tight his fingers ached.

Small fires still burned amongst the rubble, some from the air raid, others lit by the homeless for warmth. On one street, two men in tatty suits stacked mattresses according to size. In other places, tables and chairs were being collected, ready for redeployment.

A few streets away from Tiergarten Park, the road was blocked by a wooden plank perched across two oil drums. An older soldier, with sallow cheeks and greying stubble, stood guard. A door, which looked like it had been torn from its hinges in a blast, was propped against the barrier with the words 'Unexploded Bomb' painted on it in rough letters.

The sisters backtracked and took another route to the park. Feitel followed on behind, wondering when they would unleash him on this mission to find a relative.

Bomb craters and makeshift shelters littered the park. A grand old oak tree, which he remembered from Sunday afternoon walks with his parents, had been split down the middle, folding outwards with various parts of its crown resting on the grass.

At the edge of the park stood the Brandenburg Gate, its towering stone columns chipped and gnarled from the air raids. Steel-helmeted sentries scrutinised the line of haggard people streaming through, waving on those who attempted to show their papers.

Gertrud shook her head. 'I doubt those helmets will protect them when that thing collapses.'

'How long it'll stay up is anybody's guess,' Marianne replied.

They passed through and stopped, surveying the ruins beyond.

'I didn't imagine there was anything left to destroy,' Gertrud whispered.

Marianne smiled down at Feitel. 'We'll leave you here to start your search. Can you find your way around?'

He nodded.

'If you don't find anybody, wait for us in the park at the end of our street.'

'And don't go back down into the basement,' Gertrud added. 'We don't want you revealing where it is. Wait for us.'

He lowered his head and nodded again, lips pursed, seething that he needed Gertrud's permission to return to his own home.

The sisters headed south down the Ebertstrase. Feitel gazed up at the Brandenburg Gate, his mind drifting back to Sunday afternoon walks with his parents to this spot. He remembered being fascinated by its top, crowned by four horses pulling a chariot. He also remembered the first time he had counted to six. His father pointed to each column in turn and counted, *One, two, three*. The day he followed his father's finger and said *four, five* and *six* was the day his mother hurried off to find an ice cream stand on the Pariser Platz.

'Well done, my boy, well done,' she said, bending to make sure his fingers gripped the cardboard tub.

Today, he counted in silence to six, remembering his mother's touch, his father's words and the taste of cool ice cream on his lips.

Now the Pariser Platz was strewn with rubble, burnt-out cars and mangled army trucks blown onto their sides.

He thumbed through the pages of his mother's address book. His eyes pricked with tears as he read her neat handwriting, smudged onto its pages. He recognised the address on Rue des Rosiers in Paris from the letter tucked into the pages of the dictionary. He found the Schers in Berlin, his father's uncles, his brother and their families. The addresses were on nearby streets. But the names were people that had disappeared long ago. Would they have come back like he had?

He wandered through the smashed streets, trying to make sense of which street was which. Rescue parties picked over the ruins, some with their ears to the ground, listening for people. Others dragged out bodies and loaded them onto handcarts. Outside one building, a soldier trailed a hosepipe through a downstairs window. Clouds of smoke and steam bellowed back and swirled around the twisted metal frame of a burnt-out tramcar.

The walls of some apartment blocks still stood. People gazed up at what once must have been their homes. Homemade signs announcing where occupants now lived hung from some of the buildings. Ornaments, some smashed, some intact, some painted in vibrant colours, lay amongst the grey rubble.

Feitel checked every group of people and every person that he passed, hoping for an aunt, an uncle or a cousin. None were there.

Ahead, people sprinted from a building which was sinking in a cloud of billowing dust.

'Oh no,' somebody said, gasping.

Others vanished from view as the cloud and the roar of the falling building swept over them. Feitel's teeth crunched on the grit-filled air. He swung away from its choking grime and ran.

Footsteps pounded around him. Those that stopped coughed and kecked in the acrid, hazy air. Ahead, daylight teased his stinging eyes. Bit by bit, like a clearing fog, it revealed the distant Brandenburg Gate.

He smacked into somebody, coming to an abrupt stop.

Pain shot down the side of his face and into his right shoulder.

As his confusion lifted, he met the eyes of a lean, sharp-faced man wearing a shabby pinstriped civilian suit and a homburg hat.

'Careful,' the man said, giving him a curious look, like he recognised him.

Feitel recognised him too – it was Squad Leader Baer.

He stepped away, ready to bolt, but Baer grabbed at his jumper. Feitel lashed out and, with flailing arms, managed to wriggle free, then dart back towards the billowing fog of the fallen building.

In the cloud of dust and grit, he made out a pile of strewn rubble heaped to the side of the street. He ducked down behind it and lay flat on his stomach, covering the back of his head with his hands as his heart thumped in his chest.

When the cloud of dust settled, he wiped his stinging eyes with his sleeve and peeked around the pile of rubble. Baer was nowhere to be seen, so he got to his feet and hurried off in the opposite direction.

He realised he'd lost the address book.

*

Feitel picked his way along the rubble-strewn streets, glancing over his shoulder in case Squad Leader Baer was following him.

He stopped at a corner where a bombed-out church was being picked over by two men gathering firewood. Its tower half-stood, blackened and still pointing heavenwards. A pungent smell caught his nose.

'The sewer's been hit,' a tall middle-aged woman, holding a white handkerchief to her nose, said. She pointed to a group of men erecting a barrier of wooden beams from the bombed-out buildings.

Could he get into the sewer, and take food to the men

hidden beneath the road? He sauntered to where the barrier was being built, slipped through and stopped where a gaping hole in the cobbled street revealed the brick arches of the sewer. He gagged at the putrid wafts of raw sewage. Ahead, it branched into two tunnels, with concrete walkways, where foul water divided and rushed into a darkened abyss. It reminded him of the times he had spent on the underground railway system with his mother and father, stood on the end of the platform, peering into the tunnels.

The darkness and the chasm of the sewer filled him with icy tendrils of dread. It was like peering into hell and he didn't like what he saw. He'd get lost if he tried to reach the men.

With no money to buy bread, and unsure of which tunnel to take, he traipsed, head bowed with the guilt of an unfulfilled promise, back towards the Brandenburg Gate.

*

It was late afternoon. Feitel waited in the park at the end of his road for Gertrud and Marianne. He'd been sitting on an iron bench since around midday, ruing the loss of his mother's address book that vanished in the struggle with Baer. He hadn't dared to return to look for it.

A dishevelled couple with wrinkled faces and wispy white hair stacked bricks for shelter, laying floorboards on top for a roof. They reminded him of the derelict couple that had stood before him and his mother at the entrance to the camp. He brushed down his clothes, terrified of anything Gertrud might choose to chastise him for.

'Feitel,' a voice called from behind him. It was Marianne. A flash of relief shot through him – the boring wait was over and she sounded welcoming.

He stood and she gave him a friendly smile, flashing her pure white teeth. 'No luck?' she said, shaking her head.

Gertrud, holding a loaf of bread, two potatoes and a

newspaper, marched forward and glared. 'You didn't try, did you?'

'I'm sure he did,' Marianne said. 'Didn't you?'

Feitel nodded.

'Where's the address book?' Gertrud pursed her lips.

Feitel's legs trembled.

'Have you lost it?' Marianne asked.

Feitel nodded.

Gertrud's eyes darkened. 'You lost it deliberately.'

Feitel bit his lip and shook his head.

'Come along,' Marianne said, glancing at Gertrud. 'Finding a relative was a long shot anyhow.'

23

Over the next few days, Gertrud's unspoken anger stabbed at Feitel. He lay, as still as he could muster, on his bed and learnt, through a series of conversations, that both the sisters were railway booking clerks at the Potsdamer Bahnhof. Hans and Gertrud had been together since before he was conscripted into the army. Marianne had had boyfriends but nobody now.

The sisters would leave after breakfast and return in the late afternoon with food, a newspaper and the latest news of bomb damage and atrocities. In mocking tones, they read newspaper transcripts of speeches made by the Nazi leaders. Each day, they brought new rumours of how far away the Russians, Americans and the British were.

Each evening, the sisters washed at the table, flannelling themselves with cold water. Feitel always turned his head; he knew Gertrud glanced towards him to see if she could chastise him for looking. He never gave her the chance.

One of the sisters would empty the bucket. To avoid Gertrud's wrath, he always waited for the sisters to go out before using it.

He wrestled with the memories of the men in the sewer and began to tuck bits of his bread ration beneath his mattress for them. He imagined pestering the sisters for help but Gertrud would say no. The guilt of his inaction pitted in his stomach and he prayed the brick-pickers were taking them food.

Sometimes he listened to the others as one might to a gramophone playing in the background, the piece only coming into focus when a familiar note or chord was played.

'What was that story we heard this morning?' Marianne asked one afternoon.

'Which one?' Gertrud said. 'Every morning is full of new stories.'

'About the old lady who was helped out of her bombed house. You know, the old lady—'

'The half-naked one?'

'Yes,' Marianne said.

'Oh, apparently there was…' Gertrud said, glancing towards Hans, half asleep on their bed. 'Are you listening?'

'Yes,' he said, sitting up.

'A soldier was helping this old lady out of her door when he noticed all she had on was a thin night top and no bottoms. He said, "Can't you make yourself decent?" She disappeared back inside and came out wearing a hat.'

'Nothing more?' Hans said.

'No, she just popped inside and put her hat on.'

'And what was that tin opener story you heard?' Marianne asked.

'Oh, listen, Hans! This is a good one,' Gertrud said. 'A man traded his tin opener for a tin of beans and when he got home, he realised he couldn't open them.'

'Is that true?' Hans said.

'That one might be made up,' Marianne said, grinning. In a solemn tone, she added, 'The railway stations are surrounded by East Prussian refugees. They camp out in the open and were caught in last night's air raid. Many died.'

'Gertrud,' Hans said. 'Please say you won't go out in the garden again during the raids.'

'I will if I want to,' she replied.

Feitel's stomach tightened and his mind squirmed as if he had spoken Hans's words himself.

*

Later that evening, the rhythmic hum of aircraft drew closer as bombs began to crash nearby. Feitel lay on his bed, shaking with fear he drew his knees into his chest.

'This is pointless,' Gertrud said from the bed she shared with Hans. 'We're trapped here waiting for the Russians to come in on one side and the Americans on the other,' she added, her voice rising hysterically. 'And all the while the Americans and the British try to kill us first.'

'What choice do we have, other than death?' Hans whispered.

'How about the choice to try and survive?' Marianne called from her alcove.

'Fat chance,' Hans called back.

'I can't stand it. Why do they hate us so much?' Gertrud shouted, thumping her feet on the floor. She tore away from Hans, dashed past Feitel's bed and made for the door. She tripped on a step and pounded her fists against the wooden doors before clattering back to the basement floor.

Hans darted across to her. 'Are you all right?'

'Yes, yes. Leave me alone. For God's sake, leave me alone,' she said. She thrust out the words in short pants between her hacking coughs.

Hans stepped back. Gertrud rushed at the basement doors, pushed them open and slammed them shut behind her.

Marianne broke the silence, her voice a monotone. 'I don't reckon they hate us. They're trying to force Hitler to surrender.'

The bombs continued to thump the ground; anti-aircraft guns fired back. Amidst concern for Gertrud, Marianne and Hans made guesses at where the latest clutch of bombs had landed. They fell silent whenever a bomb got too close, causing the ground under the basement to quake and heave. Dust rained from the ceiling, the three beds jumped, the walls trembled. What sounded like loose masonry from the ruins above tumbled and avalanched.

Feitel grabbed the side of his bed and rode it out, like he was in a boat on a rough sea. Only when the vibrations stopped did he dare let out a breath and return his hands to his sides.

'Are you okay?' Marianne said.

'Just about,' Hans replied.

'Was that a direct hit?'

'You'd not be alive if it was.'

'Oh Jesus. Jesus, Jesus, Jesus,' Marianne said, panting. 'If I live a hundred years, I'll never forget this.'

'God, is Gertrud okay, I wonder?' Hans said.

'I reckon it hit the street,' Marianne replied.

A tugging came from the doors as crashes boomed from distant quarters of the city.

Hans stumbled to his feet. 'The floor – it's raised here!' He jogged up the steps and thumped open the doors. They gave way with a bang.

'Are you both okay?' Gertrud called from the top of the basement steps.

'Yes, we are.'

'I'll come in now.'

'Where did the bombs land?'

'In the street. Bricks were flying all over the place.'

'Are you all right?' Hans asked.

'They missed me. I had a lucky escape. I didn't hear the bombs. There was just a swish. It happened so quickly – I was on the ground before I knew it. I'm shaking. I didn't realise.'

'It could be time for a taste of that schnapps,' Marianne said.

'An excellent idea. Would you prefer it in a dirty glass or a chipped cup?' Hans said.

'Ooh, the chipped cup I think, head waiter.'

'And for you, Gertrud?' he said.

'It'll be the dirty glass for me,' she replied, sighing.

Although Feitel knew he could not drink alcohol, the isolation of not being included pricked at his eyes.

Hans scrabbled around in the fireplace and, in the glow from the doorway of Berlin burning, retrieved a bottle wrapped in newspaper.

'We can't have too much,' Gertrud said as Hans unwrapped the bottle, pulled out the cork and poured the drinks. 'We don't know when we'll need it in an emergency!'

'How are we going to do this? Down in one, or sipping?' Hans asked, passing the glasses around.

'Down in one,' Marianne shouted.

'Ready,' Gertrud said.

'Go!' Marianne ordered.

They all tipped their heads back and drank.

'My god,' Hans said, straightening his head amidst coughs and splutters. 'It's improved with age.'

'Perhaps it's the bombs.'

'That's our new patent for after the war,' Marianne said. 'We'll make bombed schnapps and it'll be the talk of the land.'

A tear of loneliness dampened Feitel's cheek: his mother and Leon always put him first. He remembered the men in the sewer and his mother's watch, imagining Gertrud dying so he could have it back. He recalled his mother's last words to him. *See those people? Run after them and find somebody to look after you.* Even without Gertrud, he doubted Hans and Marianne would be those people.

24

Late one afternoon the basement doors burst open and the sisters flew down the steps. 'The Russians are in Berlin,' Marianne rasped.

Feitel lowered his dictionary.

'The day had to come,' Hans replied, raising himself from his bed.

'We were told to leave work early, and it's up to us if we go in tomorrow.'

'And we could hear the fighting,' Gertrud added.

The brief exchange hung in the air, an anticlimax. They had no details other than finding out that the Russians had fought their way into the city, overrunning pockets of resistance.

Hans broke the silence. 'Did you bring any food?'

'No, we came straight back,' Gertrud said.

'We might need to hide for some time,' Hans said. 'We'll need food and water.'

Feitel rummaged under his mattress, checking for the bread he had saved for the men in the sewer. He hoped to get it to them, but if necessary, he could offer it back to Hans, Marianne and Gertrud.

'You're right,' Marianne agreed. 'We'd better go and get food and water before it's all gone.'

'How much can you carry?' Hans said.

'On a normal day, we would roll it into our garments. We don't have a basket. And the only bucket we have is for—'

'You're not using that!' Hans said.

'And the jugs are for water. Their necks are too thin for food anyway.'

'Let's take a blanket,' Gertrud said. 'We can hold two corners each and pile the food in the middle.'

*

Faint light seeped around the edges of the basement doors, allowing Feitel to count the bricks in the ceiling above his bed. A fly buzzed around; he followed it with his finger. When it settled, upside-down on a brick, he opened and shut each eye in turn to make it look like it was jumping around.

He tried to recall his mother but could not tease her face into focus. The harder he thought about her, the more she shrank away. He stopped then started again. Her image did not return.

For a moment he was back to the day they had stood at the top of their road as two members of the Order Police dragged his father from their house. He recalled his mother's silence and her tears as she spun him around and hurried them both through the streets. They had walked until dusk, calling in at cafés. She shook her head each time he asked what was wrong. When night fell, they returned to their house.

Instead of being taken up to bed, his mother told him to wait in the hall. She made her way upstairs, returned with two cases, then filled a box with food from the kitchen.

'Can you help me bring the beds down?'

'Why?' he said.

'We're moving into the basement.'

She took his hand and hurried him up the stairs to the bedrooms.

Standing on the landing, she surveyed the rooms. 'We need to take all three beds.'

'Why?' he asked.

'If the house gets searched and there are only two beds missing, they might realise we've taken them and gone into hiding. If we take all three, they might think the place was simply looted.'

The mattresses were an awkward size, buckling on the stairs. The bedframes were heavy, bashing against the walls as his mother took the bulk of the weight and Feitel guided them from above. He counted six trips, and on each, his mother checked all was clear before hurrying them around to the basement and pushing the bed or mattress down the steps. Once they were finished, she closed the doors and busied herself with making the basement a home.

Feitel's mind returned to earlier that night when they'd stopped in a café near his father's furniture shop.

'Are we waiting for Pappi?' he'd asked.

She had shaken her head.

He cast his mind's eye around until he found his mother's face. She was there, in front of him, dabbing the tears from her eyes.

*

As the basement doors opened, Feitel sat up on his bed. With eager eyes, he watched Marianne and Gertrud descend the basement steps, clutching small bundles which he hoped contained food. The blanket they'd taken was folded under Marianne's arm.

'Sorry we took so long, Hans,' Marianne said. 'The queues were dreadful. They're rationing what you can buy. As we've no stove, we ended up trading our oatmeal and sugar for cans of looted food.'

'Some people were coming back from the city,' Gertrud said, 'with armfuls of packets and tins.'

'One woman had a chicken strung around her neck,' Marianne added.

'Was it alive?' Hans said.

'Only if it had alopecia and was taking a rest,' Marianne said.

Gertrud gathered the two jugs and mounted the basement steps. 'I'm going for water before it gets dark.'

'Leave the doors,' Hans called after her. 'I need some air.'

Feitel settled back, pressing his head into the mattress,

and watched Marianne undo the bundles on the table.

'What do we have?' Hans asked.

Marianne gave a short laugh as she worked through the items. 'Not much I'm afraid. If there were only two of us, this could last a few days, but with four of us, who knows?'

Hans lifted a tin and examined the label. 'Ersatz coffee. We drink the coffee of the enslaved.'

Marianne ended her arranging and they both stood still.

'Was that wise, to let Gertrud go?' Marianne's voice was hushed.

'I didn't give it a thought,' Hans replied, shaking his head.

'I don't believe either of us did,' Marianne whispered. Hans slipped his arm around her waist. 'Don't, Hans. Please. I can't. Gertrud is my sister.'

Feitel remembered the men in the sewer and how they believed the war had to end before they could come out. He wondered if this was the end of the war, now the Russians were here. However, leaving the basement right now didn't feel safe.

25

Feitel jumped as Gertrud crashed down the basement steps and fell onto the floor.

Marianne dashed to her sister and knelt by her side. 'What's happened?'

Gertrud panted. 'I've… I've…'

'You've what?' Marianne said, alarmed.

'I've… I've been… been raped.'

Feitel's mind flashed back to Elisabeth running towards him on the road: the fresh bruises on her cheeks, and dried blood hanging from the corner of her mouth.

'Oh God,' Hans said, joining them.

Marianne groaned in despair. 'Help me get her onto my bed.'

'I… I…' Gertrud said, her breaths short and rasping.

'Take it easy. Take slow breaths,' Hans said, helping Marianne guide Gertrud.

'I was queueing. I was queueing for the water,' Gertrud said, as she sat on the bed, mopping her cheeks with the back of her hand. 'A Russian truck appeared. A mass of soldiers leapt out and ran down the line, grabbing whoever they fancied.'

'Oh God, I'm so sorry,' Marianne whispered, sitting next to her sister. 'We shouldn't have let you go on your own.'

'Neither of us can go out,' Gertrud sobbed, 'and I've lost the water jugs. A shoe too. I just wanted to get home.'

'Don't worry about that,' Marianne said. 'Shall I clean you up?'

'Yes please,' Gertrud whispered.

Marianne stood and stepped towards the table. 'Shit. We've no water.'

'Can I have your sponge, the one you use for washing yourself?' Gertrud asked.

'Yes, but without water, it won't be much use.'

'I'll manage.'

The mattress springs squeaked as Marianne rummaged down the side of her bed for the sponge.

'Thank you,' Gertrud whispered.

'Can you manage?'

'Yes.'

Hans lumbered towards the centre of the basement, swore and swept the books from the shelf, kicking out at the fireplace.

'*That* won't help,' Marianne said.

Feitel stood up, crossed to the steps and closed the doors. Nobody looked, nobody said thank you and nobody spoke again.

*

The hours ticked by and Feitel's stomach ached with hunger.

'She's asleep,' Marianne whispered. 'I feel so awful.'

'We shouldn't have let her go for the water on her own,' Hans said.

'You can't go out until we're certain the Nazis have stopped looking for deserters,' she replied.

'Well, I suppose—'

'No, Hans, better to be raped than dead. I should've gone with her.'

'And been raped yourself?'

'Perhaps then I'd not feel so guilty,' she said.

'You can't go out tomorrow for water. It's too dangerous.'

'And neither can you or Gertrud,' she countered with a sigh.

There was no air raid that night.

*

Feitel woke the next morning to Marianne speaking. 'I'm sorry,' she said. 'I didn't mean to disturb you.'

'No, don't worry,' Gertrud replied.

'How are you?' Hans asked.

'Dreadful. I just want a bath. I want to be clean.' Her voice broke into a hacking cough. She added, 'I hope I've given this cough to that bloody Ivan.'

'We've not got water for drinking, let alone a bath,' Marianne said, lighting a candle.

Hans settled next to Gertrud and she leaned her head against his chest. 'I feel so awful,' she sobbed.

'You need a doctor, at least to get checked over,' Hans said, laying a protective hand across her shoulder.

'No, no. I don't want that.'

Marianne opened a tin of pears and drained the fluid into a glass. She took a sip and passed it to Hans. 'Just one drop,' she said. 'The rest is for Gertrud.'

Gertrud took the glass in both hands and whispered, 'Thank you.'

Marianne returned to the table and opened a tin of meat, which she sliced and added to the pears, making up four plates for breakfast.

'Not the finest cuisine,' she said, handing out the plates.

Feitel took his, resting it on his lap, grateful he'd not been forgotten. He knew his place in the basement was fragile, that Gertrud didn't want him. Now she had been raped, would she take her anger out on him? Pushing him out?

Marianne settled on her bed and tucked in to the food. 'I have a plan,' she said, nibbling on a piece of pear.

'What?' Gertrud said.

'We wait until nightfall, then Hans and I will slip out, to see if we can find water. I reckon the Russians will be less inclined to attack a woman with a man, and at night Hans won't be recognised by any German patrols as a deserter.'

'*No*,' Gertrud said. 'I'm not going to be left here with only the Jew boy for company.'

'We could barricade you in.'

'What?' Gertrud said with a laugh. 'Entomb me? I'm not worried about the Russians down here. What frightens me is not knowing what became of you if you didn't return. No, the three of us will wait until nightfall and go out together.'

'Let's get through today,' Marianne said, 'and see how we feel this evening.'

Feitel bit into a piece of pear. It was tough and crunchy. He felt alone – he had been mentioned, but only as an insult – and his eyes filled with tears. He would need to make himself useful to keep his place in the basement.

*

Feitel waited until the others had slipped back to sleep, then reached beneath his mattress and retrieved the bread he'd kept for the men in the sewer. He made his way out of the basement and took a deep breath of the cool morning air.

He reached the street and the manhole cover. The cobbles to one side were torn away, revealing its metal rim supported by a layer of bricks. He tried to lift the cover again but it did not budge. He knelt and picked away the loose mortar around one brick then pushed it inwards, sending it into the sewer below with a splash.

Feitel lowered his face to the hole, retching at the putrid stench of the sewer. He shoved the bread through and stood and wiped his hands on his trousers.

Next to find water. He'd have to find the standpipe Marianne and Gertrud used, but first he needed to find a suitable vessel to carry it in.

He headed towards the city centre and coughed in smoke that wafted from the smouldering buildings. He made his way through the streets, the rubble and the ruins. Russian troops on foot and in armoured cars headed in the same direction, towards the gun and shell fire.

Some buildings had their façades blown away, others stood with the rooms destroyed. He peered into each one, scanning around for something to carry water in.

At the junction of a main street and a side road lay a rusting metal drum. Feitel made his way towards it, tapping it with his toe. In the open end, there was some bedding and a few belongings. He stepped back.

Feitel ambled up the side road. The buildings bore down on him, angry and misshapen. He shuddered. Perhaps people lived among them who might blame him, a Jew, for this destruction.

He reached a square surrounded by spiked iron railings, behind which stood a carriage gun, firing shells over the top of a row of burnt-out five-storey buildings. He crossed to the railings, pressed his face between them and sneezed at the reek of sulphurous rotten eggs hanging in the air. The gun, half hidden by ornamental trees standing weary, torn and forgotten, pumped out another shell. A group of older German soldiers formed a rhythmic gang – they passed, loaded and fired each shell, then waited for the gun carriage to recoil before they reloaded and fired again.

To his right, a soldier had been strung up on the railings, his arms dangling by his sides and a noose tight around his neck. Feitel remembered the hanging in the camp. The inside cover of a book was pinned to his chest. His head of thick black hair tilted forward like he was trying to read the scrawled message:

Deserter.
He who fights may die.
He who betrays his Fatherland <u>must die</u>.

Feitel shuddered, staggered back and dashed up the street. He turned left at the corner and continued until his heart thumped so hard he had to stop. He grabbed hold of a railing to steady himself and leaned forward, gulping in the heavy smoke-filled air.

When his breathing returned to normal, he took a step forward. Russian artillery guns were lined along the right-hand side of a street, firing shells back over the five-storey buildings he'd seen from the square. Each shell flashed and rasped like a saw being pulled back over a tough piece of wood.

A woman and two girls sheltered in the wide doorway of a corner building. An explosion thundered from high above. Billowing debris was spat from a top floor. A small boy, passing in the street, covered his ears. Another woman in the middle of the road, pulling a cart and followed by two women carrying cases and parcels, hesitated. She glanced back to check on her companions.

A German soldier staggered from the doorway of the next building. His uniform hung loose on his frame. His face was pale and his skin smooth, his arms raised in surrender. He scrambled over the fallen debris. Another soldier followed, then another, until there were five soldiers, hands held high, jostling their way across the mound. Smoke obscured the doorway before a Russian soldier emerged, his riffle pointing at the Germans.

Further into the street, an inferno raged from a ground-floor window, pumping out flames that snarled up to the balcony of the floor above. Black acrid smoke billowed up, lipping over the parapet of the roofline.

A line of Russian tanks chewed through the rubble-strewn road, their guns trained on the buildings, their engines revving and belching black smoke.

Feitel, heart thumping and hands clammy, pressed his back against a wall. He rued coming this far into the city. His father always warned him to be cautious, to take care when crossing roads or riding a bicycle. He needed to get away.

From a doorway, a German soldier darted, firing a bazooka into the side of the lead tank. A moment passed before the shell exploded and the hatch of the tank flew open. A Russian soldier clambered up and reached into the smoking hole, dragging a comrade out.

Another German soldier, his tunic open at the collar, stepped from a doorway next to Feitel and fired on the tanks. A Russian soldier leapt out from the opposite doorway and fired two shots into him. The *crack*, *crack* of the bullets echoed in the air as the spent shells pinged onto the ground. The German soldier tipped back and clutched his chest. His helmet tipped off and fell to the ground, grinding as it spun on a cobbled stone.

Feitel seized his chance. This would do as a water carrier. He darted forward, grabbed the helmet and sprinted back to the square. With blood pounding against his skull, he stopped to catch his breath. He clung to a railing, the helmet dangling from his left hand. He remembered the hanging man – one glance at the strung-up body set him running again, the helmet bashing against his thigh, his chest tight. Minutes later, legs aching from exhaustion, he slumped to the ground and tipped forward.

With the gunfire and shells behind him, he took rasping breaths until his heart slowed and his mind cleared. He stood and, still gripping the helmet tightly, stumbled forward.

Through tear-filled eyes, he took in the scene. A jagged end wall and chimney were all that remained across a sea of rubble. The foreground had a more formal appearance and a series of stacked bricks, forming pillars within the mound of debris. Between each set of pillars was the youthful face of a boy soldier. They stared back at him, unblinking. With a pounding heart, Feitel realised what it was to be an older boy. The stares morphed into disapproving glowers. He darted away and headed towards home.

He found the standpipe in a street to the north of his home and joined a queue of women, children and men past fighting age. The path to the standpipe twisted around mounds of rubble, piles of roof timbers and burnt-out cars.

Gertrud's missing shoe, with its flower-shaped buckle, was pushed to the side of the path, unworthy to the hundreds that must have passed it. Feitel kept his left foot on the path to mark his place in the queue and stretched until his right index finger could tease the shoe towards him. He straightened himself up, pushed the shoe inside his jumper and glanced around. Nobody paid him any attention; nobody bothered him.

When he reached the head of the queue, he placed the helmet on the wet ground and swung the handle on the standpipe. A pulse of water spat downwards, half missing its target. He tapped his foot against the helmet to line it up and pulled on the lever again. When the helmet brimmed over, he bent down, lifted it to his lips, took two large gulps and refilled it.

He held the strap with one hand and steadied the base with the other, navigated every obstacle and managed to reach the basement without spilling a drop.

Hans met him at the foot of the steps. 'Where have you been?' he asked, his face full of anger.

Feitel lifted the helmet of water to show him. Hans half closed his eyes and exhaled a long breath. 'Oh, thank you. We thought… Never mind.'

Marianne joined him, took the helmet, carried it to the table and poured out four cups. She handed one to Hans and, as she handed the second to Feitel, he pulled Gertrud's shoe from his jumper. She stared at it, disbelief written across her face.

Ruffling his hair, Marianne mouthed, 'Thank you.'

Marianne carried a third cup to Gertrud. 'It's only Feitel. He's brought us water, and your missing shoe.'

'Oh,' Gertrud whispered. 'Thank the boy for me.'

Hans stared down at Feitel, his face stern and serious.

'Is it safe for me to go out there?'

Remembering the deserter strung up in the city centre, he pursed his lips and shook his head.

Hans drew in a breath and smiled. 'Thank you for the water and the shoe. You did well.' He scanned the food on the table. 'Are you hungry?'

Feitel nodded, relaxing, pleased to have been helpful. Now he was more sure of keeping his place in the basement.

26

Feitel, preparing to go out on what had become his daily search for food, listened to Gertrud and Hans talking. 'How much longer will we have to stay down here?' she said.

Hans shook his head. 'I've no idea.'

'It's been a week,' Gertrud replied. 'How do we know the Russians are still around?'

'Feitel says so,' Marianne said.

Gertrud sighed. 'You mean he nods when you ask him.'

Feitel slipped his shoes on, grabbed the army helmet and set off up the basement steps. His scavenging now took longer as his search widened and the fruits of his labour dwindled. He preferred the escape of the city to the confines of the basement and enjoyed being the provider, returning with food, water and useful goods in exchange for praise. It reminded him of when Leon went scavenging and left him behind in the snow cave.

He spared what he could for the men in the sewer: potatoes, bread and the occasional luxury. To alert the men that food was to follow, he'd push a broken brick, a lump of masonry or a slither of roof tile through the gap in the brickwork to make a splash in the foul water below.

It had rained during the night and cloud hung heavy over the city's damp ground. People scavenged amongst the fallen buildings, the abandoned apartments and broken cars. Russian soldiers met on street corners and exchanged conversation while trading their booty.

He entered a street of once-elegant townhouses, now a mass of hollow shells, bulging walls and teetering roof tiles. A body lay half buried in the rubble with a swarm of rats scurrying over its exposed ribcage. Recoiling in horror, he choked away vomit.

He looked for a building to explore and chose one where the façade had fallen away, the first floor hanging between the walls. He made his way to the splintered remains of the front door and passed through a small hall. The door to the ground-floor apartment was a shattered opening. The stairs moved and creaked beneath him as he took long strides over missing treads. Gripping the banister, he made his way to a small landing and entered the apartment he'd spied from the street below.

The boards, damp and covered in loose grit, made a menacing creak with his every step. The chimney breast was exposed right up to the pots, where a bird stood calling out. He flinched when a small clatter of twigs and soot tumbled into the grate.

His teeth chattered and his arms trembled as he stepped into a kitchen full of bare cupboards. A two-ringed gas cooker with an attached metal splashback had been ripped away from the wall. It had been a long time since his mother cooked him a meal on such a thing.

To the right, he could make out what had been the bathroom – a large sink with chrome taps remained bolted to the wall and its pedestal lay amongst the rubble on the ground floor below.

He returned to the main room and followed the dipping floor to the front of the building. People passed by, stooped with their heads bowed.

A bald man, who wore a neat suit, lowered a camera from his eye and shouted, 'Get down! It's unsafe.'

Feitel flinched, stepped back and darted down the stairs. He turned away from the man and hurried off down the street.

*

Still in search of food, Feitel scoured the streets to the north of Tiergarten Park. After a fruitless hour, he stood despondent amongst the ruins, pressing a hand against his nose to avoid the putrid smell of rotting corpses. Everything had been looted. Finding anything was a case of being in the right place at the right time.

A crowd had formed near an unguarded Russian lorry parked on the banks of the River Spree. People slunk towards it; some peered into its cab while others examined the rear. Two men, hunched and grubby, dragged a bulky hessian sack from the tailgate, depositing it on the ground with a thud. One drew a short-bladed knife from his pocket and slit the sack, spilling potatoes onto the cobbles. The men scrabbled for them; others joined in. Feitel darted forward, scooped three potatoes into his jumper and ran.

He stopped to catch his breath outside a shop where a baying crowd had gathered. Its keeper, a man with a pointed nose and a bushy moustache, argued that his prices were fair but the crowd argued back that he had raised them beyond what anybody could afford. The shopkeeper fled as the mob closed in, leaving them to storm his shop and fight amongst themselves for the spoils.

A woman, grey-haired and thin, staggered out onto the pavement with armfuls of tinned puddings. Several clattered to the ground and Feitel grabbed two and scampered away.

With the potatoes and tins rolled into his jumper, he kept his head down and ignored the longing glances made towards his loot. Some people stopped and asked him for them, but he ignored the pleas about aged parents and young children who were starving at home.

He arrived back at the basement in the early afternoon, emptying his loot out onto the table.

'What have we here?' Marianne said, her voice full of praise.

'Well done, boy,' Hans said. 'Gertrud, look what Feitel's brought.'

Feitel then carried the army helmet to the standpipe, filled it with water and returned to the basement. Marianne thanked him as he settled on his bed. Feitel lit a candle and read from his dictionary. In the evening, Marianne chopped the potatoes and Feitel hid a share for the men in the sewer.

27

Feitel woke in the early hours to the basement doors being ripped open. Three soldiers, jabbering away in Russian, hurtled down the steps. They swung a torch around the room, painting rapid lines of light across the brickwork walls.

Feitel squinted in its powerful beam. It took him back to the evening the dreaded Order Police came for him and his mother. However, instead of being dragged away himself, the table was dragged towards the fireplace, scattering its contents as its legs scraped across the flagstone floor. Each time a leg jarred on the floor, the Russians cursed, swore and kicked the table like it was a stubborn dog.

The short edge of the table bashed against the chimney. The torch beams swung around and caught Feitel's eyes again. The soldier with the broadest shoulders, thickset eyes and a mop of black hair stumbled over and ripped the bed from underneath him.

Feitel tumbled against the wall as the claimant carried his bed to the table. Throwing it down, he used it as a seat, smashing his fist onto the wooden boards. '*Vohtkah*,' he shouted.

'They want vodka,' Gertrud whispered, her voice full of terror.

Feitel gathered the slices of potato he had saved for the men in the sewer.

Hans retrieved a bottle from the chimney breast. He handed it to the soldier who banged it onto the table and proclaimed, 'Schnapps.'

'Schnapps,' the other soldiers shouted. They swung their torches around again, picking out Hans and Gertrud's bed.

Gertrud stood, shaking her head. 'Take it.'

The soldiers ripped the bed away, kicking it across the floor until it rested on the other side of the table. They sat, glugging from the bottle.

When the soldiers had rattled its neck against their teeth to extract the last mouthfuls, it was hurled, spent, across the room. It smashed to the left of the steps, shards of glass splintering.

The man nearest Feitel smashed his fist on the table. 'More schnapps.'

Hans sighed. 'We've no more.'

He smashed his fist on the table again. 'More schnapps.' He smashed his fist on the table for a third time. 'Watches!'

'Here, take it. It keeps good time,' Gertrud said. And Feitel realised his mother's watch had been traded for no more than a reprieve.

The other two men were standing; one belched and the other broke wind. The third joined them and they tore out each alcove in search of drink and spoils. Satisfied there was nothing worth taking, they crashed their way to the steps and left.

Hans secured the door, Gertrud sobbed and Marianne tidied up. Feitel dragged his bedframe back, returning for the mattress. As he tried to lift it into place, he tripped and smashed his chest against the edge of the bed. In pain and shock, he dragged the mattress onto the bed, then hauled himself on top.

Gertrud sniffed. 'I can't take this. Is this what Berlin has become? Our bright city? I'd rather die than live like this. When will it end, Hans?'

Hans had no answers.

'They know where we are. They know Gertrud and I are here,' Marianne said, her voice wavering with terror.

*

For the next half an hour, Feitel rubbed his aching chest and tried to make himself comfortable while Marianne, Gertrud and Hans discussed whether they should move on in case the Russians returned. They didn't know where to go. None of their ideas softened the terror in their voices and everywhere else sounded more dangerous than staying put in the basement.

A thud sounded near the basement doors. Voices murmured.

'No!' Gertrud shouted.

'Oh please, leave us alone,' Marianne whispered.

The doors flew open. A crowd of soldiers piled down the steps and a crate of drinks was passed down to them. They marched over to the beds, ripping them away from their occupants. Feitel sprawled on the floor, landing on his already painful chest.

Realising the original three Russians had told their comrades about the basement, Feitel cowered against the wall, fearing for Marianne and Gertrud.

The dim figures parked themselves on the beds, sharing and passing around the bottles. Fists slammed against the table in argument, merriment and for no apparent reason.

Empty bottles were smashed and the air turned thick with foul-smelling cigarettes. The conversations became chaos, garbled and overlaid. Then a single word was audible.

'*Fräulein.*'

The conversations stopped. Feitel gulped. He knew what this meant. The soldiers stood and a beam of torchlight flashed down the side of the chimney, picking out Marianne and Gertrud. They were huddled together in the alcove to the left of the chimney, eyes wild with terror. Hans stood over them.

A soldier drew his revolver and pushed Hans to one side.

The torch went out and the Russians jockeyed for position in a makeshift queue.

'No, please! Please, no,' Gertrud pleaded.

'Get off me! Get off me!' Marianne shouted.

Feitel dug his nails into his palms as his breathing quickened and his heart raced.

The women fell quiet and, over the next half an hour, the only sounds were grunts, heavy breathing and the soldiers leaving one by one.

When the last soldier left, Gertrud's voice broke the silence. 'Don't touch me, Hans. Don't you dare touch me.'

Feitel released his nails from his palms and uncoiled his rigid body.

Marianne groaned and whimpered. Gertrud called out to her: 'Speak to me. Marianne?'

It was a few seconds before she replied. 'I feel filthy.' A minute later: 'I'm bleeding too.'

A light flashed into the basement, followed by boots thudding down the steps. A young, slender Russian soldier, silhouetted by his torch, stood there, head tilted to avoid the ceiling.

'*Fräulein.*'

He flashed the beam of his torch around until he picked out Marianne with her legs drawn to her chest and her shredded clothes hanging from her thin frame.

She raised her head. 'You can't be serious.'

The soldier repeated the word. '*Fräulein.*' It was not harsh or gruff. Instead, soft and pleading. '*Fräulein.*'

Feitel looked him up and down, relieved he would be unable to overpower Marianne and Gertrud.

'Can't you see what your comrades have done?' Marianne's face contorted with anger. 'And however much you believe you've missed out, you must be pretty desperate if you want either of us.'

'*Fräulein,*' the Russian repeated.

Marianne shook her head. 'How old are you, anyhow? Sixteen, seventeen?'

Hans pounced forward and tipped the soldier's torch,

lighting up his soft, fresh face. Hans struck him hard in the stomach. The soldier bent forward, muttering Russian words, and vomited on the floor. He stumbled forward, resting his arm against the chimney and his head against his arm. He retched and coughed until a line of bile hung from his bottom lip.

Hans swung a kick at the boy, catching him on his behind. His head cracked on the brickwork before he collapsed, sobbing, in a heap.

'Oh, see how the man protects us now,' Gertrud said. 'We're spared being raped again.'

Hans returned to his corner, chest puffed out. Feitel, sensing Hans's show of manlihood, watched the soldier writhe, groan and sob until he found the strength to crawl away up the basement steps. His torch lay on the floor, its beam shining towards Marianne.

'Hmm. We've won a torch,' she said.

28

The moon rose and shone through the open basement doors, illuminating the wall to the right of the steps. Light fanned out onto the basement floor, glinting off broken bottles, burnt-out cigarettes and mud from the Russian soldiers' boots.

The cool night breeze carried wafts of the bombed-out sewers and the clatters and cries of the city could be heard. A military engine roared by and faded into the distance.

Feitel wriggled and tried to make himself comfortable. The moonlight, the cool air, his sore ribs and the sickening memories of the evening conspired to keep him awake.

He slipped his legs off the bed, rested his feet on the floor and waited until he was sure the others were asleep. As his heart thumped against his aching ribs, he darted across the basement, skipped up the steps and pulled the doors shut.

The crack between the doors allowed a thin sliver of moonlight to shine across the basement floor. His foot caught on a bottle and sent it clattering down the steps. He froze, his stomach lurching. He felt a stab of panic as it rolled back and forth in a dip in the basement floor.

Gertrud screamed from the bed she shared with Hans.

'It's just the boy closing the doors,' Hans said, soothing her.

'God. Thank God!' Marianne said. 'We should have shut them.'

Flushed with guilt, Feitel returned to his bed.

*

The next morning Feitel stirred to Hans making breakfast. The rapes of the evening before were flying through Feitel's mind. He accepted his small ration and half a glass of lukewarm water.

Marianne washed her bruised face, changed her dress,

then took a plate, sank onto her bed and ate her slice of bread and a piece of stale-looking cheese.

'Why don't you both go out?' Gertrud said, her voice flat. 'Get some fresh air. Take the boy too. He knows how to find food.'

Feitel, surprised by Gertrud's compliment, sipped at his water.

Hans shook his head. 'It's not safe to go out.'

'The Russians won't touch Marianne if you stick together in the open,' said Gertrud. 'And if you haven't noticed, the Russians are fully in control now. So I doubt if anybody will be out there looking for you.'

'It won't be safe for you down here on your own,' Marianne said.

'Actually, if you cover the doors with lots of rubble, it'll be safer,' she said.

'I'm not happy leaving you,' Hans said.

'I need time on my own,' Gertrud replied. 'Believe me. And you both need some fresh air after being cooped up in here.'

Feitel grabbed the helmet for collecting water and followed Hans and Marianne up the basement steps and outside. He helped them pile bricks, stones and roof tiles onto the doors before they made their way onto the street. Hans stopped, staring with slack-jawed amazement at the destruction.

'I had no idea it was this bad,' he said, surveying the heaps of rubble that were once houses lining the streets.

People picked through the ruins. The stench of human waste was everywhere.

Hans flipped up the collar on his coat. Marianne smoothed down her matted hair and tightened the scarf she wore around her neck.

'Lead us to water and food,' Hans said.

Feitel's prowess as a scavenger was over. His days had

become longer – the bombed-out shops were looted bare and people hid their food well. Yet he led them, clinging to the helmet and clinging to the hope he'd stumble over a supply of food.

First, they visited the standpipe. They queued for an hour, listened to stories of unwashed Russians who reeked of alcohol, horses and cigarettes. Russians who broke into houses and basements, seeking out the most attractive women.

'It was his power,' a young woman said, perhaps not even twenty-one. 'I try and tell myself he just needed to do what he needed to.'

'And the ridiculous thing,' another woman said, in her late twenties, 'was that he left me cigarettes and a tin of meat. What was that about? Payment? Guilt?'

The women nodded.

A woman of around forty with sunken eyes and greying hair folded her arms. 'I went to the hospital and queued for five hours; it was all women. They said I was lucky because of my age, that I was unlikely to fall pregnant. Some women had done awful things to rid themselves of an Ivan. All they did for me was check for venereal disease.'

As the queue edged forward, they learnt more. How a woman had killed herself and her child by taking poison, how a man of forty-five had shot himself through the temple because he could not protect his wife. And she had since gone mad and her child was staying with an aunt. How young women and girls were hidden by their families in the most obscure places.

Feitel remembered how his mother and father protected him from what they called 'grown-up talk'. These women talked openly, not minding what he heard. Or did they want him to hear? Blaming him for being a Jew.

Another woman, with a round face and a button nose, spoke next. 'They piss and shit everywhere. The stairwells of our apartments stink of it. They barge around, demand alcohol, threaten us women and say they have orders to shoot anybody found with a gun. They're arresting party members too.'

Other women nodded.

Feitel recalled the Russians barging around in their basement, glad they hadn't used it as a toilet. But what happened to Marianne and Gertrud was happening everywhere. He thought of his mother, relieved for once she was not here.

'They don't have orders to stop,' the woman continued. 'There's no limit to their plundering. They think everything belongs to them.'

The woman who had been left the cigarettes and a tin of meat shook her head. 'It's futile to complain. We went and found a Russian officer. He just scowled at me as if I didn't understand the new order, as if I didn't understand what defeat meant.'

'I don't understand their idea of victory,' the round-faced woman said. 'They believe we should be grateful for being alive.'

As Marianne held the helmet under the standpipe, a canvas-backed Russian lorry rattled to a halt, brakes squeaking. The engine ran on for a few moments, the cab shuddering. The driver opened the door and jumped out. His rolled up right sleeve revealed a string of watches strapped to his forearm.

Feitel peered into the empty cab. A bench seat of worn brown leather stretched across to the panelled far door – its window was half wound down and its bright chrome winder was pointing upwards.

'*Nyet*,' the driver said. He grabbed hold of Feitel's collar and dragged him backwards, twisting him to the ground.

Hans helped Feitel back to his feet. The driver tugged the canvas away from the hoops at the back of the lorry, revealing two other soldiers: a woman wearing a black high-collared tunic, epaulettes and a cap, tilted at an angle over curls of dark hair, and a man who resembled the driver, thin with a flat chin and receding black hair.

The woman broke up loaves of cake and passed them to outstretched hands while the man used a large galvanised ladle to stir an enormous pot of soup simmering on a kerosene stove. Feitel remembered the day they had cleared snow from the rail tracks outside the camp and the vat of soup the commandant brought them on the lorry.

An elderly lady, with white hair and a lined face, offered up a pot. The soldier tipped in a ladleful of soup. The driver took a card from her and marked it with a cross.

'It's rationing,' Marianne said. She asked Feitel, 'Where do we get ration cards from?'

Feitel realised he had paid scant attention to the rationing and lowered his head. He wished he knew the answer.

Turning to others, she repeated her question. 'Where do we get ration cards from?'

The garbled answers – including 'Rathaus', 'registration', 'work' and 'rationing' – made it clear they'd missed out on the start of the new governance.

'I suppose,' Marianne said, 'we should go and register.'

'I don't believe we've any choice,' Hans replied.

They traipsed through the streets towards the city centre, sipping on water from the helmet. Russian soldiers glared at them as they passed. One soldier wobbled by on a bicycle. A group huddled on a street corner compared watches while others dragged along the most ridiculous objects.

'What will he do with that?' Hans said, chuckling as a soldier pushed an ebony-coloured upright piano along the street.

Marianne turned to him and pointed to her bruised face.

'Hans, please. Don't laugh at them. It'll be me that'll pay.'

Hans's shoulders tightened. His head dropped and they carried on in silence.

As they passed the familiar ruins, Feitel glanced up to his companions. However, they did not comment on the fallen buildings, but instead on the stench and flies coming from the excrement left in doorways and behind piles of rubble.

'They're animals. It's everywhere,' Hans said. 'And they're like children with their looting, taking whatever they can find and dumping what they can't carry. Did you see those two abandoning that refrigerator back there?'

Marianne nodded. 'They probably just realised there's no electricity.'

Hans stopped to inspect a half burned-out car resting on its wheel rims. Its trafficator stuck out and the open passenger door glinted in the sun.

'It's an Opel,' Hans said, kicking the front passenger wheel. 'My father had one, but his was black.'

Marianne nodded and the three of them continued, passing pale and untidy Berliners. Hans pointed to the occasional item of interest.

'They love their horses,' he said, breaking a quarter of an hour of silence. 'The Russians, I mean. That's the fourth soldier I've seen grooming his horse. If only they…'

'If only they treated the women the same?' Marianne said, raising her eyebrows.

'Sorry.'

They stopped at the Reichstag building where Soviet flags fluttered from the rooftop.

'It's like a giant has been gnawing great chunks from it,' Hans said, 'then gone on to pummel it with bullets.'

'It's smashed to pieces,' Marianne whispered. 'Hitler's flags are gone.'

They walked up Unter den Linden then Karl-

Liebknecht Strasse and stood staring at the ruins. New addresses were chalked on abandoned doors. A pale man with an untidy beard peered out of an empty window frame. Feitel dropped his head and kicked a few loose stones into a heap.

'It was so alive. We had such fabulous times here,' Marianne said, her voice hollow. 'And look at it now. Gertrud and I used to slip away from home and come into the city centre just to stroll around, watching those a year or so older than us out enjoying themselves. We admired their clothes and wondered how we'd alter our own to copy the latest fashions.'

'Berlin is the Reich's funeral pyre,' Hans said, shaking his head.

They passed a wrecked tramcar and a thin, drawn woman huddled in a doorway, her chin resting on a green skirt pulled tight over a raised knee. She stared down, motionless, and Feitel wondered about her story. He stepped forward but Hans told him to leave her alone.

At the Rathaus, they joined the back of a queue of Berliners and refugees snaking through corridors, up steps and flights of stairs.

In front, a round-faced woman wearing a loose-fitting blue headscarf said, 'In my street, the Russkis have taken the men away. And there's corpses everywhere – they only bury their own dead.'

Another woman, her bottom lip turned up, said, 'And it's not a case of whether you've been raped, but a case of how many times.'

A slim blonde woman in her mid-twenties shook her head. 'My husband used to tell me I was beautiful. I used to like that. Now I pray to be ugly and not be bait for the Russkis.'

Feitel dropped his head and scuffed his shoe on the stone floor, casting his thoughts to Canada, away from all of this. He imagined the wooden houses Leon had described. Imagined living in one with a family. His mind drifted back to the women's conversations.

'The young women try and look like girls. It's ironic. We used to dress to please men and now we dress to avoid them. They say it's better to have a Russki on the belly than a Yank overhead. But when it's your belly—'

'Do you know if Hitler is still alive?' Hans asked.

The women stopped talking.

The round-faced woman eyed Hans. 'Don't talk to me about that man,' she replied, her voice rich with venom. 'He led us into this war. We listened to his speeches. It was lies, all lies. Look at us, he has done this. If he's dead, I hope they made him suffer enough first.' And she spat on the ground.

Marianne bowed her head as her shoulders shook with laughter.

'What's so funny?' Hans said.

'I guess she doesn't like Hitler anymore. I'm sorry, it's just tickled me.'

The first woman cast a scathing eye over them. 'Why has the Jew boy got an army helmet?'

'It's our water container,' Marianne said.

'You should find yourself a bigger one,' she said, raising her eyebrows.

'What, a bigger Jew boy?' Hans asked.

'You couldn't bath a baby in that,' she said. She curled her lip, ignoring his comment.

'We haven't got a baby,' Hans said, his tone mocking.

The woman tutted. She returned to talking with her friends. Marianne bowed her head, switching back to her quiet sadness. Somewhere, a clock struck noon. For the next hour, they shuffled forward, eventually reaching a small office at the head of the queue.

Through an open window, whiffs of burning wafted in,

mixing with the odours of mustiness and wax polish.

A man in his mid-forties with thinning hair was stationed at an oak desk. A Russian soldier, with a sour face, stood to his left.

'Names, previous occupations and languages spoken, please.'

Both Hans and Marianne answered, then answered for Feitel, saying they needed a ration card for him too.

'Can I register my sister?' Marianne said.

'No, she must attend herself,' the official said, handing over three ration cards. 'Report here for work assignments tomorrow. Next please.'

'That was a bit brief,' Hans said as they left the building.

'Be thankful they didn't ask too many questions, Hans!' Marianne said. 'Now we need somewhere to actually get the food. What are we allowed?'

'It says,' Hans replied, studying his card, 'potatoes, meat, coffee, sugar, salt and bread. The amounts are different depending on what work you do. And we're both in the lowest category.'

Marianne sighed. 'Working at staying alive is the lowest of professions.'

'It seems that way,' Hans retorted.

They queued in shops and exchanged food for ticks on their ration cards. Feitel trailed along behind, wishing he had found out about the rationing earlier.

Hans surveyed the food they carried. 'Enough to keep us alive, but not enough to give us strength.'

Marianne glanced down at Feitel. 'You did well to feed us for so long.'

Feitel returned the faintest of smiles.

They made their way through the fallen streets towards home. Feitel, with his eye for food, spotted a half-crushed tin tucked amongst fallen masonry. He teased it free with the tip of his right foot, then flipped it over. It was empty.

Another gentle tap scattered it across the cobbles.

Hans jogged forward and kicked it, rattling it back to Feitel.

'Stop it, Hans,' Marianne said. 'Don't draw attention to us.'

Hans scowled and kicked it back amongst the rubble.

They stopped again for water at the standpipe, slurping from the helmet and refilling it before the short walk back to the basement.

Hans broke the silence. 'What are you thinking, Marianne?'

'Oh, only that Gertrud and I always worried about betraying the basement. We used to check we weren't being watched. There doesn't seem any point now.'

Feitel wondered if Marianne thought he was the one who had betrayed the basement. He cast his eyes to the manhole, wishing he knew how to ask for help on behalf of the Jews who hid beneath it.

29

Hans and Marianne rested the food by the basement doors, then cleared away the rubble. Feitel still held the helmet full of water, one hand keeping the strap taut while the other steadied the base.

'I hope she's okay,' Marianne said, straightening her back as she tossed the last brick to one side. 'At least nobody's been here.'

Hans opened the doors. 'You go first, Feitel.'

Feitel descended the steps and rested the helmet on the table. Marianne joined him, sniffed the air and called back up to Hans: 'Leave the doors open. It smells musty down here.'

Feitel sank onto his mattress, opposite Hans and Gertrud's bed.

'Gertrud, are you awake? We've brought food,' Marianne called out, arranging it on the table. After a second she stopped and, with concern in her voice, called again, 'Gertrud.'

Feitel's skin was cold and clammy, horror engulfing him.

Hans darted across to the other side of the chimney breast and reeled back in shock. 'My god, no,' he whispered.

'What's wrong?' Marianne took a step towards him.

'Stay where you are,' he ordered, raising a hand. 'Stay where you are.'

Marianne forced her way through and stopped, her mouth falling open. Gertrud was hanging from the meat hook screwed into the highest point of the arch. She'd torn up a blouse to make a noose, fitting it so tight and close to the ceiling that it jammed her head at right angles against the brick roof. The bed had been pulled out. She'd stepped off, and below where she hung lay a pool of urine.

'Oh no. Oh God,' Marianne whispered, covering her

mouth with her palm.

Feitel swallowed back vomit as goosebumps enveloped his body. He began to tremble, remembering the execution in the camp and the soldier strung up in the centre of Berlin. But they had been different – he hadn't known either of them. Here, the horror sank in: he knew Gertrud. And he knew her sister and boyfriend, both grief-stricken.

Hans stood on the end of the bed and picked at the knotted material tied around Gertrud's neck. 'I can't undo it. It's too tight.'

Feitel grabbed the knife from the table and dashed across to Hans.

'Hold her legs,' Hans said. Marianne did so as he took the knife and dragged it across the garrotte. The material ripped away in an instant. Gertrud slipped through her sister's arms and buckled onto the floor. Marianne bent down, took her wrist and felt for a pulse.

Hans stared down. 'Anything?'

Marianne shook her head and leaned forward, sobbing.

Feitel backed away, sinking onto his bed.

Hans stood rigidly as Marianne stroked her sister's hair. It felt like time stood still until he spoke again.

'I'll go for help.'

'From who?' Marianne sobbed.

'Anybody. I don't know. We can't leave her here,' he replied, shaking his head.

Marianne cradled her sister and, in a strained voice, whispered, 'Go on then.'

Hans left and closed the doors behind him. Feitel lit a candle, poured a glass of water and carried both to Marianne.

'T-Thank you,' she stuttered.

Feitel retreated to his bed.

'You stupid, stupid girl.' Marianne stroked her sister's hair. 'Things would have got better. I know it was terrible. Remember when we were girls? I taught you to ride a bike and you taught me how to steal apples. You told Mutti the scrape on your knee was because you slipped on the step and the apples were a present from a neighbour. And remember the walks we used to do in Berlin, just you and me, dreaming of being older, wearing the latest fashions? Were you doing this when I was remembering that today? My poor sister.'

*

Feitel sat up on his bed as Hans returned with a Russian officer, a thickset man with an officious air, and an interpreter, a native German woman with a petite face.

The officer bent down and examined Gertrud's body. The interpreter translated: 'There's death everywhere. What do you expect me to do with one more body?'

Marianne jabbed a finger towards Gertrud's neck. 'Your men made those bruises.'

The interpreter gave her a sharp glance but did not translate.

Feitel, nervous Marianne's tone would cause more trouble, eyed the Russian officer.

Hans spoke, his voice firm. 'She needs to be buried properly.'

The interpreter spoke in Russian and translated the response: 'You'll have to deal with it yourselves.'

'What?' Marianne said, stunned. 'His men *raped* her yesterday. Many of them came, and they raped me too. See my neck?' She ripped down her scarf to show the bruises. 'And look at my legs,' she added, pulling up her dress to reveal heavy bruising to her thighs. 'She's taken her life because of what your animals did to her.'

The officer tensed as this was repeated in his own tongue. He spoke for a while.

The interpreter shuffled her feet, but remained silent.

'What did he say?' Hans said.

She took a slow breath. 'He wonders what you expect. His men have been away from their families for many years and they are the victors.'

Hans's body stiffened and, veins throbbing in his neck, he glowered at the officer. 'When I served on the Eastern Front, I didn't rape. I didn't attack his women. His men are no more than vile, nasty pigs.'

Feitel, heart quickening and willing Hans to shut up, placed his hands over his knotted stomach.

The interpreter grimaced and shook her head. The officer spoke again.

'He asks, were you a member of the Nazi party?' she said. 'And for Christ's sake, deny it.'

Feitel flicked his eyes towards Hans.

'No, I wasn't,' he replied.

The officer spoke before the interpreter had the chance to translate.

'He says he has ways of checking and asks for your name.'

Hans hesitated.

The interpreter added, 'If you weren't, then tell him your real name. If you were, then tell him the name of somebody who wasn't.'

'Hans Gruber.'

The officer extracted a notebook from his tunic, wrote the name down and spoke again.

'He asks for your address, and he means before all this.'

When Hans gave it to him, the officer wrote it down, and made to leave.

'I'm so sorry,' the interpreter whispered. 'I know what you've gone through. I've been raped too. I do this job because it gives me protection and food.'

'And a warm bed for the night,' Hans added.

Feitel grunted. He wanted to tell Hans to shut up, but the words stuck in his throat.

'Oh, Hans,' Marianne said. 'Don't make it worse. She's trying to help us.'

The interpreter pursed her lips, turned on her heels and

followed the officer out of the basement.

Feitel, relieved that they'd both gone, removed his hands from his stomach. He didn't want tension between Hans and Marianne, but Hans had been stupid and Marianne was cross.

Hans covered Gertrud with a blanket and parked himself on the mattress. Marianne joined him, teary-eyed and sniffing.

'I've never felt this awful, this empty. Not even last night, after…'

'We shouldn't have gone out today,' Hans said, placing an arm around Marianne.

'Hans, don't.'

'It was only to comfort you,' he said, withdrawing his arm.

'I know,' she whispered. 'I don't want to be touched. Not now.'

Hans did not reply.

'She always took things the hardest,' Marianne said. 'She wore the weight of the world on her shoulders. Pappi called us the positive and the negative, the plus and the minus. Funny really, Mutti said I was flippant. I believed her. Now I realise it's just my way of coping.'

Marianne talked for about an hour, in a low voice with occasional tears interrupting her coherent tales of childhood. Their angst, squabbles, friendship, plans of who they'd marry and dreams of the future, now torn from them.

Feitel gathered the sliced potato he'd hidden and slipped away up the basement steps. The street was deserted save for a grey-haired man and woman, half bent with age, loading wood onto a cart. A crow, standing on the manhole cover, took off as he approached. He dropped half a brick down into the sewer followed by the slices of potato.

30

Feitel lay on his bed, hands behind his head, and stared at the basement ceiling. Gertrud's covered body sent shivers through his insides; he did not dare look at it.

As the day drifted into the evening and Hans's and Marianne's conversation drifted into silence, three Russian soldiers appeared at the foot of the steps. Hans leapt up, thrust out his chest. Feitel sat up, spinning his legs onto the floor.

One soldier spoke in poor German. 'We've come for you.'

The words hung in the air. Hans took a step back. 'What do you want from me? I wasn't a party member.'

'No, we've come for you,' the shortest and stockiest of the three said.

A waft of evening air filled the basement and Hans chose that moment to rush forward. The Russian soldier nearest the steps grabbed him by his waist, kicked his legs away and crashed him to the floor. As Hans lay panting, the soldier ground his knee into his back.

'We've not come to arrest you. We've come for the girl.'

Feitel glanced to Marianne, his heart sinking. Her eyes widened and her mouth fell open.

Hans began to struggle and with each movement the soldier's knee ground tighter into the small of his back until his legs became still.

Feitel's eyes flicked to the open basement doors, willing Marianne to run.

Hans banged his fists on the basement floor. 'Leave her alone, you pigs! For God's sake, leave her alone!' He spat out the words between sobs.

Feitel half stood, wanting to defend her. Wanting to shout at the Russians to leave her alone.

Marianne, her blotchy and tear-stained face visible in

the light cast from the open doors, got up off her bed. 'What do you want from me?'

'No, Marianne, no,' Hans sobbed. 'Don't do it.'

'Whatever you do, you can't take any more from me,' she whispered. 'There's nothing else to give. You've taken Berlin, taken my sister, taken my pride. Whatever you do doesn't matter.'

One of the Russians shook his head. 'No,' he began again. 'The... The...' He broke off, struggling for the words. After a few moments, he said, 'The *myertviye* girl.'

Feitel remembered hearing '*myertviye*' on the road and that it meant 'dead'. The words in his head built up, swelling into a crescendo. He took a deep breath and pushed them from his throat. 'They've come for Gertrud, not you!' he shouted. He fell back panting, the air stripped from his lungs.

Marianne's eyes darted towards him. Hans stopped struggling. The soldier released Hans and stood.

Marianne sighed with relief, stepped back and pointed towards her sister. 'She's there.'

Feitel raised his hand to his throat, amazed he had spoken.

Two of the Russians carried Gertrud by her shoulders; the third gripped her ankles. The blanket slipped, exposing her white face, tipped back with eyes staring at nothing. Marianne dashed forward and rearranged it, draping it over her head.

Hans stood to one side and allowed the soldiers to carry the body feet-first up the steps. He followed Marianne out into the open.

Feitel trailed along behind, expecting the soldiers to head towards the road. Instead, as Gertrud's body sagged below the blanket, they turned towards the garden. Near the furthest mound of rubble, a rough hole had been dug. The earth piled onto the grass stood neat amongst the filth and destruction of Berlin. A spade stuck up from the top of it, its handle leaning. A shadow ran through the empty grave, lighting half of one side.

The soldiers made their way to the graveside without tripping or stumbling. Marianne and Hans followed, their heads bowed. They placed her down alongside the grave then stood and straightened their backs.

Feitel blinked back tears as he wondered about his mother's last moments. In the gas chamber, in the crematorium – while he was in the barracks, getting his tattoo and tunic. She had been robbed of a grave and people to say goodbye to her.

Marianne and Hans waited as the Russians talked in their native tongue. They lifted Gertrud and lowered her into the shallow grave. Marianne reached for a handful of earth and scattered it over the blanket. Hans followed suit with another scoop of earth. The German-speaking Russian reached for the shovel and shifted the earth from the pile to the grave in regular, practised movements.

Feitel fixed his eyes on Marianne. She looked old, her face drawn and sorrowful. Hans dabbed his red eyes and hung his head low, wringing his hands together as the shroud of his girlfriend faded amongst the earth.

31

Feitel felt unnerved as the Russian soldiers finished heaping earth onto Gertrud's grave. He knew there was no returning for Gertrud; it was so final and the future now even more uncertain. Would Hans and Marianne move on? Now he could speak, should he ask for help with the Jewish men hiding in the sewer?

The soldiers stood up and bowed their heads. The youngest of the three, whose tunic hung loose on his frame, patted the earth with his spade until it formed a ridged mound. He stood, leaving the grave still and lifeless.

'Thank you,' Marianne whispered. Hans nodded.

The Russians made to leave, and Feitel took his chance. With a trembling hand, he gripped the tunic of the short, stocky soldier.

'Please,' he said, his voice croaking. 'Please.'

The soldier gave him a half-interested glance.

Feitel tugged at the soldier's tunic, leading him towards the road. 'Men are hiding in the sewer.'

He glanced to where Feitel was pointing.

'Hans, go and help the boy,' Marianne said. 'I'll be all right. I need a bit of time on my own.'

'Come on,' Hans said. 'Show us the way.'

In the cool evening air, Feitel led them out onto the street and pointed to the manhole cover.

'There are men down there?' Hans asked.

Feitel nodded, his mouth half open.

The soldiers murmured in Russian before two of them cocked their rifles, aiming at the cover. The third prised it open with the tip of the spade and, as it lifted clear of the rim, Hans stepped forward, slipped his fingers under the cover and hauled it off.

The top rungs of the ladder led into the abyss of the dark hole. Hans stepped back, covering his face as the smell

– a mix of rotten eggs and stale cheese – rose into the air. The stocky soldier pulled a torch from his pocket and descended.

'You go next,' Hans said. 'I'll follow.'

Feitel lowered himself down the ladder as the soldier splashed into the shallow water below. His torch picked out the brickwork, then a man at the foot of the ladder. His lips were pale and turned in. Flies buzzed around his cheeks. An arm, no more than a crooked stick, reached towards the rungs, the lower part of his torso submerged in the water.

Hans joined Feitel at the foot of the ladder. The torch picked out the other men: some still parked on their rickety chairs, others slumped across one another, rats scurrying across their bodies.

Hans grabbed hold of the ladder, leaned forward and vomited. When he had retched his stomach's last contents, he thrust an arm towards the dead and asked, 'These are your people? Jews, I mean.'

Feitel pursed his lips and nodded.

The soldier flashed his torch at the ladder and Feitel took the cue to leave. They climbed back up and the other soldiers helped them back out onto the street.

'*Myertviye yevryei*,' the stocky soldier said, wiping his hands on his uniform.

'Dead Jews,' Feitel repeated.

Hans laid his arm across Feitel's shoulders. 'Come on, let's find Marianne.'

They picked their way back through the rubble to the basement steps. 'You go first,' Hans said, dropping his arm from Feitel's shoulders.

Feitel descended the steps. Marianne stepped out from behind the chimney, her shoulders drooped with grief, holding a scarf of Gertrud's in one hand and a shoe in the other. The flickering light of a candle cast shadows over her puffy, tear-stained face.

'I'm sorry about Gertrud,' Feitel said.

Marianne nodded, tight-lipped. Her teary eyes glanced towards Hans, descending the steps behind him. 'What was that about?'

'We reckon we've had it bad,' Hans said, sighing as he slumped to the floor. He hung his head into his hands, muttering, 'So much death, so much death.' He began to weep.

'What was it?' Marianne said.

'His people,' he replied, shaking his head.

Feitel swelled with pride with the reference to 'his people'.

'His people? What?' She drew in her eyebrows.

Feitel, not knowing whether to look at Hans or Marianne, bowed his head.

'In the sewer. They'd been living in the sewer,' Hans said, his voice cracking. 'They're all dead, and the eyes, the bulging eyes staring at that last moment of hope… And there's poor Gertrud who'd run out of hope…'

'I'm so sorry,' Marianne whispered, turning towards Feitel. 'This bloody war. Now everybody is a casualty. Where is God?'

32

Feitel stirred from a dream – he'd found food in a nearby street, then been chased by a crowd demanding he hand it over. As the fog of sleep lifted, he became aware of Hans and Marianne leaving to report for work. Dull fragments of light peeped through the gaps around the doors and cast shard-like rays across the flagstone floor.

He hauled himself up, swinging his feet off the bed. He sipped water from a half-filled glass at the table. It tasted stale and tickled his dry throat.

Out on the street, the air smelled fresh. The Russians had gone, leaving just a few people to sift through the fallen buildings and gather firewood.

He considered venturing into the city but, with Marianne and Hans bringing food, he ambled back to the basement and lay, listless, on his bed.

*

Around midday, Marianne descended the basement steps, her matted hair clinging to her head. She looked drawn and the bruises on her face had turned purple. She spoke to him, her voice weak. 'Hello, Feitel.'

He raised himself onto his elbows, pleased to see her.

'I've brought some bread. It's not much, I'm afraid. I don't know what Hans will manage to bring so it's only one piece for now.'

She cut a slice and handed it to him. He scoffed it down then remembered to thank her.

'What did you do this morning?' she said.

'Nothing,' he replied, worried she might be cross.

'We all need days like those.'

Marianne left the basement doors open and came and went throughout the afternoon. Sometimes she passed back and forth between the garden and the street; at other times she curled up on her bed to rest. After several hours of this

Feitel swung his legs off the bed to go and see what she was doing. At the basement steps he hesitated, his courage slipping away. He retreated, settled down on his bed and pictured the days his mother had stood at the table preparing food.

*

Feitel, trying to memorise new English words, looked up from his dictionary. It was early evening and Hans was descending the basement steps.

'I lost you in the Rathaus.'

'It was a bit of a scramble,' Marianne said, rising from her bed. 'They ended up separating the men and women anyhow. How did you get on?'

'I had to go to a factory and help dismantle some steel-pressing machinery. Two Russkis stood over us. One made notes as the other labelled the parts. The other men said that throughout the city our industry is being dismantled and sent to Russia.'

'What wasn't bombed is being looted,' Marianne said, shaking her head. 'They didn't have anything for me. I've got to go back tomorrow. Now I'm officially working, they've allowed me to exchange my ration card for one with more entitlements. Though it's a moot point because I only had enough money for half a loaf of bread.'

'Everything is so expensive,' Hans said. 'The man working next to me was penniless so traded his ration card for a pot of jam and a lump of cheese. God knows what he'll eat for the rest of the week.'

'Did they feed you?' Marianne said.

'Yes, a thick gruel in the late afternoon, with bread. Here, I brought the bread.'

'Thank you,' she said, taking it from Hans's outstretched arm. She tore off a chunk and placed the rest on the table. 'Help yourself, Feitel.'

He stood, tore off a piece and jammed it into his mouth.

He scooped up a few crumbs, which he sucked from the palm of his hand.

'You were hungry,' Hans said.

Before Feitel could reply, Marianne asked, 'Did you notice that the Russians have disappeared?'

'There were plenty where I worked,' Hans said, 'but I thought it was a bit quiet when I got back.'

'I'm glad to see the back of them,' Marianne said, picking up the empty army helmet. 'Can you go for water?' She handed the helmet to him.

Hans beckoned to Feitel. 'Are you going to come with me?'

Feitel joined him and they set off through the empty streets in the dimming light of the evening. As they approached the standpipe, a line of people were bent over, tugging at a large brown body.

'I wonder what's going on there,' Hans said, pointing towards the row of raised bottoms.

'Perhaps they've found a Russian,' Feitel said.

Hans chuckled.

When they reached the crowd, a few metres from the standpipe, Hans stopped. Feitel followed his gaze to blooded chunks of meat being torn from a horse. Its head lay intact, its right eye bulged and stared, and its mane drifted down to its open torso. Blood trickled amongst the rubble and dripped from people's hands.

'My god,' Hans groaned.

A small middle-aged man clutched chunks of meat. Blood had spread onto the cuffs of his white shirt.

'We have to eat, don't we?' the man said. 'It was injured and the Russians left it behind, tied up. This evening it died.'

Hans and Feitel filled the helmet from the standpipe, then made their way back to the basement in silence.

Marianne wasn't in the cellar, so they ventured out again to search for her. She was in the garden, gazing down at

Gertrud's grave. Feitel followed Hans as he joined her. The grave was covered in cobbles, layered across the earthen mound like the underside of the brick arches in the basement. The surrounding ground had been neatly tilled.

'Did you do that?' Hans asked.

Marianne nodded.

'I'd have helped you,' he said.

'I wanted to do it for her,' she whispered. 'And it gave me something to do.'

'Yes, well, I'd have liked to,' he said, sounding a bit hurt.

'You can find us a plant or some flowers,' she said.

'Yes, yes, I'll do that.'

33

Feitel woke in the early hours, terror sucking the breath from his mouth.

'Feitel, Feitel!' a distant voice called. It was Hans, shaking him. 'Feitel, Feitel! Wake up.'

He opened his eyes. Marianne stood behind Hans, candle in hand and concern all over her face.

'You were dreaming and calling out,' Hans said.

'Take a deep breath,' Marianne said.

He remembered his mother telling him to do the same whenever he was scared. He steadied his breathing and exhaled slowly.

'Are you okay now?' Marianne said.

Feitel nodded and his basement mates returned to their beds.

*

The next morning, Hans and Marianne left together. Feitel waited for their footsteps to fade into the distance. He opened his dictionary and unfolded the letter from his mother's cousin, still tucked inside its pages. He read the address on Rue des Rosiers in Paris again, and dreamt of reaching it, then England to board a boat to Canada.

Feitel spent the rest of the day reading the dictionary. He marked off the hours using the chimes from a distant church clock. As it struck six p.m. Marianne returned, placing food on the table.

'It's just scraps of bread from my work meal, I'm afraid,' she said, dividing it across three plates. 'Let's hope Hans has had more luck.'

Hans returned with a tin of ham. Marianne opened it and cut a slice for each plate.

She handed Feitel his. 'Eat up. You must be starving.'

Feitel had never tried ham before. He tore off a piece, placed it in his mouth and chewed. It tasted soft and sweet.

He bit into a piece of bread; it was stale and tough.

'Have you heard the news?' Hans asked. 'We're now in the American zone.'

'Thank God for that,' Marianne replied. 'A woman told me today that she's living in the Russian zone and the clocks have to be set to Moscow time. And the soldiers rampage around, collecting their wedding rings.'

'People disappear there at night,' Hans said, chewing on a piece of bread. 'Young men vanish and are never heard from again. Women too.'

'It's terrible,' Marianne whispered, lighting a candle.

Feitel finished his meal and lay back with both hands behind his head, taking in the news. He lay awake long after the candle had died and their voices had fallen silent. He listened to their gentle breaths and realised he needed to move on to fulfil the dream he'd had with Leon of making it to Canada. In the stuffiness of the basement, where the night air smelled mustier than ever, he imagined heading west.

*

Feitel waited until Hans and Marianne left for work before he made his way out onto the street. He took the picture of Leon and the letter from his mother's cousin in Paris. He had no plan other than some rehearsed sentences of English, the knowledge that Paris was to the west and the hope his mother's cousin still lived at the same address. Even if he got there, would she help him reach England?

He ambled towards the centre of the city, passing light green army trucks inscribed with the letters 'USA'. Soldiers stood near them wearing pressed tunics, trousers and neat caps perched on their heads.

Two youthful soldiers pulled up in a small open-top car with its windscreen folded flat against the bonnet. Two women, walking unaccompanied, stopped to chat with them. There was cheer and excitement in their voices. Feitel assumed they were speaking English but, unable to grasp what they said, lost his courage to ask for help to get to Paris.

He scuffed his feet along the road. The trees were plastered with mosaics of cards and envelopes, pinned in place, with desperate messages written in ink or pencil. Some included drawings, others photographs. All asked after missing loved ones or offered to exchange goods for food. At one tree, a small crowd had gathered to read the notes; at another, a single person stood, jotting down details in a journal.

He read some of the messages:

Christel, I'll be waiting here each evening at eight. Franz.

Elsa, I'm at 52A Muhlheim Strasse.

Gold-leaf ornamental mantle clock, will swap for food or cigarettes, call at basement 75 Karl-Liebknecht Strasse.

Young Berlin woman will exchange favours for food, here nine each evening.

Two middle-aged women in scruffy overcoats passed with armfuls of firewood.

He sauntered on and, feet aching, passed through the Brandenburg Gate to the streets beyond. On a corner, where the ruins of the buildings had strewn out onto the pavement, a small crowd of men gathered to watch two stocky American soldiers talking and smoking cigarettes. The word 'buddy' was used more than once and he made a mental note to look it up in his dictionary to see what it meant.

As the soldiers smoked their cigarettes, the crowd murmured and jostled, anticipating a fight for the dog-ends.

When one tossed his cigarette butt onto the ground, the men tumbled over one another, scrambling for it. After a few moments, a young, unshaven, dirty-looking man stood in victory, holding the butt. Others carried on scrabbling, unaware the fight was over. The soldiers chuckled and headed off in the direction that Feitel had come from.

An old man with a head of thick white hair pushed a pram with his possessions heaped on top and firewood lodged between the wheels. He spoke as he passed: 'Got to take my belongings with me wherever I go. They'll pinch them otherwise.'

Feitel turned into a street he recognised. It was where he'd run headlong into Squad Leader Baer and lost his mother's address book. He searched around for it – it was nowhere to be seen. He wished he'd been brave enough to have come back and looked for it before.

The grand façade of one house stood as the sole survivor amongst the ruins. The blue sky glowed through its bombed-out windows and a bird swooped behind the façade, appearing then disappearing through the gaps.

He clambered up a rubble heap spewing from an arched doorway. With each step, he slid backwards. He quickened his pace and managed to grab the top of the arch. The house had no back and the side walls stood no more than a few metres above the rubble. He crawled through the gap and, using his hands to steady himself, slid down the debris into the innards of the house. The sun beat on his face and the back of his neck was chilled by a breeze funnelling through from the top of the arch.

A thin boy dressed in threadbare clothing raced towards him. 'Hey, a Jew!'

Feitel's heart thumped and he turned to leave.

Another boy with piercing blue eyes stood by the arch. 'What do you want, Yid?'

The first boy grabbed and twisted Feitel's ear. Feitel

cried out, trying to free himself.

'Why are you running off? Don't you like us?' With menace in his eyes, he added, 'We only want to talk to you.'

Feitel's ear ached, hot with pain. The boy by the arch ran forward. Feitel turned to run but the boy kicked him hard behind his testicles. Another pain shot up from his backside and spread around his abdomen before riding up his spine. He stooped forward and the first boy pounded his chest with bruising punches.

Somebody shouted from across the rubble. 'Oi, what do you think you're doing?' A woman in a blue headscarf, clutching a bundle of firewood, hurried towards them.

The beating stopped.

'He's a Jew,' the first boy said.

'Haven't you seen the signs the Russians put up? We're to leave them alone.'

'Not when they *are* alone,' the boy replied.

'Go on, leave him alone.'

The boys stepped back and Feitel dragged his aching body back through the arch and tumbled down the rubble to the road. With painful testicles and a throbbing backside, he trudged his way back towards the basement. At every lamppost, he glanced back and, heart thumping, scanned around for any sign of the boys.

He took the basement steps one by one and lay on his bed, turning sideways to ease the discomfort.

34

Feitel lay sideways on his bed, his bottom still aching from the kicking. Tears filled his eyes and he shivered. He wished for Canada, but knew, after his walk in to the city today, he wasn't brave enough to ask a stranger for help. He'd have to build up the courage to ask Marianne or Hans.

In the early evening Hans returned, followed, a few minutes later, by Marianne. She placed her hat on the table and smiled. 'I ran into Silke Klose today.'

'Oh, who's she?' Hans asked, brushing down his dusty clothes.

'An ex-colleague. I told her where I was living and she's calling by later.'

Excitement surged through Feitel. A visitor would break the monotony.

'What does she want to call here for?' Hans said, with a hint of annoyance.

'Just to be friendly I suppose,' Marianne said, raising her eyebrows. 'Why does anybody do anything these days?'

'What's she doing for work?'

'Fraternising with the Americans.'

Hans sneered. 'That's work, is it?'

Marianne sighed. 'Well, it puts food on the table, Hans. Isn't that what work's supposed to do?'

Hans curled his lip and cast his eyes towards Feitel. 'And what did you do today?'

Not wishing to admit he'd been out, he said, 'I read my book.'

'The dictionary?'

'Yes.'

'Do you have any idea where you want to go?' Marianne asked.

Here was his chance, to ask about Canada. He hesitated, dreading ridicule. Marianne was waiting for an answer.

Mustering his courage, he said, 'Canada. I want to go to Canada.'

'I don't blame you. Germany is no place for a Jew anymore.'

Hans shook his head. 'It's no place for a German anymore.'

There was no promise to help him. He wondered if she had asked because he was no longer welcome.

*

Feitel imagined Silke Klose to be a beauty, worthy of the Americans. But when she arrived, she was shorter and rounder than he had expected, with a squat nose, a pronounced chin and a plate-shaped red hat perched on a mass of thick black hair.

'Hans, this is Silke Klose. Silke Klose, this is Hans,' Marianne said by way of introduction.

'Just Silke, please,' she replied.

'How do you do?' Hans said, raising himself up from where he was positioned on the bed to shake her hand.

'Better now the Americans are here,' she said.

'So I've heard,' he said.

Marianne shot him an irritated glance.

'I mean, they treat the women better than the Russians did,' Hans added.

'You could say that,' she said, raising her eyebrows.

'And this is Feitel,' Marianne said, casting a hand in his direction.

Silke smiled. 'Hello, Feitel.'

'Hello,' he said, smiling back.

'I've brought you all some chocolate.'

Feitel's mouth watered. He'd not had chocolate for years.

Hans and Marianne murmured with approval as Silke pulled the bar from her shoulder bag.

Hans examined the wrapper. 'American chocolate!'

Marianne took the bar and glanced towards Hans, her lips pursed.

'Yes,' Silke replied. 'The Americans are very generous when you get to know them.'

Marianne opened the bar and broke chunks off, handing them to Hans and Silke. She broke off three rows and handed them to Feitel. He hesitated.

'Go on, take them,' Marianne said. 'We'll eat the rest slowly. Easier if you take your quarter of the bar now.'

Perking up, he took the chocolate, broke off a square and slipped it into his mouth. The chocolate melted on his tongue and the bittersweet taste warmed his mouth. He broke off square after square and pressed them into his mouth.

Silke spoke of how she hoped to return to her job as a railway booking clerk, and an American had been trying to arrange that for her. She promised to ask if they could take Marianne back on too. Where she lived, the electricity was back on. She did not know the fate of her husband, a soldier fighting in the east. Hitler was dead, although Hans and Marianne appeared to know that already.

Marianne explained how they were struggling for food and Silke replied, 'Why don't you come out with me later? There's a bar where the Americans go. They'll always give you food.'

'Won't I have—'

'Only if you want to,' Silke said. 'These are nice boys. They pay first and repayment is optional. And it's fun, the bar. You'll enjoy yourself.'

Marianne glanced at Hans for approval.

'Do what you like,' he said. 'After all, you're not my girl.'

Marianne puckered her lips. 'Yes, yes, I will,' Marianne said. 'Anything for a change.'

'Do you have anything to wear?'

'My summer dress,' Marianne replied. 'It's under my

mattress. When shall we go?'

'Now if you like.'

'Oh, okay,' Marianne said, sounding surprised. 'I need to wash my hands and face first.'

Hans slunk back to his bed while Marianne flannelled her face and tugged the simple dress from under the mattress. She slid off her clothes, pulled it over her head, slipped both arms through the holes and adjusted it down her body.

Feitel remembered the better times, when his mother and father used to get ready to go out. His mother would put on her best dress, his father a dinner jacket. He'd be allowed to stay up and play with the babysitter – a young Jewish woman from his father's work.

'I've lost weight,' she said.

'You look fantastic,' Silke said, heading up the basement steps. 'Worth a packet of cigarettes alone.'

Marianne followed, pulling on her shoes as she bounced up the steps. 'What do you mean, I'm worth a packet of cigarettes?'

'Looking like that, an American will give you a packet of cigarettes for a dance,' Silke replied. 'You can trade cigarettes on the black market. A cigarette butt and you eat a meal, a full cigarette and you eat for a day, a packet and you eat for a week.'

*

Feitel listened to Hans tossing and turning. He knew how angry he was that Marianne had gone out, with the intention of meeting other men. He wanted to venture outside for a pee but held on, clenching his stomach, so as not to disturb him. When he was ready to burst, he darted up the basement steps, in pain because of his bladder and the bully's kicks. He just made it to the top. He dropped his trousers and peed with relief against the bricks shielding the basement entrance.

Feitel turned back towards the basement. Hans was standing by the table holding a candle. Feitel hesitated and descended the steps.

Hans shoved the remains of the bar of chocolate into his hands. 'You eat it. I don't want the rewards of German women trading themselves with Americans.'

Heart racing, Feitel settled back onto his bed and ate the last two squares of chocolate. He unfolded the wrapper. On the front, it said 'Hershey's Chocolate'. He looked up Hershey's in his dictionary but found no such word. He looked up two other words: 'field' and 'ration', guessing Hershey's must be the manufacturer's name. He remembered 'buddy', and looked it up.

When the distant clock chimed 1 a.m., a short squeal of brakes sounded from the street above the basement, followed by the purr of an engine ticking over. It ran for a while before Marianne's voice called, 'Good night.'

A door shut with a clunk, the engine's revs picked up and the whine of its gears faded into the distance as it bumped its way out of the street.

It was a few minutes before Marianne descended the steps and crept towards her bed.

'Did you have a good time?' Hans said.

'Yes, thanks. It was a nice bar.'

'Many Americans?'

'It was heaving with them, and German girls too.'

'It's okay for you women – you have a commodity for sale.'

'*Hans*. Sometimes men don't pay. Remember that.'

He did not reply. The silence was tense. A few minutes passed before Marianne added, 'I know this is hard for you. Seeing me go out and have a good time. And yes, I have been given a packet of cigarettes and no, I didn't need to sleep with anybody to get them. I had a wonderful evening. I got fed, bought a drink, was treated like a lady and now we can eat for a week. I feel alive and more human again. Respected. They're decent young men, from decent families, a long way from home and in need of a bit of company. One showed me a picture of his wife and little girl. He was really proud of them. I enjoyed the attention for a change, even though I barely understood a word. Silke translated whenever I looked confused.'

Hans did not respond.

35

Over the next week, courtesy of Silke, the food improved. Bread, meats, and pickles became available. A small camping stove, which Marianne traded some cigarettes for, appeared along with the oily smell of kerosene. Ersatz coffee, which Feitel found earthy and bland, was boiled and drunk. Laundry powder and spare clothes became available on the black market. Silke brought them some chairs and a large enamel jug to fetch the water in. Hans found a job clearing rubble for his midday meal. Marianne went out two or three evenings a week, wearing the same dress, with bright rouge lips. Sometimes Silke called for her first; other times she met her outside. Hans seldom asked where Marianne had been. Feitel wondered what she had been doing. On other days, Silke came for a meal and they'd all stay in. Hans was more jovial on those evenings.

With the nourishing food, Feitel's strength grew, but he remained cautious whenever he went out in case he met one of the boys who had attacked him. Once, when he thought he caught a glimpse of one of them, he bolted back to the basement, his heart thumping as his body tingled with beads of sweat. Another time, he caught sight of Squad Leader Baer, and again he scuttled back to the basement.

Late one evening, he woke to Hans and Marianne talking.

'I'm pretty sure I'm pregnant,' Marianne said. 'From the Russians I mean.' She hesitated. 'There hasn't been anybody else.'

'Oh God,' Hans whispered. 'When will you know? If you don't mind my asking.'

'I'm already overdue. And, well, I just feel that I am.'

'Shit,' Hans said. 'What are you going to do?'

'Do you remember the hospital the women spoke of when we were queueing at the Rathaus?'

'Yes.'

'I'm getting rid of it there, tomorrow.'

'Just like that?' Hans asked, surprised.

'I've thought about it long and hard.'

'You don't have to. We could raise it together,' Hans said.

'It's not what I want, Hans. And remember poor Gertrud.'

'It'd be her nephew,' he said.

'Or niece. Still a Russki. If I kept it, it'd never know who its father was. Nor would I, for that matter.' Her voice broke into low sobs.

Feitel lay rigid, frightened they'd shout at him if he disturbed them or, if he reminded them of his presence, they'd not discuss such interesting things.

A long pause in their conversation followed. Lorries rumbled by on a nearby street.

'The hospitals are awful,' Hans said, breaking the silence. 'Isn't there anywhere else? What about the backstreet women who help pregnant girls out?'

'If you hadn't noticed, the backstreets have been bombed away!' Marianne replied.

Hans fell quiet for a minute. 'I am serious, Marianne, about raising the child with you. After all this, Gertrud would've wanted us to stick together.'

'I need to show you something,' Marianne said. She rustled around, struck a match, and candlelight danced against the walls. 'I haven't shown you this before. It was in Gertrud's hand when we cut her down. I didn't want you to see it. I don't know if she was angry with us or just being sweet. She knew your love had changed.'

Hans took the piece of paper from Marianne's outstretched hand and studied it.

'Shit. Do you believe that's why she did it?'

'No. No I don't, Hans. Truly. It was what happened the

night before. There have been moments when I've doubted I want to go on. Knowing poor Gertrud, it'd have been an easier decision for her.'

'She says she thinks you were in love with me.'

'That's why I haven't wanted to show it to you, Hans. I'd grown fond of you and I did sense you'd fallen in love with me. Gertrud realised that. Now, after everything that's happened, I can't… I just can't. I'm sorry. I don't love you in that way.'

'You're a beautiful woman,' Hans whispered.

Marianne ran a hand through her hair, leaving a single tuft sticking up. 'Oh Hans, please no. Look, I've always reckoned who you choose to love is the last secret of the soul. I can't explain why I don't feel the same way as you do about me. It'd be wrong of me to give you hope when there's none.'

'Are you sure the abortion is what you want?'

'Yes, yes. Motherhood… it's the most important profession in the world.' She paused. 'And I'm not that person at the moment. My mind is made up.'

Feitel thought through Marianne's words, about motherhood being the most important profession in the world. In a roundabout way she understood the loss of his own mother. He knew Hans was hoping she'd have the baby so she'd need him. He didn't want her to have a Russian baby, not after what they had done.

'Do you want me to come with you?'

'Silke's going to. You can walk us there and wait outside.'

'I'd like to,' he replied.

'It's not much. Just tents for makeshift operating theatres. I have to come home straight after. Silke kindly said she'd stay. I need a woman, Hans. There will be things to attend to that, well, I'd not want you to see.' Hans looked down and Marianne added, 'Hans, please.'

'No sorry, I wasn't… I just couldn't think what to say.'
'Oh, okay.'

'Is it safe?' Hans said, concerned.

'There's a small risk of infection but it's being done by doctors.'

'And what about the law?'

'Hmm, what law? I believe that's being quietly ignored, like the laws the Russians broke. I have a good chance of getting my old job back as a booking clerk. Silke's back there and is going to put another word in for me. I really want to go back. I couldn't with a baby.'

'That Silke does well,' Hans said, raising his eyebrows.

Feitel held his breath, waiting for an angry reply.

'I'm sure she does a few favours,' Marianne said.

'And she doesn't mind you gaining anything on the back of her favours?'

'She doesn't seem to, though it makes me nervous,' Marianne said.

'What, about whether there will be a payback day?'

'Yes. I've never had a hint of it from her. I can count myself lucky. Without the Americans, there'd be more women than men. Silke's making use of that. She says German men lost the war, so they can't expect to win in the bedroom!'

Hans sighed. 'Perhaps we'll return to normal one day.'

'It'll be a new normal, if we do. Not one we've faced before. It'll be good to get out of this place, though,' she said.

'What will we do about Feitel?'

Feitel's heart skipped a beat, and he wondered what might be said next.

'That's a tricky one,' she replied. 'I don't want to be the one to hand him over to an orphanage.'

'Nor me, but I don't see myself looking after him forever. Then there's the continual calling out for his mother in the night. I don't know how to deal with that.'

Feitel cringed to hear he'd been calling out for his mother at night – they must think him a baby. His heart sank with feelings of loss. They didn't want him. He'd sometimes dreamed of being adopted by them. Now they wanted him to go.

'Where did he want to go?' Marianne asked.

'Canada, I believe. Poor kid.'

'At least he has a dream,' Marianne said, sighing. 'I wish I had a dream. I wish I knew how to help him. There are no Canadian soldiers around and I worry the Americans might handle him like any other kid.'

*

Silke called the following morning and left together with Hans and Marianne. They returned late in the afternoon, Hans and Silke guiding an ashen, tear-stained Marianne down the steps. Feitel wanted to rush towards her, but that would not be allowed.

'I reckoned the worst of the pain was over when they used that bloody syringe,' Marianne said, wheezing. 'The pain shot right up inside me, but this…' And she buckled forward, gasping. 'My god, my god.'

Sweat dripped from her face and her hair was tangled across her brow. Silke led her to the bed.

'Oh Silke!' She screamed out in pain. 'Oh my god!'

Feitel listened to her breaths shortening. Wishing he could help her.

'I'm going to have to—' Silke said.

Hans looked the other way.

'Can you get some warm water?'

Hans glanced at the table. 'We can't heat any, we're out of kerosene.'

'Go and beg some. From anywhere.'

Hans grabbed the water jug and darted out of the basement.

'Please, oh please,' Marianne sobbed, 'just get that fucking Ivan out of me.'

'Can you push a bit?'

'I'll... I'll...' she said, panting through laboured breaths. 'I'll try.'

The basement echoed with her piercing scream.

Feitel raised his hand to his mouth and flinched.

'That's it, that's it. It's all come out,' Silke said.

'I don't want to see it. Please don't let me see it. Oh, please.'

'Don't worry, you don't have to.'

Silke stepped back into the main part of the basement and glanced around. Feitel rose, took a few steps towards her and pointed to the toilet bucket. She grabbed its galvanised handle, pulled off the lid and returned to Marianne's bed.

Hans came back covered in sweat, carrying the jug of water. 'I begged it from people living in the street,' he said, catching his breath. 'How is she?'

'It's over, but she's exhausted and sore. Get rid of this, will you?'

Hans left the basement carrying the bucket.

*

Silke stayed and Feitel lay awake while Marianne sobbed and panted. 'It's cramps,' she said, gasping. 'Think of the worst cramps you've ever had and times them by ten... Oh Christ.'

'You don't need to talk,' Silke said.

'I'm going to be sick,' said Marianne. She retched and coughed.

'It's okay,' Silke said. She crossed to the table and poured some water into a glass. 'Here, sip this,' she said, returning to Marianne's side.

'This could put you off sex for life,' Marianne whispered.

'Even with an American?' Silke asked, chuckling.

Feitel remembered the woman on the road to Berlin, washing at the trough, breasts exposed. He remembered how he felt then. The word 'sex' gave him the same feelings again. Ashamed, he bowed his head.

Marianne scoffed. 'Americans or Germans, or Canadians for that matter.'

'Why Canadians? We've not met any.'

'Oh, it's just that Feitel wants to go to Canada,' she said, panting, 'so I was hoping to find a Canadian to talk to, with you translating of course.'

'There are none that I know of. He'd have a better chance in Paris.'

'Could you get him there?' Marianne said, her voice tight with pain.

'What?'

'On a train. Could you get him there on a train?'

'It might be possible. It won't be easy though. The trains are full of Americans and British troops.'

'But it might be possible?'

'Well, yes, it might be. I'll look into it.'

Feitel shuddered with excitement – there might be Canadians in Paris. And perhaps his mother's cousin would still be there. She might help him.

*

The following evening, a group of American soldiers visited. Amongst their booming voices and concerns, it was clear they did not know what had happened to Marianne. In on the secret, Feitel felt, for once, that he belonged in the basement.

Silke translated their good wishes and divided the chocolate, coffee and cigarettes they'd brought. She gave Feitel more chocolate than the others, explaining he wasn't getting a share of the cigarette ration. She translated this into English; the American soldiers laughed and said they bet he'd like some apple pie. Hans and Marianne said they'd love some apple pie too and when the soldiers left, Hans shook hands with them.

As Marianne's strength grew, Hans returned to work and Silke called round every other evening. Feitel was desperate to ask her about the train to Paris but if he did, they'd know he'd been eavesdropping.

Sometimes Silke brought Americans to the basement with her to play cards. They included Feitel and he tried to pick up a few words of English. Though he found the card game Chase the Ace easier to play than learning English. Whoever ended up with the ace of spades lost. The Americans would drink beer and share around chocolate and cigarettes. Silke gazed at one of the men across the table – the most clean-cut and boyish of his colleagues. When he caught her gaze, he'd smile, blush, then bow his head.

36

One evening, while Feitel was reading his dictionary, Silke descended the basement steps accompanied by a well-dressed, sharp-featured man with grey hair and a large nose. 'This is Philip,' she explained. 'He is a British journalist and is writing a novel about the fall of Berlin. He'd like to interview Hans about when he deserted the army, how you both came to live in this basement and what happened to poor Gertrud.'

Hans shot Marianne a worried glance. She shook her head and shrugged.

'Sorry,' Silke said. 'I should have warned you. I only met him this afternoon. He interviewed me and I thought you'd like to tell him your story.'

Philip drew some papers from an inside pocket.

Hans examined them. 'Philip Gibbs,' he said, nodding as he returned them. 'What does he want to know?'

Silke spoke to Philip. Feitel, unable to follow what she was saying, had a heavy sense he wasn't going to be able to master English.

Philip took a seat and replied.

'He asks how you deserted,' Silke translated.

'Easy. My unit returned from the Eastern Front. I visited my girlfriend, Gertrud, and asked her to find somewhere for me to hide. She found me this basement. She later joined me with her sister,' he nodded towards Marianne, 'when their house was bombed-out.'

'Philip asks why you deserted,' Silke said.

'The war with Russia had become futile. I didn't want to die for no reason.'

'But you knew the risks?' Silke asked, translating.

'Of being executed?' Hans said.

Silke translated and Philip nodded.

'I felt I had a better chance of surviving this way,' he

said, shrugging.

Philip produced a packet of cigarettes and handed them around.

'Senior Service,' Hans said. 'A good brand.'

Philip gestured for him to keep the packet then pulled an unopened packet from his coat pocket, speaking for a moment.

'You can trade these,' Silke said.

'Thank you,' Hans said, taking the packet.

'What are conditions like in Canada?' Marianne said.

Silke translated and Philip spoke again.

Feitel held his breath, waiting for the answer.

'Good. They've not been bombed,' Silke said.

'And Paris?' Marianne asked.

Again, Silke translated and Philip replied at some length.

'Better than here,' Silke said. 'With the Russians in Berlin, this is the new front. The further you head west, the better it gets.'

Feitel was glad they didn't mention him, but grateful Marianne had checked what it was like in Paris and Canada. The interview went on. Marianne, knees together and wringing her hands, spoke of their time in the basement, the rapes and Gertrud's suicide. Silke translated how sorry Philip was. He'd heard similar stories throughout Berlin. He added that she looked to be coping well.

'The thing with grief,' Marianne said, 'is that it comes over you in waves. Some you can manage, then a big one crashes on your shore and you are left floundering.'

'Philip asks whether you have family,' Silke said.

Marianne explained how her mother had died from cancer the year before they were bombed-out. Feitel glanced at her. She'd lost her mother too.

'Are conditions as bad in London?' Hans said.

They weren't. It was bad in London during the Blitz, but things had settled.

Hans took a breath. 'Did the British and Americans need to bomb us so much?'

Silke translated.

Philip nodded and spoke, his foreign voice sounding sympathetic.

'He says that question comes up a lot,' Silke explained. 'While Hitler wouldn't surrender, the Allies felt the need to keep bombing.'

Feitel allowed his mind to wander off and was relieved when Philip left without asking him any questions. He didn't want to tell a stranger about his mother.

Hans left to visit friends and Silke went out with Marianne. Alone, Feitel started to read but, finding his eyelids heavy, rested the dictionary on his chest and fell asleep. He came to in the small hours. A wisp of a breeze from the open basement doors tickled his face. Hans and Marianne were speaking in whispers.

'She reckons she can get him on a train tomorrow night. A relief-troop train is returning to Paris. There's always less demand on them in that direction.'

A rush of excitement flooded through Feitel. Could he be about to go to Paris?

'Won't he stick out?' Hans asked.

Feitel, afraid Hans was about to put Marianne off, clenched his fists, digging his nails into his palms.

'There will be other civilians on board too,' she said.

'What time does it leave?'

'Silke reckons about eleven in the evening, but it's best to be there for ten.'

'When will she know for sure?'

'By 5 p.m. That's when the official tickets will have been allocated. She can then steal any unallocated ones.'

'Shall I talk with him?' Hans said.

'If you wish to,' Marianne said. 'Don't go raising his hopes.'

Feitel's rush of excitement ebbed. This train trip to Paris wasn't for certain. But he wanted it so much.

Marianne and Hans fell silent. He dozed until a lone aircraft droned across the skies and the shadows of the night became the first tentacles of morning light.

Marianne rose and lit the kerosene stove. The flame roared then settled and hissed unnervingly like people whispering. She poured some water into a pan which fizzed and gurgled until it boiled. She poured two cups and he detected the sickly odour of the ersatz coffee. Hans drank his at the table and shared a slice of bread and a thin piece of meat with Marianne.

*

Feitel lay on his bed, wondering if Marianne's talk about the train to Paris had been a dream. Convincing himself it was real, he pondered if 'tomorrow night' meant tonight or the one after.

It was a painful wait with the distant clock chiming the morning away. He dared not venture out, concerned he might be detained and miss the opportunity of catching the train to Paris.

The clock struck one. He flicked through his dictionary, unable to concentrate. He paced around the basement, tapping the walls and chimney breast in turn. The clock struck two, three and then four.

Hans arrived back early, half tripping down the steps. Feitel stopped his navigation of the basement.

'Do you know where Paris is?' Hans said.

'Yes,' Feitel said, giving an eager nod.

'There are Canadian soldiers there who might be able to help you. Silke might – just might, and we can't promise – be able to get you on a train there tonight. At eleven o'clock. Do you want to go?'

'Yes,' he said, trying to contain his excitement.

'Marianne has been with Silke all day so she can bring

the ticket straight back, if it can be issued.'

The clock struck five.

Hans paced. The clock struck six and, after another long wait, Marianne trotted down the basement steps.

'I've got it,' she said, panting. 'Have you told him?'

'Yes,' Hans said.

Feitel clambered to his feet.

'Feitel,' she said. 'You're going to Paris. We have to be at the station for ten. Are you pleased?'

'Of course he's pleased,' Hans said.

She bent down and held his arms. 'Are you sure you want to go?'

He smiled and said, 'Yes.'

She drew him close, wrapped her arms around him and squeezed him tight. 'I'll miss you. Write and let me know you're safe. Care of Potsdamer Bahnhof. It'll be sure to find me.'

He rested his head on her shoulder and nodded. She pulled back and looked at him through tear-filled eyes. 'Oh dear, how stupid of me,' she said. 'It feels like I'm giving up my own child.'

Hans looked awkward and rocked on his heels.

'Okay, let's get you packed,' she said, springing up. 'You'll need a bag.' She rummaged around at the back of the basement. 'This was Gertrud's. It's a simple canvas bag, not too much like a girl's. Let's see now. What have you got?'

Feitel gathered his belongings and laid them out on his bed.

'Of course – the dictionary,' she croaked. 'You'll never be without your dictionary, will you? What food can we spare, Hans?'

Hans scanned the table. 'The best part of a loaf and a few slices of meat.'

'He hasn't got a knife, so slice the loaf and wrap it with

the meat for him. Who's this picture of?' She picked up the photograph.

'Leon,' Feitel whispered. 'He was in the camp. He's dead.'

Marianne nodded, her mouth half open. 'And who are these with him, his *mutti* and *pappi*?'

'No, Leon's the man, not the boy,' Feitel said. 'I think the boy is his son and the lady is his wife. I never met them.'

'And what's this letter?' she asked.

'It's to my mother, from Paris,' he replied.

Marianne picked it up and read out the address. 'Will you go there?'

Feitel nodded, eager to reassure her he had a plan.

Hans handed Marianne the meat and bread he'd wrapped. She tucked it in the bag then gave him a quizzical look as he handed her the packet of Senior Service cigarettes left by the British journalist, and an Iron Cross.

'Pop those in his bag too,' Hans said. 'He can trade them in Paris.'

'Where did you get the Iron Cross?' Marianne asked.

'I didn't win it, if that's what you think,' Hans said, snorting. 'There are lots of them circulating Berlin. They're worthless here, but it might be worth something in Paris.'

As the distant clock chimed its eight peals, Feitel climbed the cellar steps to get some fresh air before he had to leave for the train. He glanced around at the piles of rubble – once the houses on his street – and wondered what Canadian streets, with their wooden houses, looked like.

Hans's voice drifted up the steps. 'I thought you wanted him to go.'

'I do,' Marianne said. 'I've just realised how much I'm going to miss him. He's become part of our basement family. When he was packing, I imagined how it'll be when we come back tonight – his bed will be empty and we won't have to whisper anymore. It made me very sad, that's all.

This bloody war has torn people apart and also thrown people together.'

Feitel coughed, then skipped down the steps.

'Hello, Feitel,' Hans said. 'Shall we make a start for the station? Better to be early.'

'Do you mind taking him?' Marianne asked. 'I have things I need to do.'

'No,' he replied, sounding surprised.

Feitel took Gertrud's bag, opened it and fingered through the contents.

'Got everything?' Marianne's eyes turned misty.

Feitel nodded.

'Come on then,' Hans said. 'It's a bit of a walk into the city centre.'

Marianne grabbed Feitel and pulled him towards her again, holding his head close to her chest. 'You'll find somebody to look after you, won't you?'

'Yes,' he said, recalling his mother's last words to him in the camp: *Feitel. See those people? Run after them and find somebody to look after you.*

A tear leaked from his eye. Marianne pulled a handkerchief from her sleeve and wiped it away, her own eyes glazed with tears. It reminded him of his mother's soft fingers, wiping away his tear at the camp. He tried to recall which eye it had come from; still the memory did not come.

'Run along before I…' Marianne said. And as Feitel followed Hans up the steps, she called out, 'Make sure you find somebody to look after you.'

*

The streets were quiet and the evening air cool as Hans walked Feitel to the station. A few people sifted through the rubble and a group of men played cards on a rescued table. American soldiers patrolled but nobody asked them their business. Near the station, the streets became busier. Refugees were camped out in makeshift shelters. A woman and three children lay beneath a railing, their scruffy heads poking out of a blanket. An old man and woman huddled cross-legged with their backs to a wall.

At the station, Hans showed the ticket to a burly, black American soldier who took it and studied it. Feitel rocked from foot to foot, tugging on his earlobe. He was uneasy. Was the man going to allow him to travel? After a few more anxious seconds, the soldier gave a broad grin, handed the ticket back and pointed towards the platform they needed.

Throngs of people hung around the iron-gated entrance to the platform. Some protested to railway officials while American soldiers pushed away anybody who could not produce a ticket.

'I must get to Paris – my wife and child…' a man said. An official shooed him away, saying he must have a ticket. The man shouted back, 'Where's the ticket that says I have to be here?'

Somebody barged into Feitel's back. Hans grabbed him as he staggered, clinging onto his cloth bag.

'Steady on,' the official said. 'I'll deal with you one at a time.'

Hans managed to show him the ticket. The railway official studied it and nodded to the soldier, who opened the gate. Feitel stepped through and Hans began to follow.

'The ticket is for one person only,' the official said, raising his palm.

Feitel took the ticket from Hans's outstretched hand.

'Cheerio, Feitel,' Hans said.

'Bye,' Feitel replied. 'Thank you.'

And with that Hans was consumed by the crowd. Feitel scanned the faces but could not steal a final glimpse of him.

The train was not yet in and Feitel wandered back and forth along the platform, weaving amongst the masses of people. He clutched his bag and his ticket until he thought to stow it away. He opened the bag, tucked it in, closed it, opened it again, and checked the contents.

Feitel remembered his mother and the last time he'd been at this station – the night the police had come. Under torchlight, they'd been dragged from the basement and shoved into the back of a truck. In the shadows, he'd made out the silhouettes of others huddled under the watchful eye of a soldier with a handgun, cocked and pointing, looking for any sign of resistance. His mother's hand had trembled as she gripped his tightly. She'd asked where they were being taken.

Someone had replied, 'Forced labour. Death. We don't know.'

There was resignation in the voices of the others as stories were exchanged about how they'd escaped the main roundups and hidden for years in attics, sewers and basements. One man explained how he'd avoided the last of the main roundups in April 1943, then hidden in plain sight, pretending to be a non-Jew. That evening, he'd been captured. Feitel's mother asked how they knew he was a Jew. 'They measured the width of my nose,' he said, 'and they made me lower my trousers to see if I had been circumcised.'

When they'd arrived at the station, the platform was empty. They were herded, tightly packed, into a single waiting wagon. Over the next hour, the door was slid open and shut as more people were pushed in. The soldiers grumbled they needed another wagon but a superior officer, speaking in clipped tones, ordered them to push everybody on board.

They'd waited, crushed into the wagon, taking desperate breaths of stale air. A man had called out the time on the hour. At midnight, there was the hiss of a steam train and the wagon jolted. They fell silent, listening to the voices of men coupling the wagon to a train. They lurched forward and the train rattled through the night to the camp.

Feitel wandered along the platform, his eyes filled with tears. He longed for his mother. The pain bit deep. He was about to leave Berlin and head west, further away from her. But she was dead. Leon was dead. Berlin offered nothing, Paris offered hope.

The train came in at midnight, an hour late. People had become concerned and the mood turned hostile as rumours spread it was not coming, or it had crashed.

The train slid to a standstill and exhaled a rush of steam like a massive sigh while the wagons concertinaed to a clattering halt. The throngs of people surged forward. Men elbowed their way through and women with babies and flailing baskets lost their tempers. The old tried their best, but fell to the back. Feitel ducked his head and followed in the wake of a group of men hauling themselves aboard. His mind flashed back to gripping his mother's hand as they were shoved aboard by soldiers and prodded with rifles.

The train, already packed with troops, smelled foul with the stench of sweat and cigarettes. Railway officials forced people up the corridors until they met people being thrust the other way.

Feitel held his bag tightly and, when the pushing settled, sank to the floor with his back to a compartment. Others settled around him, complaining of the delay and the cramped conditions.

The train lurched into life. Arms flew out as people steadied themselves.

The train rattled through the night, stopping only to refill its tanks with water before it jolted back to life. Feitel's back and bottom ached against the hard floor and compartment, each bump of the train sending a shockwave up his spine.

As the sun rose and beat on the roof of the carriage, the heat became stifling. Some people vomited into their handkerchiefs, a few urinated on the floor and others shoved and jostled for room.

The train did not stop at any station and no announcements were made. Instead, as telegraph poles flashed by, its progress was signalled by passengers calling out the names of stations that the train thundered through.

He remembered Leon's words. *Follow the tracks. They lead west.* He remembered the train ride with his mother to the camp. He remembered her wiping away his tear, but he still couldn't recall which eye it had come from.

In the mid-afternoon, the train rattled its way through the sunlit rundown suburbs of Paris.

37

The train came to a halt. Somebody called out, 'At last, we are in Paris.' People stood, gathered their belongings and queued along the corridors for the door. When Feitel reached the doorway, a waft of fresh air took away the suffocating stench of stale urine.

Up and down the train, people spilt out onto the platform. He shook with dread. It felt like the day he'd arrived with his mother at the camp. He glanced out across the sea of bobbing heads and froze as he caught sight of the lean, sharp-featured face of Squad Leader Baer.

His stomach knotted and somebody slammed into his back. Stumbling, he half fell onto the platform. He regained his balance and, clutching onto his canvas bag, found himself funnelled towards an exit.

Feitel stepped out of the station into the light of a late spring afternoon in Paris. The boulevard was busy with clean-looking people wearing short skirts, suits and tunics. He glanced around, trembling, relieved Baer had disappeared.

All the trees were intact. None were shattered or smashed, and none were plastered in cards offering items for sale or notes for missing loved ones.

A rich blue sky filled the gaps between the buildings surrounding the station. Birds swooped and hovered, with the sun lighting their bellies.

The buildings, with their grand façades and irregular rooflines, stood intact. Birds perched on chimneys, silhouettes against the skyline.

The dampness and smell of the charred remains of Berlin slipped away. The clear, fresh air of the city filled his lungs.

He started to wander. Piano music drifted across a square from the open windows of a café.

He peered at the blue enamel signs on every street corner in the hope of stumbling across Rue des Rosiers, the home of his mother's cousin. The church clocks chimed each passing hour and, when one struck seven, he was relieved to find a wooden bench overlooking a wide river. He sat and rested his aching feet.

Men and women ambled past, arms linked. The sunlight cast long shadows on distant buildings. Tears pressed against his eyes. Now he was alone, the loss of his mother bit deeper, piercing through his stomach. It stabbed at his heart.

He headed up a narrow cobbled alleyway in search of a place to sleep, slumping inside a porch. Tiredness pulled at him and he gave way to a yawn.

A chill rose through his bottom from the cold stone step. He shivered and leaned back against the door. The sides of the porch were made of corrugated wood and, to pass the time, he ran his fingers back and forth across their ridges and troughs, counting as he did so.

The light in the alleyway slipped away and the road it was joined to faded into shadows cast by the moon. He slept and woke whenever somebody passed or when lovers stopped to kiss or a distant cry echoed from the city.

One couple stepped into the alleyway. She lifted her dress while he tore at his trousers, dropping them to his knees. He lifted her onto his waist and pounded back and forth as she clung to his neck, gasping. Feitel knew they were having sex – he'd heard his parents, heard Gertrud and Hans. He remained still, scared they'd be angry if they saw him. When they'd gone, he shed a tear, missing Marianne and Hans.

He next stirred when a church bell chimed four times. Something brushed his feet. His stomach tightened and his skin tingled. In the first light of dawn, he made out three cats a yard from his feet. One had mounted another, while a third waited, poised for its turn.

He slept again and woke with the church bell chiming seven times. The door behind him opened and he tipped backwards.

An elderly woman – dressed in an ankle-length brown fur coat, with a small poodle tucked under her arm – stepped over him. She wore heavy makeup, covering wrinkled skin, a headscarf, and dark brown-rimmed glasses. She swung round and scolded him. He did not understand the words, but understood she did not want him there.

She lowered her dog to the ground and beckoned it to follow her.

Feitel set off in the other direction. A street cleaner swept the pavement, tipping his pan into a small handcart, allowing a square of paper to flutter away in the breeze. Feitel ran and grabbed it. On one side was a flag – three rectangles with waved edges: one blue, one white and one red, bordered by a blue patterned band. He flipped it over. *ÉMIS EN FRANCE*. A five was in each corner. It looked like money.

He sauntered over to a street vendor, an older man with a pitted nose, selling bread from an open-sided wagon. The man took the note from Feitel, examined it and shook his head. With a cigarette sprouting from his grimace, he handed it back.

Feitel stopped by another man with grey hair protruding from below a wide-brimmed felt hat. He squatted, legs crossed, on a blanket covered in items Feitel recognised from Berlin: guns, bullets, lumps of metal, knives, Iron Crosses and a coat similar to Muller's. A sign, crayon on corrugated cardboard, read *Souvenirs pour les soldats américains*. A number and the letter F was tied on each item. He recognised a German helmet identical to the one he'd carried water to the basement in. He reached forward to touch it. The man gave him an icy stare and he snatched his hand back.

Rummaging in Gertrud's canvas bag, he teased out the Iron Cross that Hans had given him. He withdrew it and showed it to the man, who pursed his lips and plucked a wad of scruffy notes from a pocket. He counted out a few and handed them to Feitel in exchange for the Iron Cross.

Feitel returned to the bread-seller and showed him the notes. The man took one and, after slipping it into the wide pocket of his apron, dropped two iced buns into a paper bag. He scooped three coins from a metal dish and handed them to Feitel along with the bag.

Feitel settled on a bench, his back to the wide river, while he munched his way through the sticky bread, wiping his hands on his trousers. He walked on a bit further until he gazed upon a dark brown tower with four legs, which tapered and joined so high up he wondered if they connected at all.

He puzzled over why there was only one watchtower. Was it tall enough for the soldiers to watch over the entire city from?

An American soldier, arm in arm with a young woman wearing a lampshade skirt, laughed as they approached a rundown wooden kiosk. The vendor, a man with a pointed nose and a scruffy mop of greasy black hair, sold them a pair of tickets and pointed them towards the tower.

Feitel pulled his mother's cousin's letter from his bag, unfolded it and, heart thumping against his ribcage, approached the kiosk. The vendor tore a ticket off a roll. Feitel shook his head and handed the man the letter, pointing to the address on Rue des Rosiers. The man took the letter and studied it. Shaking his head, he pointed to a row of bicycle taxis parked nearby.

The taxis were standard bicycles towing two-wheeled wooden boxes covered in a makeshift hoods and cellophane windscreens.

Feitel showed the address to the driver of the first taxi in the row, a spotty youth of around seventeen who proceeded to gabble away in French. Feitel replied in German. The youth raised his eyebrows then indicated the price by drawing number shapes in the air. Feitel pulled the notes and coins from his pocket and offered them from the palm of his hand. The youth surveyed them, took two notes and all the coins, and pointed to the cab.

*

The bicycle taxi lurched forward as the youth pedalled towards a bridge crossing the river. The cellophane windscreen made the city appear vague with a yellow tinge. Feitel peered out of the uncovered sides, first at the river then, as the taxi bumped its way off the bridge onto a road, the buildings overlooking the river.

They reached a hill where a roar of engines, music and a cheering crowd swept over them. The youth pulled up to allow tanks, trucks and a marching band to pass. He stood on his pedals and pointed to a brigade of parading troops.

'*Soldats français*,' he called out.

As they passed, the youth clapped his hands above his head and cheered. The passing army trucks and tanks were draped with French flags which flapped in the breeze and revealed the letters USA.

When the parade had passed, and its cacophony of sound faded, the youth pedalled off, faster than before, throwing Feitel around in the box.

The taxi branched further away from the river then raced along narrow streets lined with drab four-storey grey buildings – shops and apartments. When the taxi drew to a sharp halt on a cobbled street, the youth pointed to a tatty narrow door and jabbered something in French.

Feitel hauled himself out and, still dizzy from the ride, steadied himself against the side of the taxi. The youth thrust the palm of his hand towards him. Feitel was unsure of what he wanted. The youth shrugged and cycled off.

Feitel checked the letter and the number on the door. While he was poised to knock, a woman emerged, dressed in a threadbare fur coat. She brushed past him, puffing on a cigarette from an old-fashioned Bakelite holder.

He entered a tiled hallway. A door to the first apartment and a worn stone staircase led to the upper floors. He checked the apartment number on the letter and climbed the stairs, treading through dust and flakes of green paint peeled from the walls. On the first floor landing, he stopped and peered upwards, through the metal balustrades.

A familiar voice, speaking German, echoed down the stairwell. 'I'm looking for my family.'

It was Squad Leader Baer.

A woman's voice – German with a French accent – replied, 'They don't live here anymore.'

'Do you know where they are?'

'No,' she said, sounding agitated. 'They left in July 1942. They were sent east along with many other Jews from the city.'

'Do you know if they've ever come back?'

'No,' the woman said. 'This is *my* apartment. It was allocated to me. Go away.' In a half-scream, she added, 'I don't know where your family is!'

The door slammed shut. A few seconds later, footsteps clomped down the stairs. Feitel took his cue and darted down the first flight of steps, out onto the street, ducking down behind a window cleaner's handcart.

Baer, thin and shabby, appeared in the doorway. Feitel held his breath until he strode off towards the river.

He remained ducked down, his heart thumping, wondering why Baer had claimed his family lived there.

A sharp voice, speaking French, interrupted his thoughts. He stood up, trembling. The window cleaner, chamois leather tucked into his belt and carrying a galvanised bucket, glowered at him, curled his lip and shooed him away.

Feitel, not relishing the narrow side streets, sauntered back towards the river. He stopped at a news stand by the steps down to the Saint-Paul Metro Station. Men in shabby suits whispered to every passerby, '*Chocolat? Le tabac? Gauloises? Cigarettes anglaises?*'

The rumble of a train echoed up the steps. People emerged. Room was made for a group of men, stick-like, with greyish-green waxen faces and reddish-brown circles around their eyes. Feitel recognised them as Jews, in worse condition than he'd seen in the camp.

He scanned over the magazine and newspaper pictures on the news stand. The vendor, with a thickset face and a tatty cigarette swinging from a pendulous lip, cast a suspicious eye over him.

A hand pressed down hard on his shoulder. Feitel's heart leapt and thumped inside his chest. He wanted to run, run for safety, but his feet were rooted to the spot.

He tried to turn. The hand tightened its grip.

'Feitel Scher.'

It was Squad Leader Baer.

Fear crippled every muscle in Feitel's body.

Baer loosened his grip. 'I'm not going to hurt you. I need your help.'

38

Feitel sipped a fresh coffee and tucked into a sweet-tasting bread roll. Baer was across from him at a café table. 'I've been searching for you everywhere.'

The words hung in the air. Baer lit a cigarette, holding it between his stained ochre fingers. Feitel gazed up to a menu, chalked on a blackboard mounted on the wall.

Baer half closed his eyes. 'I never killed a Jew. But we Germans who worked in the camps are wanted, like we're *all* criminals. They're hanging us. I'd only been there a month. I hated it, hated Muller. Nobody is going to believe me.'

Feitel took a large bite of his bread roll and chewed it.

'Did you see me kill Muller after the Russian plane attacked us?' he asked.

Feitel thought hard before answering with a nod.

Baer smiled and lowered his head, taking a sip of his coffee. He didn't look much older than Leon. 'I did that to let you all go,' he said. 'I need you to tell the Americans that.'

Feitel remembered hiding with Leon as Baer rounded up the survivors. Baer was lying.

Baer pulled a small book bound in pink cloth from his pocket. Feitel stared, slack-jawed, at his mother's address book.

'I saw you on the road, then in Berlin. You dropped it. I hunted everywhere for you. I visited every Berlin address in it. Where were you?'

'I went home,' Feitel said.

Baer closed his eyes for a moment and sighed. 'Of course, of course. The one address that's not in an address book is where the owner lives.' He shook his head and groaned. 'Why didn't I think of that? Why did you come here?'

'To look for my mother's cousin.'

'On Rue des Rosiers?'

Feitel nodded.

'She's not there,' Baer said, his voice firm.

'I know,' Feitel replied.

'You've been there already?' Baer said, his voice lifting.

'You were there too,' Feitel whispered. 'I was on the stairs below you.'

Baer sat up straight, a scowl flashing across his face. 'Did you hear me talking?'

'Yes,' Feitel said, wondering if this would make Baer cross.

Baer, deep in thought, took a puff on his cigarette, then another sip of his coffee. 'I'm staying in a hotel nearby. It's a bit run-down, but do you want to stay with me until I speak with the Americans?'

Feitel gave a half-hearted nod.

Baer stubbed out his cigarette.

*

On the street in front of the café, they stopped as a soldier tossed a packet of cigarettes from a passing American jeep. It landed near them. A picture of a camel below the words *FILTERS CAMEL* adorned the packet. Baer kicked them towards a pouncing crowd and hurried Feitel away.

They made their way to the river, reaching the Hotel de Ville with its grand façade of stone peppered with bullet holes. A group of young women cycled by, clutching elaborate hats to their heads as their skirts billowed in the wind. Two American soldiers stood by the entrance, admiring them. A French flag fluttered from one of the upstairs windows of the hotel.

A wave of excitement enveloped Feitel. Was this the hotel they'd be staying at?

Baer caught Feitel's gaze. 'Sorry to get your hopes up, but we *aren't* staying there.'

He led Feitel through some sunless slums of narrow

side streets with a multitude of shops either empty, closed or boarded up with rough bits of wood.

Baer took a left turn. 'This is the street,' he said, pointing into the distance to a ramshackle hotel.

A man hunched over a stick limped by, his shoes resoled with wood.

*

The hotel room contained a cast-iron bed, a worn rug and a washstand with an enamel jug, yellowing with age. Feitel dumped his canvas bag down. Baer indicated he should sit on the rug, with his back to the wall. As he sank to the floor, the mustiness of the room teased his nostrils.

Baer parked himself on the bed and glowered at him. 'You didn't see me kill any Jews, did you?'

Feitel shook his head.

'You saw Muller kill Jews in the workshop and on the road?'

Feitel nodded.

'Good. That's good, Feitel. And you told me in the café you saw me kill Muller. That's good too.' He hesitated. 'And you saw me let everybody go after the Russian plane attacked us?'

Feitel hesitated.

'I *did* let everybody go,' Baer said, balling his fist. 'The next day.'

Feitel knew he was lying. Knew he was frightened.

'I can give you money,' Baer said. With that he pulled a wad of notes from his pocket, holding them out. 'Tell the Americans I was good and there's enough money here to keep you fed for a few weeks.'

Feitel did not move. 'Can I have my mother's address book?'

Baer pulled it from his pocket. Feitel reached for it. Baer snatched it away, smirking.

'It's mine,' Feitel said.

Baer furrowed his brow. 'First promise you'll tell the Americans I never killed a Jew.'

Feitel didn't answer.

'What else do you want?'

Feitel hesitated. 'I want to go to Canada.'

Baer tipped his head back, shoved the notes back into his pocket and raised his eyebrows. 'I thought you Jews loved money.' He paused. 'Okay, if you tell the Americans I never killed a Jew, I'll tell them you want to go to Canada. They'll arrange it for you. Deal?'

Feitel nodded, knowing Baer was lying.

Baer tossed him his mother's address book.

*

Baer lounged on the bed all afternoon. Feitel sat with his back to the wall and stared at the curtainless window. An occasional bird swooped past, and one or two perched on the windowsill, pecking at insects caught in spiderwebs.

Feitel considered his options. He could dart for the door, seek out some Americans and report Baer, find somebody to look after him, or try fending for himself. His mother's cousin had been his real hope. Now none of the options appealed. However, the thought of staying with Baer made icy tendrils of unease grip his stomach.

When the sunlight turned to the warm glows of early evening, Baer sat up and twisted his legs off the bed. 'Let's go out and find something to eat.'

Feitel bent down to pick up his canvas bag.

'Leave it there,' Baer ordered. He waited a second before adding, in a more mellow voice, 'It'll be safer here.'

They stepped out onto the landing, passing an ancient brass tap over a once-ornate basin. A sign pointed downstairs to a toilet.

They strolled back to the river and to the front of the Hotel de Ville. A group of men and women, clad in grubby worn-out clothes, dragged a well-dressed woman out through its main entrance. She clutched a baby as they pinned her to the ground. She kicked and screamed, with terror flicking across her eyes. One of the women spat in her face while another produced a pair of scissors and hacked at her brown hair. The baby tumbled to the ground, screaming.

'What are they doing that for?' Feitel asked.

'I think she's a collaborator and the child is a German officer's,' Baer whispered. 'Best we don't speak. We don't want them knowing we're Germans.'

Feitel's stomach stabbed with unease – Baer was allying him as a fellow German.

When the remains of her hair was left in uneven clumps, they dragged her to her feet and ripped at her dress and bra, then underpants, until she stood naked, hands clutched over her hairy crotch, breasts leaking milk.

Tears pricked Feitel's eyes as he gazed at her trembling body.

A woman spat in her face.

Another shouted, '*Traîtresse!*' at her while one of the men took a photograph with a small box camera.

The men and women left.

Feitel stepped towards her. Baer grabbed his shoulder and whispered, 'Don't get involved.'

The woman gathered up her screaming baby and the remains of her clothes and hurried back into the hotel. She left behind her clumps of hair, tumbling in the breeze.

Baer marched Feitel across the road to a line of street vendors selling produce from stalls under striped cloth canopies. He pulled two notes from his pocket and exchanged them for a baguette and two apples.

They relaxed on a bench overlooking the river. A small boat chugged by, puffing out black fumes from a short funnel. Baer broke the baguette in two and handed Feitel his share along with an apple.

'I can't face hiding all my life,' Baer mumbled. He took a bite from his apple. 'I don't want to be on the run, always fearing capture and execution. If I give myself up, explain myself, get you to vouch for me, give them as much help as I can, they might not even send me to prison.'

Feitel ate his bread then munched his apple down to its core.

'Come on,' Baer said. 'I need a drink.'

*

Baer led Feitel down a set of curved steps to a basement bar with a low vaulted ceiling. Above the bar, *Caveau des Paris* was painted in red and black letters. Long benches ran down the middle of the room. Parisians joked with American soldiers who bought them drinks with cash, cigarettes and bars of soap.

Baer took one of the offered drinks and nodded his thanks, not giving away he was German. He sipped the froth from the golden beer and gestured for Feitel to sit opposite him at a bench.

The basement was airless and Feitel rolled up his sleeves. A group of young women, with short skirts and bare legs, sat in a corner, laughing with some soldiers. Two men dressed in shabby pinstriped trousers and jackets, worn through at the elbows, sipped at their beers.

A woman in her early twenties, with brown curls bobbing over her ears, took a glass of wine from a soldier. She stopped, her eyes widening at the tattoo on Feitel's arm.

She came over and spoke in French.

Feitel gazed up at her.

'You were in the camps?' She was now speaking in German.

Feitel lowered his gaze.

'You poor boy, and your papa too,' she said, glancing at Baer.

Baer spoke before Feitel could reply. 'Yes, I was in the

camps too.'

'There are many like you coming back to Paris, flown back by the Americans in transport planes. Some are Jews. Some are from the resistance. They look so ill with their sunken faces and hollowed eyes.'

Feitel cast his mind back to the group of stick-like men he'd seen earlier at the Saint-Paul Metro Station.

'People are returning from the countryside too. They carry cardboard suitcases and sacks of flour to trade. There's so little food around, they get a small fortune for it—' She broke off. 'Why come to Paris when you're German?'

Again, Baer spoke. 'Germany is no place for Jews. We want to make a new life here.'

'I wish you luck,' the woman said. She flashed him a sunny smile and turned away.

Baer took another sip of his beer and muttered, 'I've missed having fun.'

They sat for another hour. Feitel, bored and tired, was wishing they could leave. Baer gazed at every woman who entered the bar. When he ordered a bottle of brandy and slipped it, unopened, into his pocket, Feitel sensed they were about to leave.

'Come on,' Baer said.

*

Back in the hotel room, Baer grabbed the bed, uncorked the brandy, tipped his head back and took two large swigs. 'Good stuff,' he muttered.

Feitel settled on the floor and shielded his eyes from the naked lightbulb, drifting in and out of sleep as Baer drank.

He woke to Baer slurring, 'You Jews got me into this mess.'

His heart beat fast.

'If you'd not been so selfish, we could have lived side by side. But you wanted the riches. Now they want to punish me.'

Feitel did not dare to move.

Baer swigged from the bottle again, turned it upside down to check it was empty, then hurled it, spent, across the room.

'Can't they turn that light out?' Baer said, glaring up at the bulb.

Feitel contemplated reaching for the switch but at that moment Baer pulled his Luger from his pocket. Every muscle in Feitel's body screamed at him to flee. He remained frozen, paralysed to the floor, as Baer's menacing aura held him in a vice-like grip.

Baer waved the gun in the air. Feitel opened his mouth but no scream came out. Baer pulled the trigger and Feitel winced at its sharp crack. Plaster tumbled to the floor. He'd aimed at the lightbulb, but missed. He fired twice more and hit the bulb, plunging the room into darkness.

Shouts came from elsewhere in the hotel; people ran up and down the landings.

Baer began to snore and Feitel closed his eyes, covering his ears. Somebody rapped on their door and his heart leapt, thumping inside his chest. He only settled once the shouts and the footsteps had stopped.

39

Feitel woke to morning light streaming through the hotel room window. His face was stiff and sore from being pressed against the hard floor. Baer lay on the bed snoring, his Luger clutched in his left hand.

Feitel stood up and crossed to the window, treading over the fallen ceiling plaster and fragments of glass from the lightbulb. He gazed down at the narrow, crumbling, sunless street. A man and woman breakfasted in an opposite apartment. Through another window, he made out five adults sharing one small room.

Baer stopped snoring and took a deep breath. 'When were you born?'

Feitel swung around, surprised at the question. Baer was lighting a cigarette he must have taken from an open packet of Senior Service on the bed beside him. Feitel checked his canvas bag – the packet that Philip Gibbs, the British journalist, had given Hans was missing.

'I mean, what's your date of birth?' Baer asked. 'And you're too young to smoke.'

'They were mine to sell!' Feitel shouted.

'Keep your voice down,' Baer whispered. 'I've got plenty of money. What's your date of birth?'

Feitel lowered his head and spoke in a whisper. 'It's the 21 September 1934.'

'Speak up,' Baer said.

'The 21 September 1934.'

'Good. And you were born in Berlin?'

Feitel nodded.

Baer pulled a chewed pencil and a notebook from his trouser pocket, flipped it open and made a note.

'And what was your father's name?' Baer asked, glancing up.

Feitel hesitated. 'Simon Scher,' he whispered.

'Good. And when was he born?' Baer said, scribbling down the previous answer as he drew on his cigarette.

Feitel, wondering what this was about, tried to remember, but could only recall the year 1907.

Feitel made up a date. 'June 27 1907.'

'Good,' Baer replied, recording it with a nod. He slipped the notebook back into his pocket.

'Why do you want to know?' Feitel asked.

'Come and sit on the bed,' Baer said, patting the mattress beside him.

Feitel did as he was told, his mouth turning dry. Baer grasped his arm and held it tight.

'You're hurting me!' Feitel said, twisting to try to escape.

'Shut up and stay still,' Baer said, his nostrils flaring.

He rolled Feitel's sleeve up, then his own and, after peering at the tattooed camp number, proceeded to pencil it onto his own arm. He went over some of the numbers more than once; for others he licked the tip of the pencil to darken the print. When he reached the last digit, he deviated, writing a number one less than Feitel's.

'We need to find a tattooist to ink this over for me.'

'Why?' Feitel asked.

'I'm now your father, Simon Scher,' Baer said. 'We entered the camps together and we're now refugees.'

Feitel lowered his head. He recalled the barn where Leon died, and the despair he felt when Abraham said, *Stay with me, boy. We can find food together and make our way to a city.* This felt the same, but Baer was stronger and this time there was nobody to encourage him to flee. And no crowd of refugees to hide amongst.

'We entered the camps together and we're now refugees,' Baer repeated. 'Have you got that?'

'I thought you were going to find the Americans,' Feitel said, sniffing, 'and give yourself up.'

'Change of plan,' Baer said. 'So, we are father and son, okay?'

Feitel nodded while keeping his head bowed.

'Good boy. Do as you're told and I can keep you fed. We might even make it to Canada.'

Feitel interlocked his fingers, gripping the backs of his hands as tight as he could. This was nothing more than a false promise.

*

Baer bought breakfast – bread rolls and jam – from a street vendor then marched Feitel through Paris. They took in boulevards, narrow side streets and the promenade alongside the river. They managed to find streets with open shops, some drab and rundown, others neat with wealthy customers and American soldiers browsing through the goods.

As a clock struck 1 p.m., they came across a double-fronted shop with a half-panelled door. Above, a blue and gold painted sign announced, *Paris Tatouage*.

'At last, a tattooist,' Baer said. He opened the door and gestured for Feitel to follow him inside.

The walls were painted light green, and the floor was made of dusty bare boards. A stocky middle-aged man, with tattoos up his arms and a round face sprouting a walrus moustache, folded his newspaper over and stood to greet them.

'*Bonjour.*'

'Do you speak German?' Baer asked.

The tattooist nodded.

'Can you tattoo over this?' Baer rolled up his sleeve to reveal the number written in pencil.

The tattooist's face sank. '*Camp de concentration?*'

'Yes,' Baer replied. 'I managed to escape when they were doing the selections at the camp entrance. They took my son,' he added, pointing towards Feitel. 'The Red Cross managed to trace him. I've come to Paris so we can be reunited.'

The tattooist raised his eyebrows, as if unconvinced.

Baer snatched Feitel's arm and rolled up his sleeve, revealing his tattooed number. 'I want my number to be one less than his, so he doesn't feel the number singles him out.'

The tattooist took Feitel's arm and studied his number. 'I could tattoo over the number instead.'

Baer thought for a moment. 'No, I don't want that. I want a tattoo one number less than his.'

The tattooist shook his head. 'It'll be six thousand francs.'

Baer nodded and the tattooist pointed to a black leather barber's-style chair. As Baer settled down, the tattooist opened a drawer and pulled out a set of needles, a bottle of ink and a metal syringe. He began to puncture Baer's skin, filling the holes with the ink.

Feitel gazed out the window, across the road to a grocery shop with prices chalked on miniature blackboards. Further up the road, a jeep with two American soldiers inside pulled to a halt, brakes squeaking. They jumped out, glanced up and down the street, dragged out a canvas holdall and began to sell packets of cigarettes. A small crowd formed. One soldier handed out the packets. The other collected the money.

Feitel turned back to the shop. The tattooist curled his upper lip as Baer winced with each prick of the needle. Feitel remembered getting his tattoo and how the needle had bit into his skin – the day he lost his mother. He was glad it was hurting Baer.

Feitel glanced out the window again. The crowd around the jeep had swollen. A young woman chatted with the soldiers.

After a few more minutes, the tattooist said, '*Fini.*'

Baer stood and, under the watchful eye of the tattooist, wiped his arm with a towel, drew a wad of notes from his pocket and counted out the money, returning the rest to his pocket.

'Thirty thousand francs,' the tattooist said, half sneering.

'We agreed on six thousand,' Baer said.

'I won't make trouble for you or report you if you give me thirty,' the tattooist whispered.

Baer curled his lip. 'You're a cheat.'

'And you're *not* a Jew.'

Baer fumbled in his pockets, extracting the rest of his money. It wasn't enough. The tattooist stretched out his hand. Baer stuffed the money back into his pocket and rooted around, pulling out a small cloth bag, fastened with a drawstring at its neck. He loosened the string and tipped two gold fillings onto his palm.

Feitel's mouth was half open. His mind shot back to his mother's tooth, the one with the two gold fillings. Then to breaking the teeth in the workshop. Separating the gold. Baer must have pinched some for himself. His mind thundered forward to Leon, the road and back again to his mother as she wiped away his tear.

He pounced forward, yelled, screamed and shoved Baer in rage. He kicked him in the shins and pounded his stomach. Baer tried to wrestle him away. Feitel's energy rose as he punched, kicked and screamed.

Baer grabbed him round the neck with the crook of his elbow. Feitel wriggled but Baer pressed his other hand hard against his chest. In his crushing grip, Feitel stopped.

The tattooist darted towards the door.

Baer tightened his grip. 'You let me go or I'll break the boy's bloody neck.'

The tattooist flung open his shop door and flashed his eyes along the street. He pointed back into his shop, shouting, 'Nazi, Nazi!'

Seconds later, the two American soldiers appeared, sprinting towards the shop door.

Baer removed his arm from Feitel's chest and pulled out his Luger from his pocket. The cold steel of its barrel pressed into Feitel's temple.

'Nazi, Nazi!' the tattooist repeated.

The soldiers glanced through the window and rushed inside, guns at the ready.

Baer increased the pressure of the barrel against Feitel's temple. 'You let me go or I shoot the boy!' he shouted.

Feitel tensed. One of the soldiers flicked his wrist and a bright flash came from his gun. Fine droplets of blood spattered along the wall of the shop. A sharp pop stabbed in Feitel's ears. His head spun and his legs became heavy as the barrel of the gun slipped away from his forehead. Baer tipped backwards and Feitel slipped to the ground.

*

Feitel opened his eyes and, in a foggy haze, realised he was being wheeled into a hospital ward. He was lifted onto a bed. The sheets – firm and crisp – were fresh, the mattress and pillow soft. The windows were tall and half open, with patterned curtains swaying in the breeze.

Two nurses peered down at him. Both were dressed in white aprons over dark blue tunics with white hats flowing back from their temples. They asked him something – he reckoned they were American. He shook his head and the one nearest to him asked, '*Deutscher?*'

He wanted to speak English with them but instead nodded his head, confirming he was German.

The one who had spoken flashed him a warm smile, revealing a row of neat, bright white teeth. The other pulled up a sheet and thin blanket, tucking it around his neck. He took short breaths and slipped off to sleep again.

*

Feitel woke to distant voices coming from a corridor. A wheel squeaked on a trolley and wafts of disinfectant hung in his nose. He patted his chest – his old clothes, the ones he'd taken from the boy on the road between the camp and Berlin, had been replaced by soft pyjamas.

He kept his eyes closed until a woman's voice spoke German in what sounded like an American accent. 'Hello. My name is Dorothy Aaron and I'm with the Canadian Red

Cross Corps.'

He opened his eyes. A young woman with shoulder-length brown hair perched on a chair next to the bed. She wore a dark blue tunic with a red cross on a small white circle stitched to the left arm. A patch with the word 'CANADA' written on it was sewn on her upper arm, beneath the shoulder seam.

She offered a polite smile. 'I've been sent to look after you. How are you?'

'I'm okay.'

She nodded, looking pleased with his answer. 'Can you tell me your name?'

'Feitel Scher,' he whispered.

She pulled a notebook and pencil from her breast pocket and jotted it down. 'And can you remember what happened to you today, Feitel?' she asked, glancing up.

Feitel nodded.

'Can you tell me?'

He liked her gentle voice. 'Baer was getting numbers tattooed on his arm. Two soldiers rushed in.'

'And who was Baer?' she said.

'Squad Leader Baer,' Feitel replied. 'He was a guard from the camp.'

'Do you know his first name?'

Feitel thought for a moment, recalling how Mrs Baer addressed him when they were leaving the camp. 'Karl.'

She made a note. 'Do you know which camp?'

'No, but it's the one I went to with my mother.'

'And what numbers was he having tattooed?'

Feitel rolled up his sleeve, exposing his camp number. 'One less than these – he wanted to be my father.'

She fixed her eyes, stunned, on his tattoo. 'And was he your father?'

'No, he was pretending,' Feitel replied. He shook his head and trembled, believing he was in trouble.

'And you're Jewish?' she asked.

He nodded vigorously.

'I am too,' she said, beaming. 'Well, to be exact, I'm half Jewish on my father's side.'

'Oh, that's good,' Feitel whispered, relaxing.

She leaned forward. His arm tingled as her gentle fingers traced over his inked tattoo.

'My name is Feitel,' he began in English, 'and I want to live in Canada.'

Her head tilted back in surprise. 'I can't wait to live back in Canada myself!' she continued in German. 'I'm hoping to go back soon. You speak English.'

Feitel shook his head. 'Only those words,' he said, speaking in German.

'You've been practising them?' she said.

His cheeks burned as he nodded.

'Have you lost your papa?'

He nodded again.

'And your mama?'

His mouth crumpled and a tear leaked from his eye. She reached forward and the brief touch of the edge of her thumb followed his tear down his left cheek. He remembered the tear – the tear shed for his mother, the day she wiped it away, and she was with him again. It had come from his left eye.

He remembered his mother's words at the camp gates. *Find somebody to look after you.* He smiled up at Dorothy. 'Will you take me to Canada?' He blurted out the words.

Her eyes widened. 'You've no other family alive?'

He shook his head.

Her face broke into a broad smile. 'It might be difficult. But let's try, shall we?'

Epilogue

Eighty Years Later

I think I've found the spot where I said goodbye to my mother. It's peaceful, with neat lawns interspersed with the remains of brick foundations and information boards marking the locations of huts, chimneys and crematoria. One of the guards' quarters still stands, with a chapel room set aside for whatever faith offers comfort. There are piles of shoes and spectacles. No sweet smell, no screams. No despair. A museum piece. I worked out the spot from memories I'd assumed had vanished. But they were there. Time has healed this site from the horrors it once witnessed. Yet my memory is replaying it. A mortal's pain only ceases at death. Inanimate objects have no memory, no pain. Instead, they serve to remind the living.

My wife, Pearl; our daughter, Grace; our grandchildren; and one great-grandchild stand ten metres behind me. She never met them. All of them are silent and respectful – they allowed me to wander around. When they sensed a purposefulness in my stride, they stopped and looked on. I know they wonder how I cope, with yesterday always peering over my shoulder. I know no other life. Know no other existence. Humans have the ability to live with whatever life throws at them.

I didn't know my mother beyond the age of ten. I can only guess what she could have given me. My past is so out of sorts with my own prosperous Canadian family that yesterday, when I mentioned my mother spoke no English, there was real surprise on their faces. It was there again when I spoke to the receptionist at the hotel in German.

My eldest granddaughter, Esther, who studied the Holocaust at the University of Victoria, discovered my father died in Auschwitz in April 1943. She worked through my mother's address book. None of my relatives survived the war.

She traced Marianne and Hans's families using social media. Marianne married in 1951, had three children and died in a care home in 2011. Esther is Facebook friends with her granddaughter, Gertie. Gertie sent her a YouTube clip of Marianne being interviewed in 1967 on German television. She looked much the same, but sad, as she recalled her sister and the violation of the Berlin women by the Russians in 1945. I'm glad the darkness of the basement spared me the sight of her being raped, but my imagination was never spared.

Dorothy, my adoptive mother, wrote to Marianne in 1946 (care of Potsdamer Bahnhof) to let her know I'd made it to Canada. We got a reply saying how delighted she was. Esther also discovered Hans was living in East Berlin when the Russians put the wall up. He moved to the west in 1993 and died in 2003. He had one son. She couldn't find any trace of Elisabeth Seeler or Silke Klose.

Encouraged by Esther, some five years ago I began reading about the Holocaust. With the German authorities trying to root out the surviving perpetrators, my memories of Germany mellowed.

Esther found a copy of *Thine Enemy* – a book the British journalist, Philip Gibbs, who visited Hans and Marianne in the basement, wrote just after the war. I saw hints of Hans, Gertrud and Marianne in his story.

Esther also discovered, in a Holocaust archive, the picture of Leon and me in a group clearing the snow. I treasure it, along with the photo of Leon and his family.

Now, as I stand here with my family, I recall my mother's words at the camp gates. *Find somebody to look after you.*

I close my eyes and whisper, 'I did, Mama. I did.'

I've never forgotten Marianne's words either: *Motherhood… it's the most important profession in the world* and *I've always reckoned who you choose to love is the last secret of the soul.*

I sense Pearl's presence – she's the last secret of my soul. A tear leaks from my left eye, and she traces it down my cheek with the edge of her thumb. Slowly – no rush due to guards and now delayed by my whiskery old face.

I smile. She knows what she is doing. I'd told her the story years before, repeating it many a time. Ever since I retired, she's encouraged me to come here. Only now, as I'm growing frail with age, have I wanted to face this place. I think 'closure' is the English term for this.

'You must go one day, Feitel,' she would say. It felt like a betrayal to Dorothy. But now she's gone… both my mothers are gone.

'Thank you,' I whisper.

When I turn, I find Pearl is not with me. She's still standing with the others. She approaches, sliding her hand gently into mine.

'It *was* the left eye,' I whisper.

Can you spare some time to give me a review?

Your honest opinion matters to me. You can rate this book on www.amazon.co.uk (under 'Your Orders' then the 'Write a product review' button) or www.goodreads.com

Many thanks.

Stephen P. Smith

Acknowledgements

Many thanks to Rachel Rowlands, Debz Hobbs-Wyatt, Dinah Ceely (Cornerstones Literary Consultancy), Jon Stock (author of The Sleep Room), Suzanne Bellenger, Steven Hampton, Cait Clear and Patrick Gale and Romesh Gunesekera (via The Arvon Foundation), who gave me much valued feedback.

Thanks also to Reg Hazel for sharing his memories of the liberation of Bergen-Belsen and to Esther Fairfax (who escaped the Holocaust but lost her grandparents in Auschwitz) for her unstinted encouragement.

And to Alvin Lewis who, in February 2018, was staying in the same New Zealand Backpacker's hostel as me. He glanced at the cover of the book I was reading – Schindler's List – and, in his American accent, announced, "My dad was on that list." The room stopped, everybody looked on. His father, Victor Lewis (Wiktor Lezerkiewicz), and his mother (Regina Steiner) were in the concentration camps. I'm grateful to the time Alvin gave me, telling their story. Their survival was good will, good survival skills, good timing and good luck. It's worth a Google.

Source Material

1. Shoah – a film by Claude Lanzmann.
2. Thine Enemy – Philip Gibbs.
3. Alone in Berlin – Hans Fallada.
4. A Woman in Berlin – Marta Hiller.
5. Schindler's List – Thomas Keneally.
6. The Destruction of the European Jews – Raul Hilberg.
7. Paris After the Liberation – Antony Beevor & Artemis Cooper.
8. Numerous television documentaries and online accounts of survivors.

About the Author

Steve (as he prefers to be known) has a first-class honours degree in Computing and Electronics, a field he worked in for thirty years before retiring in 2017.

His career highlights include designing the server transaction management system for the NSPIS (National Strategy for Police Information Systems) Command and Control System and taking on the role of system architect on the NSPIS HOLMES2 project. He prides himself on having taken the technical lead on eight £1m plus public sector IT projects and made a success of them all.

He is a keen hillwalker and, despite having chronic asthma, has climbed the 282 Munros (Scottish mountains 3000ft and above), the 443 Nuttalls (English and Welsh mountains 2000ft and above) and many other mountains. He has also walked coast to coast across Scotland seven times and walked in The Alps, The Canadian Rockies, The Adirondacks in the USA, New Zealand and Australia.

Accounts of his walking are published in his two autobiographies, 'The Munros' and 'Walking it Through'.

He has written a novella, 'The Veteran and The Boy'. He has also had books published on computer programming and Charlie Chaplin, (a biography entitled 'The Charlie Chaplin Walk').

He is a seasoned rail campaigner and in 2013 he received Rail Future's Clara Zilahi Award for Best Campaigner.

Steve has Ashkenazi Jewish heritage and is married with one child.

Read the opening chapter of Stephen Smith's novella

The Veteran and the Boy

Available on Amazon

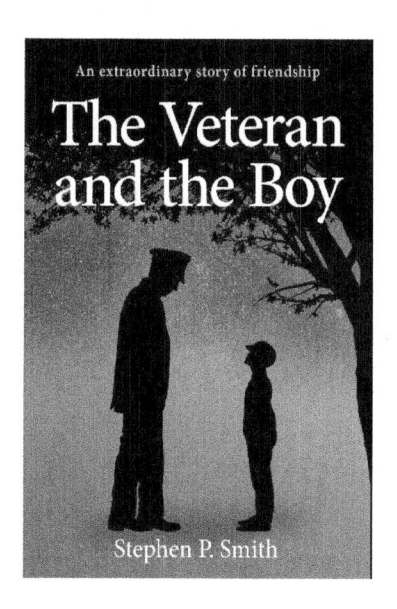

It's the 1930s and the Great War still casts its shadow over rural England. One ex-soldier, 'The Veteran', is suffering from shellshock and spends his days wandering between the market town of Devizes and the surrounding villages.

He's as outcast as the bullied schoolboy, Billy Shelton, who he befriends and protects. But when The Veteran is accused of a crime can Billy protect him?

'A compelling and well written piece' Debz Hobbs-Wyatt, Winner of the Bath Short Story Award 2013

1

There were two things the talk of Devizes Market Place at four o'clock on that Tuesday afternoon.

It wasn't market day so the price of things was not discussed.

Nor was the weather – the sky was clear and there was no wind. The shops, a mixture of redbrick and stone, were busy and the smell of the brewery hung over the town, but the locals were used to that so nobody thought to mention it.

The coal merchant's steam lorry puffed its way through, but they'd run it for years and the black hessian sacks of coal, propped on its flatbed, and the men with their caps, dirty faces (some stern, some cheeky) and brown leather flak jackets, were an everyday sight too.

The fishmongers, with its red canvas canopy, dulled by the sun, had fresh stock and a pig hung in the butcher's plate-glass window. The greengrocer, wearing his khaki shopkeeper's coat, weighed out apples and tipped them into brown paper bags.

The agent's office, next to the cinema, advertised the land that was for sale, what it was good for and whether it was tenanted. But there was always land for sale so the window only attracted those looking to buy or those who were just plain curious and liked to keep up with these things.

As for the Veteran he stood in front of the ladies window of Sloper's Drapery Store admiring the mannequins as they were stripped and dressed. It was the same every Tuesday. He gathered comment, the usual comments of disgust and suspicion, and was one of the two things that were the talk of the market place on that Tuesday afternoon. And the other? Just about anybody that was not talking about the Veteran was talking about the shiny new school bus parked in the middle of the market place.

*

Billy Shelton liked the new bus, liked its dark green paint, large black tyres with white hubs, radiator and the ever present starting-handle. The number plate was AM1921, and 1921 was the year of his birth: a simple connection that made him feel special. He pulled a pencil and a blue clothbound notebook from his trouser pocket and added AM1921 to a long list of numbers he'd collected. When something bad happened his father would ask him for the numbers he'd seen, when he'd seen them and who was about at the time. And when Mike Hillier, a sandy-haired boy with sharp, piercing blue eyes, found out he would clip Billy's ear for being a policeman's snitch.

And on this Tuesday afternoon, when the shop assistants had finished dressing the mannequins in their new outfits, the Veteran turned and shuffled towards the children. His gait was so strange they always stopped whatever they were doing when he hobbled by: a conker fight would cease, the brown chestnuts left to swing on bits of string in the breeze; the trade of a dead frog for a tuppenth of boiled sweets; the reassembly of a bicycle chain and the skimming of a pebble on a dew pond hung as if an artist had painted them.

Billy was glad that no car backfired today, and no fork of lightning lit the sky as these would cause the Veteran to cower and his strange mumblings to become frantic cries. Then the children would laugh and jeer, but none was brave enough to go near him. And Billy would look on the man, wondering about his past and whether he felt as alone as he did.

Nobody was sure where the Veteran slept at night, but the rumour was he bedded down in hedgerows in the summer, and barns in the winter. Billy sometimes saw him in Market Lavington, the village where he lived. Sometimes he saw him up on the plain – a large area of flat land above his village. But more often he was seen here in the main town, Devizes.

When Billy asked his father about the Veteran, all he would say was, "The war affected him." But he never added any more to his pleas of, "What war? What happened? Was he blown up?" other than to warn him to stay clear of him.

Mike Hillier had once announced, "It was the Great War and he'd been taken prisoner and tortured by the Germans." And then some older boys beat him up for being a know-all and he, in turn, beat up Billy Shelton for simply being Billy Shelton.

He watched Paul Redshaw, a boy who lived in the town but hung around with Hillier, load a peashooter and catch the Veteran on the cheek then laugh as he flapped and attacked the air. Mike Hillier gathered some small stones from the gutter then peppered the Veteran's greatcoat. He jeered as the Veteran jumped.

Billy looked towards the bus, hoping the driver would open the doors and call the children to board. But there was no sign of the doors being opened, instead the driver sat at his steering wheel and turned the pages of a newspaper.

"Leave him be," yelled Billy.

Redshaw turned towards him, his face full of threat. "You what?"

Billy stared into Redshaw's dark black eyes. There was menace in them and he wished he'd said nothing. He wished he'd walked around the market place again, or hidden behind the market cross, to chew the time up and avoid the rage of the bullies between the school bell and the driver opening the doors to the bus.

"What did you say?" asked Redshaw, flicking back his dark hair and pressing his face into Billy's.

"Shelton's got a friend," jeered Hillier.

"He's your friend now is he?" asked Redshaw.

Billy's legs felt heavy and he trembled.

"Shelton's got a friend," chanted the other boys. The other boys always joined in the jibes, but never the hitting.

He felt Redshaw grab hold of his ear and twist, a hot burning feeling rode up his head. He didn't really see what happened next: the Veteran had somehow waded towards Redshaw and now, with his stick flailing, struck the bully across the side of his head. The boys backed away as the Veteran attacked the air, keeping Hillier and Redshaw at bay like a lion tamer at a circus. With each protest the Veteran jabbed his stick, and Billy rubbed his ear.

The driver unlocked and opened the doors to the bus. "You," he yelled, pointing at the Veteran, "Clear off."

The Veteran stared and appeared to shake his head, but it was more of a tremble than a shake. He backed away and only then did the driver beckon the children towards the bus.

The boys allowed the girls to board first. They always did – it was a rule of the driver. Then they jostled and shoved and took up their seats as Redshaw ran along the outside of the bus, yelling at Billy that he was going to get him tomorrow.

Billy took a seat but Mike Hillier dragged him out and shoved him towards the back. He sat on the boards of the gangway, still rubbing his ear and patted his pocket to make sure he'd not lost the shopping list which his mother had given him that morning. He dreaded losing his mother's list, dreaded any incident that might unleash her anger and dreaded getting off the bus where Hillier was sure to punch and kick him.

As the bus pulled away he listened to the roar of the engine, the whine of the straight cut gearbox and guessed when the driver would change gear. The gear changes were smooth, sending a slight rumble below the deck. The old bus used to lurch and the driver held back for as a long as he could until the engine screamed or laboured for a different cog. He listened to other boys list the new bus's virtues, the size of the engine, its top speed (if only it were unleashed) and Billy felt peeved the girls were learning about the bus from somebody other than him.

At a small village at the foot of a steep hill the bus pulled up and half a dozen boys and two girls alighted. Billy parked himself on one of the hard brown leather seats set in a chrome frame. He watched an elderly man look upon the new bus, and Billy now felt important to be on that bus.

The next stop was at Black Dog Farm (where a friend of the driver's hitched a ride) before it trundled along the lanes and came to its final stop outside the church in Market Lavington. As soon as the doors opened Billy dashed off to get ahead of Mike Hillier, to disappear before he got a final cuff of the day.

Hillier's mother and sister, Molly, were waiting for him. Billy was safe, the tension sank and even Molly smiled, through her freckles, as if somehow she knew she'd saved him. She had long, dark locks and always wore a white dress with a red bow. Molly was a pretty girl, and her mother would beam with pride whenever anybody mentioned it.